13 COUNTY ROAD 666

13 COUNTY ROAD 666

TRAILER PARK CRYPTIDS
BOOK ONE

C.L. MCCOLLUM

Charlotte, NC

FALSTAFF
BOOKS

WWW.FALSTAFFBOOKS.COM

For Eric, because I love you even more than books.
Yes, even this one, and that one, and that series, and that stack by the
bed and...
Look, you knew what you got yourself into long before you built me custom
bookshelves.
But seriously, even more than books.

1

The werewolf from the next row over and five trailers down had slipped his leash again, howling bloody murder and knocking over the neighbors' trash cans.

Full moons weren't meant for a good night's sleep. Even in the mundane world, something about that big ball in the sky set folks on edge. Ask any ER nurse—the full moon was anything but relaxing. I knew that better than most of the population, as did all people living hip deep in the supernatural world.

No, full moons meant sleepless nights for me and damn near always had.

Now, had I ever learned to nap during the day so I was coherent after moonrise?

Of course not; that would be proactive and intelligent, and most times I was unfortunately neither of those things.

Thus, it was sometime around midnight when I jerked awake on the couch where I'd fallen into a doze, fully dressed, waiting for...well, for *exactly* what had awoken me. I sat up to listen as the sound came again, then groaned as sure enough I recognized the noise. "Damn it, Harvey."

I scowled and forced myself up. I pulled a hoodie over my tank top, not bothering with a bra, then grabbed my shotgun and shoved a couple extra shells in the hoodie's pocket. I'd loaded the witch-silenced gun before I crashed out on the couch after my regular check of the calendar. I'd hoped I wouldn't need it—he'd been warned before and more than once—but Harvey Stephens, our resident stubborn-ass werewolf, often ignored my scolding, along with the rest of the community rules for Asphodel Estates at No. 13 County Road 666.

I scrubbed my free hand across my face and fumbled for my boots. If I didn't hurry, the whole damn trailer park would get involved, and I did not have the energy to talk down an angry group of residents even during daylight hours. At this time of night, I'd be hard pressed to talk down one person at a time, honestly. It was bad enough that Harvey'd likely woken half the park by now. Oh well, that meant I didn't have to worry about how loud I was in dealing with him. Our tenants would prefer the matter handled quickly as opposed to quietly in a case like this. It didn't mean they were going to be civil about it, though. As the managerial goddesses knew, one of them would end up filing a complaint, and a visit from the boss rarely ended well for me.

Something to look forward to *after* sunrise.

At least the trailer park was far enough out of Tartarus, Texas's tiny town proper, that it was unlikely the local sheriff would be called. Not impossible, but unlikely. As long as gunshots weren't heard, we tended to get away with more than we didn't; thus the silencer on my shotgun that Mama had paid a witch for as a Yule gift a few years back. It wasn't a perfect solution to the noise issue, but it helped.

Regardless, Harvey's dumbass was my responsibility as property manager. I'd deal with him and then hopefully get a few hours of sleep before my alarm went off.

Please Mr. Sandman, I needed some sleep.

I pushed out the door to my trailer, wincing as the hinges squeaked something fierce. I made a mental note it would need some WD40 in the morning. Tonight though, I could be a little thankful for the noise as the screech of metal did some of my work for me, or so I found once I got to the edge of my wooden deck. It attracted one angry, and more than likely drunk as a skunk, werewolf away from whichever trashcan was prey for the evening.

The massive fur ball crouched about two trailers away over by Miss Ginger's place, his dark hide a black blur blending into the darker night. I hefted the shotgun up to my shoulder with the muzzle aimed at the ground and took the few steps down to the gravel and pale caliche clay road between the two rows of mobile homes, careful to keep my balance on the rocks slick from rain earlier in the day. I made another mental note to be wary of mud puddles, if this went the way I expected it to and I had to venture farther back into the community.

"Harvey, what do you think you're doing?" I hissed, trying to keep myself to a whisper despite my annoyance. "You know damn well you're supposed to stay in the shed on full moons as per the rental agreement." The werewolf tossed his head and growled, clearly unimpressed and unwilling to cooperate. "Don't give me that shit. I read the thing out loud for you, and you initialed after every single rule, including the Full Moon Clause."

If Harvey'd been a regular dog instead of a mangy werewolf, I might have found myself facing a pair of deeply ashamed puppy dog eyes by this point, belly crawling achieved with the scolding tone in my voice. But no, not Harvey. He gave zero shits about the dressing down I was giving him.

I missed regular dogs. They were so much easier to train.

Harvey growled again, low and vicious, and pulled himself up to his hind legs to loom over me, looking more like an angry bear in the moonlight than a wolf. I sighed and pointed the shotgun at him, leaving no question about what would happen if he moved forward. "Last chance, man. I really don't want to have to wake everyone else up when I fire. Think this through. You don't want to do this, do you? You know what happened last time."

The growls got louder and somehow even meaner. Oh yeah, he remembered the last time. Shame he hadn't learned from it. He bent his knees, then lunged straight at me as I'd expected him to.

The shotgun barked in my hands, the sound thankfully muffled by the sound-dampening spell, rocking me back a little from the impact to my shoulder. Harvey yelped and abandoned his charge, twisting in midair with a whimper as he smacked full on into the side of Miss Ginger's trailer. I cringed; maybe I'd get lucky and she'd be in town for the night. Otherwise, I'd get an earful in the morning. Harvey kept whimpering, his fur and skin smoking where the consecrated rock salt mixed with silver shavings had hit him. There wasn't near enough silver in the salt to actually cause major damage; for all his flaws, he paid his rent on time every single month, and the landlord wouldn't approve of me killing his tenants even if they were running amok in spite of their rental agreements. Non-fatal didn't mean it didn't hurt like a bitch, though.

"See what happens when you misbehave?" I asked, stepping closer. Harvey whimpered and made to retreat past me toward the entrance to the community. I shot him again, this time across the left side of his body to force him back the way he'd come, wincing at another high-pitched yelp. Some nights I hated my job. But he was my responsibility whether I liked it or not, and I had warned him. "You know where you need to be, Harvey. Either you get, or I have to keep firing. You know how this works."

Making sure his eyes were on me, I loaded another pair of shells and snapped the shotgun closed. "Well?"

Harvey finally started edging back down the gravel road in the direction I wanted him to go, clawed feet barely slipping on the wet at all. I followed, trying not to trip over anybody's driveways in the dark or end up sinking into the mud. There was only so much moonlight could do for human eyes. I wished the boss had agreed to install better lighting, but he'd argued that too many of his tenants would be offended by artificial light when they all could see perfectly well in the dark, thank you very much. To hell with those of us who couldn't, I supposed. I kept after Harvey as he made his slow sulking way back toward his trailer at the very end of the road. I only had to use the shotgun twice more, both times due to him making like he planned to knock over another trashcan out of sheer spite.

The trashcans would definitely cause the most clean-up. I, on the other hand, was much harder to knock over than the cans, as more than a few of the tenants decided to test from time to time. It got old fast.

We finally reached Harvey's rented trailer and the small shed slash dog house the boss had insisted on Harvey paying for us to install when he moved in. Some of our tenants owned their own single- or double-wide or RV or airstream or whatever the hell they'd decided to live in, and they only rented a spot with all the basic utility hook ups. About half the trailers and mobile homes on-site belonged to the property itself. Rental contracts were stricter on those lots, and often edited based on the individual tenant who'd be moving in. Harvey's once-a-month-shenanigans required somewhere contained to shift where his decidedly less intelligent wolfy-self could screw around without damaging Asphodel Estates' property. We'd had werewolf tenants in the past who insisted on being allowed to stay in a rental during the full moon, and we ended up completely gutting and reno-vating the battered shell of a mobile home they'd left behind. Thus, Harvey's shed/werewolf house. He'd protested being "punished" for the previous renters' behavior, but beggars couldn't be choosers. If he wanted to live here, he needed to suck it up and deal with the boss's decisions.

The shed was firmly secured to the ground, with a small concrete slab and walls and roof anchored by fence posts buried a good three feet down with more concrete keeping them secure. It looked cold and sparse and uncomfortable as hell, but it wasn't like his wolf needed much in the way of comfort and it was only used once a month. I'd actually tried to add some outdoor furniture cushions to soften it up a bit, but Harvey tore through them like a tornado his very first full moon in under ten minutes. The boss hadn't been willing to reimburse me since I was dumb enough to buy them without approval on the purchase, so I sure as hell wasn't going to replace them for Harvey. If he wanted a nicer shed, then he could fix it up himself.

Harvey reached the edge of the shed and crouched down by the tangle of a chain and collar snaking in to attach to an iron ring securely mounted to the concrete slab. He whined pitifully and showed me his throat like he should have done in the first place. I waited a beat, not sure whether I believed his "please don't hurt me, alpha" act, but then sighed and eased down to lean the shotgun against his trailer. With my hand still on it, I eyed him and directed him to lay all the way down. "And don't think about getting mouthy with me 'cause the weapon's down. You know how that will go."

I let go of the shotgun and stepped forward. Gritting my teeth, I quickly leaned down and picked the collar up by the buckle, biting back a scream as the curse activated and sent a nasty shock through my palms. The curse was an impressive piece of work, designed to only activate when someone touched the buckle while the full moon was up. Any other time the collar was a normal, if sturdy, collar, but if Harvey tried to remove it, he'd get the same jolt I was feeling now. Most nights, it was plenty to deter him from an escape attempt, but when he'd been drinking, his pain receptors were dulled enough that he could stand the shocks long enough to get free.

Which meant I had to be willing to stand the curse myself to get it back on him. This wasn't our first such full moon dance, and it always hurt as much as it did the first time. I turned, still holding the damned collar and trusting my ability to hold out against the pain, then reached out and under Harvey's head to get the collar into position around his neck.

This was the most dangerous part of our little ritual: the part where I had to lean nice and close to Harvey's very sharp teeth. Sometimes, he behaved himself, but sometimes—"Son of a bitch!"

I ducked as he tried to lunge, those teeth snapping shut close enough to me that some of his slobber slimed across the shell of my ear.

So, I did what anyone in my position would do: I lunged at him in turn, sinking my blunter human teeth into the skin across the top of his muzzle. He yipped and shook his head, trying to dislodge me, but I held on, forcing my arms up and the buckle of the collar closed by feel. Only when I knew it was secure, did I let myself spit out the nasty tasting fur and release the cattle prod of a collar. I staggered back and almost fell, the sudden relaxing of my unknowingly tensed muscles nearly giving me whiplash. I forced myself to reach for the shotgun, but Harvey collapsed onto the ground outside the shed with a terribly wounded moan at the unfairness of his life.

"Fuck you," I told him and turned my back on him, surveying the route back through the trailer park with a groan.

My hands still stung like a bitch, and I knew they'd be red and blistered for an hour or so. Picking up the knocked over trashcans would have to wait until morning, damn it all. I gingerly lifted the shotgun and near juggled it until I had it held steady in the crook of arms. With another glare over my shoulder at the little shit who'd cost me my beauty sleep, I trudged back between the line of mobile homes and down the row back towards my place.

Someone waited there, leaning gracefully back across the stairs up to my deck, the protection amulet I'd given her glowing in the moonlight.

2

___

At this time of night, my best friend, Iris Johnson wore only a silk sleep scarf protecting her hair which normally spilled out like a halo around her head, rain boots due to the mud, and a fuzzy robe unbelted over a cotton nightgown hanging loose from broad shoulders down to just above her knees.

She pushed to her feet and put her hands on her hips as I trudged up, already eyeing the awkward way I held my hands. "Will you never learn to wear gloves?"

Iris shook her head and waved me past her to my front door as if it was her place instead of mine. She was over so often, it might as well be. "You stocked up on burn cream like I told you, right?"

I rolled my eyes and set the shotgun against the sofa, reminding myself to lock it back up in the safe in my bedroom before I crashed out. "I don't see the point—the boon'll have it gone in an hour."

"An hour in which you'll be wincing and unable to undress yourself. Don't try that shit with me, sugar." She lightly shoved against my shoulder, arching dark eyebrows over darker eyes when I winced. "And how much is the boon going to do for that bruise?" I shrugged, immediately regretting the action. Youth model or not, a shotgun gave a beating after firing several shots. Iris committed to her unimpressed look, and I surrendered to the inevitable and lowered myself to the sofa.

She was right anyway; the boon wasn't going to do shit for the shoulder soreness even if I was willing to wait a solid hour for my hands. Satisfied with my compliance, Iris grabbed the first aid kit she'd insisted on stocking for me, setting it at my feet and then fetched a familiar blue gel pack from the freezer. "Where'd you move the new dishcloths?" she asked after opening one drawer and then another. "I know they were here last week."

"Yeah, because you put them there when you brought them over," I shot back, amused despite the nagging aches in my body. "I had a mishap making soup a couple days ago and had to wash 'em. They're in the dryer. Haven't had time to fold laundry."

Iris retrieved one of the soft, linen cloths and folded up the cold pack, placing it over the top of my shoulder and then shoving me gently back against the cushions so my body weight held it in place. Exhausted all of a sudden, I let my eyes slip closed as she gently began tending my blistered hands even as they healed around her work.

The "boon" or so my family tended to call it. Sometimes the legend reciting went another way, but the most accepted version had the one who granted it calling it a "boon." Honestly, I wasn't sure if it was more a boon or curse, and I'm not sure any of our family members were sure, either. But for polite company and lack of a better word, we called it a boon.

The story goes that once upon a time way back when our ancestors were still traveling Europe, one of my forefathers stumbled upon some kind of spirit or fae or vampire or witch—I swear my mama used a different creature each time she told the story and if I had a buck, I'd bet my granddad did the same thing back when he was telling the story to her—losing a battle against a deadly foe. Not understanding that both of the combatants were paranormal in nature, or else not caring, my blacksmith forefather hefted an iron bar from his cart and dove into the fray, choosing to protect the first creature. Whether it was because that supernatural being looked more human or because it looked weaker no one knows, but once iron was thrown into the mix as a weapon, the other fighter was defeated and retreated back into the wilds. The first fae or witch turned to my ancestor and decided they owed a debt. And as most supernatural hate to be in a mortal's debt, they granted what they called a boon to my ancestor: he and all who came from him would be granted the ability to "see and survive the supernatural."

I would doubt the wording, but it and the iron are the only details of the story that never changed. And however it came to be, whether we were blessed or cursed by one creature or another, there was no denying that the members of my family, tracing back from my mama all the way up to that long ago and name forgotten forefather, were no longer garden-variety humans anymore. We were still mortal, but we had something extra in the tool belt as it were.

We had the Sight—an ability to "See" past the glamor keeping regular humans in the dark about the things that go bump in the night beyond the stories they tell themselves about the things they swear couldn't possibly be real. The Sight meant I could generally tell what was "normal" versus "extra," and I had to learn not to react to scales on somebody at the grocery store if nobody commented on their "awesome makeup." And considering most supernatural folks wouldn't see anything special about me, it gave me a leg up when it came to any possible confrontations. Being underestimated could be annoying, but it was better than the alternative for damn sure.

Then there was the "survive" bit of the boon. That part was trickier. For one thing, our healing wasn't a full-time gig the way the Sight is—it kicked in only for injuries or illnesses that fit the proper qualifications, i.e., those caused by supernatural beings or means. Thus, my hands would heal within the hour as they were injured with a curse, but my shoulder with its plain ole' kickback bruise would take the same number of days it would for a normal human. With an enchanted sleep, we'd wake up long before the expiration date on the spell. Cursed dolls could hurt like hell but only for a moment, and the connection between my family member and the doll in question would wear off sooner rather than later no matter how long the caster thought it was supposed to last. A vampire would have a hard time drinking from one of us as the wounds would try to close around their fangs, and if Harvey had managed to bite me, he'd only tear the skin without turning me into a werewolf like anyone else he bit. Those sorts of things.

Mortal sicknesses though: cancer, stroke, the damn flu, those could kick our asses like any other mundane human. My mama was in an assisted living facility thanks to a drunk driver T-boning her car and paralyzing her from the hips down. And me? I caught the flu every year no matter whether I got a shot or not.

But my hands would be fine. I'd heal from the spell damage faster than half the non-human residents of Asphodel Estates.

I still hadn't figured out how I felt about the boon, honestly. Iris knew that. She also knew that I had a nasty tendency to dwell on the pain as I healed for as long as I could, like it was some sort of penance for being here while my dad wasn't, and while my mama's hips would continue to pain her on the regular for the rest of her life.

Lucky for me, Iris didn't agree with me punishing myself. Or sort of lucky, I guess? Lucky she'd be here to doctor my wounds whether I liked it or not; less lucky she had the silent lecture down to an art form, all thinned lips and raised eyebrows and pointed glances. I always told myself I'd be able to ignore her ire and quiet disappointment, but me, myself, and I all knew better. That was the downside of having a friend who'd known me since before either of us went through puberty or transition.

I kept myself quiet, biting back the words that always bubbled up during these moments between us. Did she know how important she was to me? I wondered sometimes. I knew what I meant to Iris, or thought I did: I was the first person she'd shared the name "Iris" with, the one she'd trusted to take bra shopping with a foam chest shaper for the first time, and the one she'd called from New Orleans in a panic trying to decide if she really dared take the first of the hormone pills she'd gotten from her doctor there before finishing up grad school. We were supposed to go off to Tulane together—to say screw the world and greet it as a pair of two freshmen girls, the way we'd always been, but Iris had never felt she could live as openly under her parents' roof. I was supposed to be there for her when she needed me.

Instead, Dad got sick and started chemo, and I'd stayed behind to help out Mama, first only deferring enrollment for a semester, then a year, then canceling my acceptance all together when it became clear they were going to need more help than they wanted to admit. I'd gotten one crap job and then another and finally landed the property manager position here, trading on our family history with the boss, doing anything I could, doing my gods be damned best to help keep Mama ahead of the medical bills and house payments. My best didn't end up quite good enough, not with the complications in Dad's condition and treatment on and off for a good five years. She hadn't told him, not wanting to trouble him in those last weeks in hospice, but Mama let the bank foreclose on the house the month before he passed, and then filed for bankruptcy after he was gone to get out from under the medical debt and the credit card bills she'd racked up while turning into an accidental full-time caregiver for him.

I'd wanted to help them, done all I could, and in the end, it wasn't enough to let Mama keep the little house they'd lived in since they got married.

And I hadn't been there for Iris the way I'd promised.

She didn't blame me. She never did have that kind of spitefulness in her. Iris just promised to keep calling me on the regular and forgave me for sending her off alone in the pretty sundress we'd picked out together. She'd faced it, though, and damned if she hadn't taken the campus by storm, the way I always thought she could. I was so proud of her, ridiculous as it sounded, but I wished I'd been there to see her do it. No, she didn't blame me, but she likely knew *I* did, which was yet another thing she silently scolded me for.

Said silent scolding was the reason I bit my tongue instead of thanking her for being there for me yet again, and as always. She'd come back to Tartarus with a four-year bachelor's degree and a bonus master's under her belt and found a job as a youth counselor at a shelter for LGBTQ+ kids up in south Austin. Then she'd casually applied for a rental spot here at Asphodel Estates and moved in the nicest renovated airstream I'd ever seen in my life. She could afford a real apartment in Austin and something better than a forty-minute commute both ways every weekday, especially after weeknights like this one, where she lost sleep to patch me up after another round of "what'd my idiot tenants do this time?" and never said a word about it.

But she chose here. She chose to stick close to me.

Damn, I loved the woman, I thought with a tired smile. I felt Iris pat my wrapped hands gently and then carefully push me sideways to stretch out on the couch since we both knew I was unlikely to make it down the hallway to the bedroom in my post-healing energy crash. A blanket slipped over me, and I mumbled something like a thank you, knowing Iris would understand what I meant. Then the lights went out, and it was dark in my trailer. The part of me still barely awake hoped I'd get to sleep more than a couple hours this time.

To my surprise, I fell immediately into a deep dreamless sleep and didn't stir until a hesitant, but unceasing knocking on my screen door woke me.

3

The knocking came again, insistent enough that I couldn't ignore it and crash out again. I blinked hazily and sat up, wincing as my back and neck protested the hours crashed out on the couch. Comfy though it might be, it still wasn't the best place to sleep for more than a short midday nap. Iris was conspicuously absent. Either she'd taken my guest bed or let herself out after I'd fallen asleep. Either was possible, and if she'd stayed, she would have lit out early to make it to work on time. The knocking kept going, and now that I thought about it, I could hear a quiet repeating mumble of my name. "Mel, you up? Come on now, Mel. I know you're mad, but you don't have to keep me locked out. Mel?"

I stumbled to my bare feet and glanced around, pleased to see the shotgun missing. Iris knew the combination of the gun safe, too. One less thing to worry about. I scrubbed a hand across my face and walked a few feet to the door, unlocking it to see the man I'd expected. Harvey stood on the other side of the screen, looking hung over and this side of sheepish.

"Morning, Harvey," I said, not bothering to unlock and open the screen.

The dark-haired man rubbed the back of his neck under his

hideous orange trucker hat. You could not convince me werewolves weren't color blind with some of the eye-searing color combos I'd seen them wear. He forced a smile on his face under bloodshot green eyes. "You gonna let me in?"

"I don't know. You gonna try to claw my face off?" I crossed my arms and leaned against the door frame, not willing to give him an inch.

"Aww hell, Mel, you know I didn't mean it. I brought a peace offering?" He pulled his other hand from behind his back revealing a familiar plastic cup topped with whipped cream and a green straw. "Caramel frap with almond milk. Your favorite, right?"

I sighed and opened the door to let him in, making sure to snatch my sugary caffeinated fix before he made it through to the living room. Never let it be said I'm above taking a bribe, especially when I'd earned it, by all the gracious barista gods. "Take your shoes off. The ground'll be muddy as a damn swamp after all the rain yesterday afternoon, and I am not going to clean up after you."

He nodded and did as I told him. I waved him over to the stools by the tiny kitchen's breakfast bar. "You want coffee?" I asked, hovering in the space between the kitchen and the living room. "It's generic, but it's dark roast. Or the HEB brand of dark roast anyway. Has a decent kick."

"No ma'am, I'm all right. Got me a cup at Starbucks when I ran by." Ugh. He was 'ma'am'-ing me. I preferred it when he acted his age. He was at least thirty or so, though with the way werewolves aged, it was hard to tell for sure. I'd heard it explained as a sort of reversed dog years, but it didn't sound quite right. The last werewolf family who stayed here included a little boy, and he seemed to age the same as the other children in the trailer park. Maybe their aging slowed as they got older or something. Regardless, he was well past old enough to be calling me ma'am like I was some old lady, especially when he was a few years older than me.

"All right now, you've come with a bribe to get through the door. Just like last time." His shoulders sank forward, trying to shrink his leanly muscled 5'11" form into something smaller, mostly likely in hopes he'd be small enough to escape my ire. It'd be a neat trick, but sadly for him, it wasn't one that werewolves were capable of. I took a long sip of my frap, trying not to visibly wince when brain freeze hit.

Show no weakness, I reminded myself; that was the way to deal with a predator, even one in a less furry form and who clearly suffered from a hangover. Good. He deserved it. "What do you have to say for yourself this time?"

"Come on, don't be like that, Mel. I didn't mean to cause trouble." He didn't look nearly as contrite as I'd like. Typical Harvey. It never did occur to him that his idiocy on full moons meant other people lost out on sleep. Or if it did, he didn't care. I preferred to think it was the former rather than the latter, if only so I didn't have to be more pissed off with him in general. I gave him a flat stare, and a bit of comprehension seemed to get through his thick skull. A hint of contrition entered his voice as he went on. "I—I get confused when I'm shifted, sometimes."

"And by sometimes you mean when you're drunk prior to the shift." Now he did look a little more sheepish, though only a little. "How do you even manage to get drunk? Isn't that hard for y'all?"

He waggled his hand back and forth. "It's hard, not impossible. Takes a specific combination of alcohol and mixer is all. You have to have a high enough booze percentage with some sugar and caffeine to metabolize it right."

"So, what you're saying is you deliberately worked at it. On a full moon. When you know it fucks with your control." His shoulders were sinking more and more with every word I spoke. "And when you know I have to deal with it when you lose said control." I sighed, too tired to have this conversation yet again, but knowing I couldn't avoid it. Not when maybe he'd listen this time. "You can't keep pulling this, Harvey. What if you get out of the trailer park one of these nights? A regular civilian won't have a chance against a full-grown werewolf. You're gonna get someone maimed or killed, and then the State Council'll have to get involved. You know what that will mean, Harvey."

He sat back against the stool's high back and threw up his hands, his face stubborn. "Look it was just some Bailey's and hot cocoa. Why you getting so worked up about this? It's not like it's your responsibility to police my drinking now. I'm a grown ass man."

"Cocoa too? Oh good—let's throw chocolate induced food poisoning into the mix along with the hangover. You start barfing, you do it outside and clean it up, you hear me? And I am getting worked up over this *again* because I've had to get up in the middle of the night three months in a row now because *you* feel like it's too much to ask to stay sober and in control during your shift. I'm exhausted, Harvey, and my hands still ache like a bitch after having to re-fasten the collar. And you knew I would be. You *had to know* I would be because the same thing happened last time!"

My rant ran out of steam, and I slumped down against the counter and put my head in my battered hands. "I'm tired, Harvey. You're right: your behavior is not my responsibility, but the safety of everyone in this community and the mortals outside the park *are* my responsibility. Do you honestly not get why I'm pissed right now?"

His eyes said he did, but I could tell from the stubborn way he crossed his arms across his chest he wasn't prepared to admit it. "Look, I'm a grown ass man," he said again. "You're not my mother. You can't tell me what to do."

Harvey bared his teeth, showing his one crooked canine, and pushed off the stool to loom at me as best he could from across the kitchen counter. In response, I slowly pushed up to my 5'6" of height and braced my hands on the edge of the counter. No, I wasn't his mother, and I wasn't his damned alpha. *He* wasn't an alpha either, though, else he wouldn't be living in a rundown trailer park alone. There was a word for werewolves who weren't welcome among their own kind, one my boss preferred I didn't say out loud around certain of our tenants as it set off their pride like nothing else.

Omegas were the lowest of the low, pitied by the rest of the pack at best and openly driven away at worst. I didn't know which of those Harvey had been, but I knew he wasn't welcome back in his old pack. Much as he hated to admit it, if he hadn't been an omega before, he was now. And he needed this place far more than we needed him.

If this were a pack, I'd outrank him in every way that mattered. I had to remember that, and more, convince *him*, or this could get ugly. Maybe not today with his posturing bullshit, but eventually. And I was tired of trying to stave off yet another eventually.

I held his gaze, refusing to blink or look away and burying how the slightly submissive part of myself *hated* having to take control this way, even when a low growl built in his throat. Convinced I finally had his attention, I spoke. "I'm not your mother, no, and you *are* a grown ass man. However, you're a grown ass man who's acting like a toddler bitching about having to clean his room. You are an adult, you're responsible for yourself, and you need to act like it. This is your last chance, Harvey; I'm not going to have this conversation with you again. Either you get your shit together at the next full moon, or you're out."

"What, you gonna evict me? You can't! Your boss would never let you—"

"My boss would *expect* me to evict you." He stared at me dumbfounded, but still I held my gaze at him. I ignored my eyes starting to burn for a blink; I had drops, and I'd use them once he'd left. "Evicting clients who violate the rental agreement is literally a part of my job. If you continue to cause a danger or an inconvenience to the other tenants, then I would be required to kick you out."

He looked away and shook his head, trying to maintain his looming stance, but it was all over. I'd won when he lost our staring contest, and we both knew it. "You can't do this to me, Mel. Where am I supposed to go? You know how hard it is to find a place I can afford these days?"

I did know. Rent along the I-35 corridor anywhere from Waco to San Antonio could be much more than the state average, especially the closer you got to the Austin area. Add in his monthly fuzzy tantrums, and he'd be a no-go on a lease for most places. That, however, wasn't my problem, and I told him so. "I can do this, Harvey, and will if you force me to. That's my point—*you* are the one risking your rental contract, not me. You know the rules; you've obeyed them in the past. You seem to think they no longer apply to you lately, which doesn't work."

I shrugged and took another drink of my frap to give him a little time to mull it over. He still didn't look repentant, but I was too tired to keep arguing with him. "That's all I've got, Harvey. Either work with me, or don't and leave. It's up to you."

I turned my back to dismiss him and heard him growl softly again at the implied insult, though he didn't say anything else.

"Oh, and make sure you pick up the damn trash cans if you haven't yet," I called over my shoulder, ready to shift the task onto the shoulders of the one who actually deserved it. I waited until I heard his stomping feet cross the living room to snatch up his shoes and the front doors creak and slam behind him before I turned around and slumped against the counter again. I listened as he muttered to himself while he put on his work boots at my picnic table, only truly relaxing when I heard his heavy boot heels tromping down the steps. Then and only then did I sigh heavily and take another drink of my caramel goodness. If the day kept going like it was, the frap was likely to be the only bright spot of my morning.

Even if Harvey had only gotten the Tall. Cheap ass. I finished it off with a frown.

Glad to be caffeinated but wishing for another couple hours of sleep, I dragged myself into the shower, wrinkling my nose as I peeled off the tank top that now smelled ranker than I'd like. It would definitely need a wash, post-werewolf shenanigans *and* sleeping in it after. I probably needed to toss in the throw blanket too, I realized. I washed my shoulder-length brown hair on autopilot, then lathered up, letting the smell of pomegranate put me in a slightly better mood as it always did. Call it a Persephone complex or something, but *damn* did I love me some pomegranate. A quick check of the pits and legs said I could get away without shaving this morning, something I always appreciated.

Thank the fuzzy deities, it was getting closer to something like winter, too. We were in the Texas Hill Country version of autumn: meaning mornings in the 50s and afternoons up to the 80s, and more rain than we were ever used to, all of which would likely last a month, tops, before dropping into the 30s from December to February. Granted, it wasn't 100 plus degrees anymore, which was always a relief, and with the chill, I could wear jeans damn near every day. Thus, shaving would happen even less often as long as my no-dates streak continues on its rather lackluster path.

The world thought being bi…or pan (I was still working out labels for me, but bi worked well enough) meant having more opportunities to date, but not so much in my experience. Shitty "slutty bi" stereotype aside, when a girl still lived in the tiny ass town she grew up in, the number of folks she still *wanted* to date after knowing them her whole life was a surprisingly small number. Of those few in our graduating class that I'd been at all attracted to, less than half had stuck around here, instead going out of state for college or to work in one of the bigger cities if they'd decided to bypass a degree. I wished them all well. Anybody who could make their escape deserved to find some scrap of success, but damned if I didn't envy them more than a little. And also, occasionally, miss the way their butts fit into a pair of jeans, be they skinny ones over Missy Jones's lovely rear, or a worn-out pair of Levis filled out by our various varsity baseball boys.

I'd never been an athlete myself, but you can bet your ass I was there at every single game, as much for the view as for love of any of the sports. Besides, there wasn't much else to do on the weekends in this town back in high school.

With my dismal love life in mind, I said fuck it and pulled on my fave pair of black denim jeans and a bra that never failed to make my B-cup girls look more voluptuous than they actually were. I topped it off with a sniff-test-passing button-up shirt in the queer uniform standard of red and black plaid—OK yes, I *definitely* needed to do laundry—and I figured I looked both casually hot and relatively professional, or as professional as I needed to be for this job, anyway. I forewent shoes for the moment, knowing I'd want my tall boots when I headed out to brave the mud and the wet to see my mama at lunch, and headed to the second bedroom I used as a combination office and guest room. I opened the door slowly, trying to be quiet on the off-chance Iris hadn't left after all, but the coast was clear. Nobody in my trailer but me, which was the way I mostly liked it, right? Mostly?

I settled down at my laptop and logged in to check my work emails, unsurprised to find not one, not two, but *three* complaints about the noise level last night. Only one had my boss copied, praise the fluffy lords, but that one was sent by Miss Ginger as I'd feared. Boss had responded to her personally and scheduled a meeting with all three of us for later this morning at his place.

I liked Miss Ginger—it was hard *not* to like her to be honest—but damned if she wasn't one of those stout older Southern auntie types who didn't put up with anybody's shit and never failed to remind me of my late grandma giving me a *look* when I'd done something stupid. I gave one more self-indulgent sigh and then put the meeting in my Google calendar and set a reminder. No need to show up late and add insult to injury. I gritted my teeth and answered the other two complaints, placating them as best I could, and promising Harvey should be cleaning up the mess he'd left, entirely unashamed to throw him under the bus.

Whether or not a mere email would put my tenants off remained to be seen. Hopefully they'd wait to show up at my trailer in person until after my meeting with the boss. Honestly, I couldn't be bothered to worry one way or another on a dreary Thursday like this one would be, judging by the gray outside the window. I took care to keep said window clean and the blinds open if only so I'd hopefully see said annoyed tenants coming and be able to hide in the bathroom until they went away.

I was kidding about that. Most days anyway. No matter how much it seemed like a good idea at the time.

Resigned to a damp chill and the likelihood of more rain later to make my day that much better, I fiddled about a little longer, answering the rest of my more typical and less irate work emails, scheduling some repairs I could handle on my own with my tool bag and a trip or two to the Home Depot down the way, and checking my handy list of in-the-know plumbers to make yet another maintenance appointment.

Rent had been due two days prior, so I sent out reminders to the few folks I hadn't gotten either a check or an online bill pay deposit from. We always had a few people who were late as freelance and under-the-table jobs didn't always pay right on time. Having too many fingers or scales for a human made regular work difficult to find, after all. But while the nature of the boss's contracts meant I could give them a little more leeway than a regular place might, it did mean more work on my part to keep track of all of it, and spread-sheets would never be anything but a stone bitch. The upside of the contracts meant I'd only had to send two people to collections in the entire five years I'd worked there, and damned if those two hadn't deliberately set out to screw us over, so I felt no shame there. In all other cases though, the more I could avoid evictions, the better in my opinion.

Updating my Word doc of a to-do list took me right up to my meeting alarm on my phone, surprising me out of a fatigue-induced daydream. I lightly slapped my cheeks, trying to wake up without resorting to any more caffeine, knowing I'd be up all night if I drank more than three cups in a day. I wasn't exactly sure how much a tall frap equated to in boring cups of coffee, but I figured the sugar alone had to add up to an extra mug's worth or two. Then I shook myself and closed my laptop, sending it to sleep in a manner that made me envious. I moved myself out to pull on my boots and gather the small backpack that doubled as a purse when out and about on personal errands, and as a tool bag when hard at work about the Estates.

Mama hated the bulky thing, but she'd always had far more in the way of style than I did. I didn't doubt that sooner rather than later, she'd insist on either ordering a prettier replacement online or convincing Iris to help her venture out to the Outlets for the day. Whenever said trip occurred, I'd loan them my minivan and wish them the best. I shop on occasion, but the crowds in the Outlet Mall were easily my quickest route to the rare anxiety attack. Paired with the Sight, it equaled an incident I wanted to avoid, to say the least. Mama understood, thank goodness, though she'd never had the same issue tied to her own boon-fueled abilities. She loved crowds when she was younger, back when I'd been in school. She'd be more excited to attend the packed football games with the stands full of students from the various tiny towns all bussed into the local high school than I, the actual high school student in the family, was. She made it more fun though; even when stressed over Dad, she'd made a point to try to make it fun.

And contemplating my mama's opinion of my accessory game, or lack thereof, would not make the meeting I was avoiding suddenly disappear. I shook myself and swung the backpack on and then, loins girded as best they could be, headed out the door and into the damp. I immediately ducked back in for a hoodie as much to allow myself to procrastinate another moment as to keep off the drizzle.

Then, it was time to face the music, or in this case, Miss Ginger's abject disappointment and disapproval.

Unfortunately for me, facing her didn't remotely happen the way I hoped it would. And my day got decidedly worse, too.

4

They say the name of the thing can summon the thing, and I gather that's what happened with my boss specifically at some point in the past. It was the reason I'd done my best since meeting him to avoid giving any consistent call to a god or creator, even when cussing, which made my personal curse words a bit unusual at times.

In any case, semi-benevolent though Boss's landlord-ship might be, there was no denying that he was an out-and-proud demon of the incubus variety. He was also out and proud in the local gay scene which was…unexpected given the lore, and likely the reason he'd stuck around on our plane after his accidental summoning due to Hell being "tragically allocisheteronormative," in his opinion. According to the lore, in the usual way of things, incubi preyed upon the sexual desires of women, while succubae went for dudes as their prey of choice. Boss was an exception, blatantly homosexual and completely unattracted to women as a whole or even the more femme-presenting enbies, as it happened.

It didn't mean it was any easier to stand in his presence as a woman. Some of the incubus allure kicked in whether he liked it or not. Even without him actively intending for panties to drop, they did anyway. It got awkward in public. He'd taken to having his flavor of the week go with him whenever he needed to go off of the trailer park's grounds. Still, even with one of his string of flamboyantly gay lovers hanging off his arm, incidents occurred at least once a week with him at the middle of it. It happened less often around our home-town, as the neighbors knew Boss's preferences and could mostly keep their wits about them whenever they were tempted to wander over and sit in his lap.

The boon offered me a bit more resistance than most women, too, thank all that was good in the world, but it was only a bit. Any time we had to have a face-to-face regarding business, he was usually kind enough to do so in the strongest daylight hours possible and leave his windows and doors open so to disperse the effect of his allure like a perfume fresh air could chase away.

I'd still more than likely on most days end up going for a nice, cold swim in the small in-ground pool we had for the residents, some of whom required more time in the water than others, if only to cool off the heat in my cheeks. Dang, but Boss's allure was *potent* for anyone who wasn't full-on ace.

I'd discovered it helped when he was angry or just irritated about something; smoldering though he could be when pissed off, my lizard brain recognized him as a predator and thus a threat far easier when he frowned than when he smiled. If he had really good news for me, he tended to call, or more preferably as occasionally his voice could summon the libido without his face to add to it, use email. Maybe not the most efficient of boss to employee communication, especially when we literally lived on the same property, but it left me the least embarrassed and him the least hit on accidentally. It was a work in progress, but after the past few years, we were functional enough.

All of this meant using his real name was out of the question. If it had been used to summon him, I didn't want to think about what repetitive use might do for his strength on the mortal plane. We did not want to start a riot of sex starved soccer moms by accident one of these days. Instead, he was just "Boss," to me and everyone else he talked to from what I could tell. His various lovers kept to the trend, though they gave it an entirely different connotation. Which was none of my business, even if some of them liked to brag to whoever was around. Granted, the ones who bragged rarely lasted long. Boss's current honey definitely wasn't a braggart, which might have been why they'd been around the longest of any I remembered: a solid six months so far with no sign they planned to go anywhere, nor that Boss wanted them to leave.

Boss lived in a ramshackle old farmhouse he'd painted a glorious blue and white on about an acre of land the Estates' residents could access across a weathered footbridge spanning the narrowest part of the creek at the edge of the trailer park. Both properties were owned by him, but they technically were *not*, I repeat were not, the same property, something he felt very strongly about for some reason and had given more than one lecture on the subject to me or simply within my hearing on multiple occasions over the years of my employment. Mama figured it was something to do with contracts both legal and infernal, keeping his business and his *business* separate so as to make it easier to stay on this plane. I'd learned over the years not to argue with her when it came to legal terminology and contract law. She'd worked as a paralegal for years prior to Dad's cancer cropping up—I still hadn't forgiven her long-time employer for basically hanging her out to dry when it came to time off and insurance coverage—and absolutely had picked up more than a few little tidbits of knowledge. It amused me more than it should how often mortal plane law ended up twisted for supernatural purposes. Hell, the trailer park rental contacts alone made more of a difference in the lives of our tenants than I'd ever guessed they would. And never let it be said those tenants weren't grateful for the binding protection of said contract. Our occasional vampire renters in particular were always gracious about their appreciation of the ongoing open 'invitation' to rent. There were several RV spots located under a protective pole barn connected to our tenant bathhouse to keep out the sun and in a posted "garlic free zone" of a good twenty feet around said barn. It was one of the reasons that food wasn't allowed in the pool area proper, and instead relegated to the picnic tables past the pool itself.

Yes, garlic was actually deadly, apparently, along the lines of an EpiPen-requiring allergy. I was still getting used to how oddly accurate some of the legends could be, and yet completely inaccurate at the same time. One of our favorite vampire tenants—for his prompt payment and quiet nature—had been a Catholic priest back in their mortal days. You can bet your ass he never failed to remind us how silly the supposed aversion to crosses was. He said that rumor started originally as folks who might be thought to rise as vampires after death were staked and buried at a cross*road.* Thus, the myth. Though, only the staking through the heart kept the dead from rising. It was not anything to do with the crossroad. That part of the legend was due to making sure the dead and possible resulting vampire couldn't be considered a citizen of any of the townships intersecting at those crossroads.

Legality strikes again I suppose.

In any case, I actually loved visiting the boss's place, though I preferred doing so when he was off on a romantic road trip or something and I was watching his cats. The house was damn near my idea of a dream house: all old Victorian farmhouse lines and wraparound porches on not one but two stories of the three-story structure. If I ever won the lottery, I'd buy up an old house like his and fix it up nice. Knowing my luck, I'd buy a haunted one, but on the whole, I've found ghosts made for decent tenants as long as you negotiated with them properly. Really, half of those old houses always seemed like they were spirits themselves, holding so much long forgotten personality. They simply *felt* like they were haunted, even if they weren't. Boss's place certainly did, though I still wasn't convinced he didn't have a ghost or two. I'd never been in the third floor—he strictly forbade the casual guest and/or house sitter from venturing up there, and all the fiery lords knew one did not argue with a demon when they made those sorts of decrees, or at least I didn't. But that didn't mean I couldn't go up to the *second* floor and stand at the bottom of the final dimly lit and cramped as hell set of stairs and just…listen. And while yes, older houses do tend to creak a bit, they do *not* do so in the pattern of footsteps pacing back and forth across the length of the garret room above.

I lived in eternal mystery there, but oh well. I was fairly sure he wasn't pulling a Mr. Rochester and keeping a tragically mentally ill husband locked away up there. No moaning or wailing for one thing, and no sudden fires for another.

Fairly sure.

Either way, the walk out past the southeast corner of the property and his place was usually a nice one. I never turned down a chance to get some fresh air, but with the cold ass drizzle having picked up strength, I would have preferred to stay nice and dry inside.

Glad again for my sturdy boots, I sighed and set out, free hand in my pocket and a smile carefully calculated to be properly polite to any residents who poked their heads out of their trailers, while at the same time gently implying I had somewhere to be and couldn't chat. My success rate with said smile was about 50/50 to be honest, and I had a feeling they only waved and ducked back inside today as much to do with the weather as any respect for my "on my way" stride.

Reaching the creek that loosely marked the edge between the community and Boss's land, I carefully walked across the footbridge, the boards slick from the wet and mud someone else had already tracked across it at some point. I made a mental note to once again beg the boss to let me put rails up, but doubted he'd be any more ready to let me do so than the previous times I'd asked him that same question. "It would ruin the aesthetic, Melanie. You can't underestimate the appeal of a proper look to a footbridge. I mean, you wouldn't want us to attract a troll now, would you? I didn't think so."

It was another of those things I couldn't argue with him about, no matter how much I wanted to. And he wasn't wrong about the bridge troll issue either. The more elaborate a bridge was, the more likely it would attract one of the ornery creatures. Least we'd probably only end up with a *small* troll considering the size of creek and bridge respectively, but it wouldn't be any less of a pain in the ass trying to keep the thing from eating whoever crossed without paying said troll whatever they wanted. And considering how often those tolls included the "marrow from your bones!" we wouldn't be able to pay it anyway. So yeah, the boss was probably right, but damned if I cared on days like this where I felt sure I was going to end up sliding off and falling ass over tea kettle right into the creek. It only came up to my waist under the footbridge anyway, but it was sure to be cold this time of year. It moved pretty darned fast too, which meant I could end up swept farther down where the kids in the trailer park used it as an extra swimming hole which was far more than waist deep.

Don't get me wrong, I can swim and all, but these boots would weigh a girl down more than is strictly safe in fast moving water.

I stepped off the footbridge with a sigh of relief on the other side of the creek, narrowly avoiding the muddy puddle collecting at the base of the bridge. I blinked, thinking I'd seen a flicker of movement out of my peripheral vision, but before I could turn to look, Boss was calling out to me from one of the chairs on the porch. I waved and trotted over, wanting to be out of the rain, and glad we were having the meeting in something like open air. Once up on the porch, I shook my hair out of my face and turned to my boss to find him smiling softly. He waved me to one of the other well-cushioned wicker chairs and handed across a mug. "Tea? I've a mood for pumpkin chai. Must be the weather I think."

I nodded, letting him fill the mug with tea and then doctor it with sugar and almond milk, as I always preferred in the rare times I went in for tea instead of coffee. I wrapped my chilly hands around the blissfully hot mug and breathed in the scent that meant autumn the same way hot apple cider did. I blew on the tea, then sipped, glad to find the milk had cooled it enough that I wouldn't manage to burn the shit out of my tongue like I often did. Then I leaned back, trying to relax as much as it looked like he was and hoping that was a good sign for the meeting to come.

Boss looked different today, as he always did as time passed. I thought the turtleneck and soft looking tan leather jacket highlighted how different he looked than he had six months ago and prior to meeting his current lover, Terry. Most folks didn't mention or even notice his slow metamorphosis, but about a year into my employment, I'd gotten tipsy enough at a trailer park-wide potluck to ask him about it. I didn't know if it was all incubi, but he tended to shift based on the desires of those he was involved with or was interested in being involved with. It was almost imperceptible, tiny changes in his appearance over time until he'd look completely different six months later, though he'd consistently looked Latino as long as I'd known him.

The last look he'd sported had been one of those massive 6'4"-ish leather daddy types, sporting a truly ridiculous beard as well as tattoos littering the hulking biceps under white tank tops and cut off denim vests. Now though, he was lither, still tall, though a few inches shorter than the leather daddy had been. His skin and hair were a rich brown leaning towards black at the hair and eyes. He had that "is he really Latino or is he an Italian model hired because Hollywood 'couldn't find' an actual brown guy with enough 'name recognition'" thing going on for now.

It was definitely a good look on him (they were *all* good looks on him), though I personally missed the tattoos, if not the beard and build liable to challenge a literal bear for sheer size. I didn't doubt this was more to the taste of his current enby lover though. I wondered if he'd keep changing this time, or if with him being settled into a slightly more stable relationship, his looks would stay semi-stable too as long as they were together. Who knew?

The lover in question—and my standing pedicure date—Terry, in contrast to the boss's tall model look, stood on the short side at only an inch or two taller than me with the chest hair and round tummy of a proper bear. Though with their open, welcoming smile and diminutive height, they were more of a cuddly care bear than a grizzly like Boss had been in his last physical form. Hollywood would have taken one look at the pair of them and decided they didn't "fit" together, but for those of us in the real world, the way the pair of them looked at each other told how well suited for each other they really were.

I really hoped they'd stick. Terry deserved to be part of that kind of adorably hot couple.

Boss smiled at me, slowly smirking as if he'd read all my thoughts on my face, and I fought down the expected blush and tingle in my belly. No time for that, and no use in it either considering I was single. I could always head home to my trusty vibrator afterwards, but masturbating to my boss's face was creepier than I could handle, incubus or not.

I shook my head and took another long drink, trying to lose the dryness of my mouth in the hot spicy taste. Somewhat calmed, I looked out across his backyard toward the creek and the park beyond. "It's a bitch of a day, isn't it? I'll have to switch the damn heater on at this rate."

"This time of year does seem to play for unpredictable, doesn't it? You'll need to call about getting a tech out here to check everyone's systems in the next week, I'd suggest. Want to make sure they won't catch fire or have the system shut down completely when they try to run their own heaters," Boss mused, closing his eyes and breathing in deeply as if to test the very air around us. "Yes, I think we'll finally get our first freeze soon. Best to be prepared."

I nodded, then pulled my phone out and made the note to make the call tomorrow. Sooner was always better than later when it came to maintenance calls, and Boss had a way of reading the weather. I figured that was as much due to being alive for centuries in Texas than due to any uncanny ability related to his demonic self. Sex demons rarely had much to do with forecasting the weather, I'd guess. Since I had my phone out, I checked the time. "Miss Ginger's running a little late. That's unlike her."

"No, no, she's right over there. Just past the creek," Boss commented, waving a languid hand in the direction he meant.

I looked and saw the green clad figure he meant. She stood there on the bank of the creek, looking across it. Was she waiting for us to come to her or—

Miss Ginger screamed.

5

Her voice rang loud and terrified enough to have Boss and I both leaping to our feet, mugs dropped carelessly on the porch as we ran down the porch steps toward the creek. "There!" Miss Ginger yelled, seeing us coming. She waved a hand madly towards a spot on our side of the creek. "She's right over there. Get her!"

We ran to where she was pointing and stopped short at what we found, the shock of it paralyzing us in our tracks. There, half in the water, half sprawled across the bank was the bloody form of a woman. "Oh shit," I murmured, then threw myself forward to pull her from the water and check her pulse. "She's breathing!" I shouted at both Boss, who'd shaken off his own shock to come to my side, and Miss Ginger across the way. "She's hurt—get Sadie!"

Miss Ginger waved and shot off at a run toward our resident witch's RV, leaving me to get a closer look at the woman I'd pulled from the water. Four sluggishly bleeding wounds slashed across her pale skin, starting up under the line of her dark hair and slanting down across her forehead and cheeks, coming dangerously close to blinding her. Claw marks if I was right, and considering how often I'd caught claws with various parts of my body in the course of my duties, I figured I was probably correct. The worst though was a vicious bite mark on her forearm near to the elbow. I could see the teeth marks clearly and felt bile rise in my throat as I realized the teeth had gone almost completely through her arm. There was a terrible chance she would never use that arm again, I realized. "We've got to get her to a hospital," I muttered, only to trail off as Boss forced his face into my line of sight and shook his head. "Huh?"

"We cannot take her to a hospital, Melanie, not until we figure out who or what bit her." He nodded toward the wounds. "I could be mistaken, but those look like werewolf bites. As far as I know, there is only one were close enough to be the perpetrator."

"No," I breathed, his meaning sinking like a stone in my stomach. "No, it couldn't have been Harvey. It's been hours since moonset. There's no way."

He studied me, dark eyes sympathetic but unyielding. "You would bet your life on it? Her life?"

"No, I mean, yes, I... Fuck, Boss, he might piss me off, but he's always been harmless except for the occasional trashcan. I can't believe he did this. I can't." My employer looked like he wanted to argue the point, but a flash of color and a shout cut us off short.

With Miss Ginger and some of the other residents trailing behind her, Sadie came at a run almost graceful enough to be a dance. Everything Sadie did was graceful, as if she refused to be seen doing anything clumsy. She leaped across the footbridge, then loped over to us, her long red curls streaming behind her like a banner along with the ties of the unseasonal silk dress she wore skimming the top of her knees. Even in the circumstances, I couldn't help but be struck again by how damned stunning she was.

She knew it, too.

Lips perfectly done up in scarlet lipstick twisted at the corners as she sank to her bare knees beside us, taking a moment to shoot me a wink with her heavily lined blue eyes. I looked away, back down to the victim, trying not to scowl with irritation she'd gotten to me yet again.

OK, so yes it was possible I'd had a drunken hook up with her once, or, well, more like three or possibly six times, but she'd made it clear following each of our encounters that there was nothing resembling a relationship ever to happen between us. "Someone like me can't afford to settle down for just anyone. You understand, don't you?" That was a direct quote, and one she'd paired with a patronizing little kiss on the cheek.

So yeah, she was basically a stone bitch who'd broken my heart and enjoyed continuing to tease me with what she wasn't interested in giving up again (until her next whim anyway), but she was still the closest thing to a medic we had at Asphodel. She was one of the most talented witches I'd ever met in my life. Right now, we needed her, and I'd deal with my discomfort until the girl was taken care of. "Miss Ginger saw her half in the creek. No idea how long she was down there, but she's awful cold to the touch."

Sadie delicately laid her hand against the woman's neck, checking both her pulse and the temperature of her skin. "Her pulse is thready. We need to get her out of the wet."

"My porch—the long chaise should work," Boss said, already sliding his hands under her ankles, ready to lift when we were. "There is hot water in the kettle as well."

"Perfect. Mel, if you would take her other side, please, dear?" I bit back a retort at her using a pet name but did as she bid, sliding my arms under the girl's shoulder and hip to link across with Sadie's own, forming something almost like a basket around her torso. "Harvey, get her head, would you?"

I blinked to realize our werewolf had come with Sadie. His face was ghostly pale and his eyes wide and terrified. He wouldn't meet my gaze, only focused on the girl in all our arms. His voice shook when he answered, but his hands were steady as he carefully secured his broad hands cradling her head and neck so it wouldn't loll back when we carried her to the dry. "Y-yeah, yeah, I got her. Lift on three."

On his count, the four of us rose as in sync as we could. Predictably, I was the only one who struggled with the movement, my mortal clumsiness fighting with the slick grass and mud I was standing in. I didn't drop her though, and that was what mattered in my book. It occurred to me as we were shuffling towards the steps that really Harvey could have carried her easily all by himself, but a quick look at his face had me second-guessing. He was still pale and trembling almost imperceptibly. Whatever had happened to this girl, it had him all shook up, no matter if he really was the one who'd hurt her or not.

We got her settled on the chaise, and Sadie reached imperiously behind her for the embroidered canvas bag one of the stragglers had apparently carried for her from her trailer. I knew from prior experience the thing was far, far heavier than it looked, Sadie having done some sort of spell to make the bag with its compartments far larger on the inside than it was on the outside though the bag retained all of its actual weight even if the size didn't change. It carried all of her workings and individual spell components, dried and fresh herbs in some sort of stasis spell side by side with jars of pond scum and teeth, bloody and otherwise and also human and otherwise—I never asked where she got them. She also had a collection of teas and tonics already brewed and ready to be either added to hot water or simply drunk down as they were. She pulled out one of the latter and gently tipped up the woman's head to trickle it down her throat, then reached for one of the bags of dried teas, handing it over to Boss to add to the hot water in the kettle on the table. A quick chant and the kettle began to steam, the water reheated to the boiling temperature she wanted.

"The first was a general blood pressure potion—it'll help with the effect of the blood she must have already lost. The tea will aid in replenishing said blood, as well as getting her body temperature back up with the heat. And this," she reached back in the bag for a fat mason jar with a thick rust colored salve inside, "will help fight off infection and get the wounds to close. I'll bandage up the arm for sure, but any on her face will likely block her vision, and I don't want her panicking when she wakes."

She began to carefully spread the salve onto the bleeding gashes with a single finger, hesitating each time the unconscious woman stirred and whimpered in her sleep at the pain. "She's still got decent sensation. That's a good sign. A blanket and some towels wouldn't go amiss."

She turned those blue eyes up to Boss who nodded, heading inside to get what she'd asked for. It was a sign of how bad Sadie's patient looked that he hadn't blinked at the imperious redhead giving him, of all beings in the trailer park, orders.

"Can you tell how long she was out there?" Miss Ginger asked, her eyes drifting to Harvey's hunched shoulders and stricken face. I felt for the werewolf. Even if I didn't think he was guilty, he sure looked it.

Sadie followed Miss Ginger's gaze to its destination and raised her perfectly plucked eyebrows, clearly getting what Miss Ginger was implying. "It's hard to tell. I'd say the wounds happened sometime earlier this morning, but couldn't give you an exact time. Something in the wound is slowing the healing time—they look fresh, but with her having been in the water, they couldn't possibly be, and indeed the bleeding should have slowed too." She tapped a clean finger against her chin, then shrugged elegantly. "No, I think the wounds occurred this morning, and she either ran from her attacker and fell into the creek or was dumped there to hide the body."

"So, it could have been a werewolf then," Miss Ginger pressed, her habitual mirrored sunglasses still leveled at Harvey.

At her words though, he looked up from the ground slowly, shoulders still hunched. "No, it couldn't," he said softly but resolutely, clearly having no doubts about his answer. "Look, I—I know you're thinking I done this, you're all thinking it, but I didn't. And it wasn't another wolf neither."

"How do you know?" I asked as gently as I could, trying not to spook him into clamming up again.

He gave a low sigh that almost sounded like a groan and shook himself once, twice, and then spoke. "A werewolf during the shift isn't mindless, not really, not like the movies tell ya. We're more instinctual, true, but not raving monsters. Giving someone the bite," he hesitated, then forced himself to continue, "it's a big deal. It's a contract between a pack and an applicant. It's—it's *not* supposed to be used as a punishment or an attack. Pack is family, is protection. A wolf in their right mind doesn't want a new pack member who's terrified off the bat, you know?"

"What about a wolf who *isn't* in their right mind?" Miss Ginger pressed. I wanted to strangle her for the suspicious tone still in her voice.

Harvey looked her dead in the eyes, not hiding behind the brim of his hat any longer. "A werewolf out of their mind, one gone feral... Yeah, they might have bit a girl this way. But they wouldn't have stopped. A bite is either a turning, or it's just what it sounds like: a bite. The start to a fucking meal. And a predator doesn't leave their food in mid-meal. You get me now?"

I certainly did, and I fought down a shudder at the thought of dying that way: eaten alive by a werewolf stronger than I could ever be. Could the boon heal that? How long could I last if my wounds tried to close themselves as fast as a monster tried to eat me? This time I did shudder; I couldn't help it, and I tried not to see how Harvey's shoulders hunched farther forward as his eyes darted away from me. I swallowed and tried to recover the conversation.

"So, it's unlikely she's gonna turn then, right?" I managed, and Harvey gave a short jerk of a nod. I bit my lip thinking, then turned back to Sadie. "If she's not going to turn, the wounds aren't going to heal on their own, are they?"

Sadie gave me a deliberately disappointed look. "I believe I already said something's slowing the healing down, didn't I? If she was turning, the wounds would be healing faster, not slower."

"So, you don't think it's a werewolf either, then?" I mentally begged her to agree with me, not wanting to deal with the low-key supernatural riot that might start if she said otherwise.

She rolled her eyes. "Anything's possible around here. *But,*" she stressed as Miss Ginger looked about ready to interrupt, "it does seem less likely it's a were bite. We'll only know for sure if she turns on the next full moon. It's possible, if improbable, that her reaction to a were bite could be slowed for some reason, but I can't tell for sure one way or another until then."

"Packs can't either," Harvey added softly, his eyes now glued to the young woman on the chaise. "The bite doesn't take with everyone. With a willing applicant, they're bitten and then cossetted up some for the rest of the month until they've got a chance to change with the moon."

"And if it doesn't take?" Miss Ginger asked. "What will we be dealing with then?"

Harvey growled a little under his breath. "If it was a werewolf bite, which I told you it isn't, and it doesn't take, it'll go two ways. Either the applicant survives, or they don't. It's a fifty/fifty shot with anyone resistant to the bite."

He shrugged. "Best thing for her now is to take care of her wounds and hope they heal over time."

Sadie eyed him, apparently surprised to find the redneck wolf she'd often dismissed could have such insight into one of her patients. "But if she *is* going to change... Are there any signs or treatment we should be giving her?"

Harvey hesitated, looking around at those gathered by us, and I nodded to him, encouraging him to answer and get it over with.

"If she's accepting a bite, she's gonna need meat, lots of it when she wakes up. She'll be craving raw, but it'll fuck up her stomach something awful. It's like the stomach doesn't realize a werewolf's still mostly human when they wake up. Best to make sure cooked meat is right in front of her when she wants it, then she'll take what she can get no matter what she actually wants."

Each word sounded painful as Harvey spoke, and I wondered again what he'd run from in his home pack. Blame the look on his face when the girl was discovered and the accusations started flying, but I no longer thought he'd been the one to screw things up with those other wolves he never talked about instead of the other way around. If I was honest with myself, I never actually thought that, not really— he'd just been pissing me off more than usual with the full moon shenanigans.

I studied the young woman again, then turned to Sadie. "Can you keep her out until someone gets back with food?" She nodded. "Excellent. I'm thinking a Rudy's run would prolly be best; we can order up a shit ton of barbecue for her for a late lunch. If you think she'll go for that," I added with a raised eyebrow to Harvey who nodded. "Anything better for her than the rest?"

"The moist brisket will prolly go down easiest, but a new wolf will gorge their way through any of it." He rubbed at the scruff on his jaw, his brow furrowed in thought and worry. "Their ribs might not be a bad idea either. It'll feel more like a kill with the bones to gnaw on."

I blinked at that particular detail but was careful not to say anything.

"OK, Rudy's it is then. Group order?" I asked, looking at the other residents who'd hovered around while we tended to the injured woman.

One of them, a barrow wight called Alex who'd mostly kept to themselves since moving in only a few months prior, hesitantly held up a hand before anyone else could answer. "If she needs food sooner rather than later, should we maybe buy from The Smokehouse? It's much closer..."

They trailed off as most of us stared back at them, unwilling to scoff when the shy wight so rarely felt comfortable speaking up, but still doubting their taste and struggling to agree to subject ourselves to sub-par barbecue.

The barbecue joint in question called "The Smokehouse"—in Texas, there's almost always a barbecue joint in every small town and seven out of ten are named something similar to "Smokehouse"—got some decent traffic as it was right off the highway. But they were technically outside our town limits and were a little too proud of that fact for most of Tartarus's residents, our folks included, to be willing to head there very often. The "we'll support our local businesses but you specifically said you aren't local so screw you" kind of attitude amused the hell out of me except for those days when I craved ribs, but didn't dare get caught heading to The Smokehouse. If it had been a Rudy's, that would have been another thing entirely. Like Dairy Queen and Buc-ee's, Rudy's was damn near a Texas institution, and one could be forgiven for venturing out of our corner of the world for it. Fairly often after announcing an HEB run, the resident attempting the grocery trip in question ended up coerced into taking a collection of around dozen or more orders for a stop off at the Rudy's a few exits past the aforementioned HEB. What can I say—we've all got our priorities.

I bit back a groan. Our preferences weren't the priority right then; the wounded woman was. Luckily before I could force myself to agree with Alex, Sadie spoke up. "It's fine—she'll hold under the sleep spell for at least an hour or so. Plenty of time to get to Rudy's and back, and their beans and coleslaw are far superior to anything The Smokehouse has. And I deserve lunch after all of this."

Of course she did, I thought wryly. "That works then—anyone else want to share the order?" At the expected nods from everyone including Alex who seemed relieved to be overruled, I reached out to snag Harvey's trucker hat and flipped it. I pulled out a precious twenty from my wallet and tossed it in the hat, then passed it on to Miss Ginger to get the collection going. I tried not to sigh as I saw my longed-for lunch at Elysian Fields with Mama and afternoon nap vanish in the face of either a road trip or observation of our mystery guest. "Someone's gonna need to go and get it and I—"

"I can get it! I can drive!" Khoi, a lanky Asian who looked late teens but was likely older than any of the other residents within view with the exception of Boss, and possibly Miss Ginger though one didn't dare ask a lady her real age around here anymore than they did in the rest of the South, bounced on the balls of his feet at the thought. He rarely drove and certainly didn't have a vehicle of his own as far as I knew though I didn't know why exactly, and each opportunity to drive someone else's car was a treat in his opinion.

I eyed him. "If someone goes with you, you could drive my van, maybe. How's your hands looking?"

He shoved back the sleeves of the hoodie he wore everywhere but the pool and waved his hands in front of my face, letting me see he was scale free and his fingers didn't sport any webbing. Khoi was something like a mermaid, though I imagined what he actually was answered to a name none of us would recognize. This part of Texas had pretty solid Asian populations with pockets in the not too far off Austin of Vietnamese, Korean, and Indian especially, though there were families of Bangladeshi and Chinese, as well. With them had come their nations' supernatural residents, but those tended to be policed by their own, thankfully, as the more benevolent of those supernatural communities, kitsune and garuda and the like, made sure the more vicious, the kappas and oni and mogwai and who knew what else, didn't threaten the mortals in their community if at all possible.

Khoi was... Well, I felt fairly certain he leaned to the benevolent side, but on the other hand, Boss had had a very pointed conversation with him about how "yes people will be in the pool with you but that does *not* make them acceptable prey" when we had the new resident meeting and contract signing with the Vietnamese supernatural. Occasional cannibalism aside (though was it technically cannibalism when we weren't the same species as he was? Inquiring minds did not *at all* want to know), he was a relatively helpful tenant, taking on the pool cleaning duties by choice since he spent the most time there in his koi-tailed and finned form. He was certainly pretty for sure, but that didn't make him any less lethal, nor did it mean his sort of middle of the road form with scales and razor-sharp teeth under a barely-there nose would be any less upsetting to the general public.

"As long as you remember to keep the scales under wraps, you can go," I affirmed again with a nod. "Harvey, you good to go with him?" I asked, guessing he might want some space about now. He nodded, eyes painfully grateful. "Thanks. I appreciate it. We got all the cash tossed in we're gonna get?"

Miss Ginger passed the hat back, and I did a quick count before passing it back to Harvey, bills and all. Over a hundred bucks this round. Nice. I made a note in my phone to keep anyone from claiming to be cheated when the food arrived. Harvey nodded to me and stood to go "Everybody text me what ya want. I'll get as much of everything as I can with this."

"You sure you trust your vehicle with that one driving?" Miss

Ginger asked, folding her arms across her chest and ignoring the wounded look on Khoi's face at her words.

I resisted the urge to snap at her. She wasn't usually this dismissive of the more visibly non-human members of the community. But then, we usually didn't have strange young women bleeding all over my boss's porch. I guessed I could give her a pass this time, though it was straining my patience to do so.

With that in mind, I shrugged, deliberately careless and unconcerned, and nodded. "Khoi's driven Velma before, and Harvey knows where to go. Keys are hanging by my door by the way, Harvey. But yeah, they'll be fine."

"Fair enough. We'll keep an eye on her 'til they get back."

6

Like a queen, Miss Ginger turned away dismissing 'her' new delivery drivers, and began to order everyone else about, directing them in the best way to carry the girl and to get the bed clothes in Boss's ground floor guest room turned down as she decided that would be the best place for the girl to rest while we all got a trailer prepped for her. It was more than a little presumptuous with Boss and me right there, but frankly as exhausted as I felt, I was more than willing to let her take charge if she wanted to. I waved as Harvey and Khoi headed out, and idly thought I'd need to grab a snack if I wanted to hold out until they got back with brisket. A Frappuccino did not a breakfast make, and even if it had, I'd finished it off hours ago.

Had that only been a few hours ago? With all the commotion, it seemed like days since the morning started with its face off against Harvey and the exhausting round of mundane day job tasks and the discovery of a bloody woman half in the creek. Remembering, my stomachache eased, hunger chased away temporarily by the image of her still oozing bloody face and arm. Hopefully she'd have woken up by the time they got back, I thought. Whatever I thought about her otherwise, Sadie was a damn good witch, and her salves could heal a wound up quick like. I couldn't imagine they wouldn't be working on our new foundling.

Granted, I bet the wounds would still scar, though they would heal faster than usual under Sadie's ministrations.

Unless the stranger *had been* bitten by a werewolf, as everyone seemed convinced of, or everyone but Harvey and me. If that was the case, the wounds would heal, but the scars should fade to a silvery pale before the next full moon and her subsequent trans-formation.

Those would be the only scars a werewolf ever had again. Even old human injury scars would be annihilated by the werewolf virus, but the mark that turned them—it was theirs to bear for the rest of their extended unnatural lives. Born werewolves never had any scars at all, which was another matter entirely.

No, the girl might never lose her scars, but hopefully she'd be strong enough to survive them, to refuse to let the attack define her, whatever the long-term effect was.

The rest of the afternoon passed fairly calm. I barely remembered to text Mama I'd be missing our standing daily lunch date at her apartment at the local assisted living center, Elysian Fields, and promising I'd call her either later or the following day to give her the details on all the drama.

Once Harvey and Khoi arrived back at Boss's place, they handed out the barbecue to everyone who'd chipped in, along with some resi-dents who hadn't been there to contribute as always happened—I made a mental list of those individuals to make sure they ponied up next time—and everyone scattered to their respective homes to eat out of the now steadily falling rain. Before the guys headed off too, I made the careful introduction to the young woman who'd awakened some twenty minutes before their arrival, and then the five of us—the stranger, Boss, Miss Ginger, Sadie, and I—settled in to eat at Boss's gorgeous farmhouse kitchen table.

She wasn't talking, which worried me, but she didn't seem too utterly terrified. Wary as hell, and who could blame her, but not flat out scared beyond belief. She had her ID tucked away in a pocket to show us: "Inna Ivanova" with an address in an apartment complex on the very edge of the next town over.

To my surprise, she wasn't panicking about being asked to stay on site for the next few weeks. I wasn't sure if Boss was the cause—he'd turned on the influence deliberately for once, offering to cover her apartment's rent and that of a small furnished RV we kept open for short-term residents—but it seemed likely he was pulling out all the stops to near-hypnotize her into agreeing with what he wanted her to do. I didn't want to think about whether or not I'd been talked into my job the same way. That had worked out for me after all, hadn't it? Regardless of the cause, she agreed to the rental without any complaint and swooned in his direction during dinner, though Sadie was the only one she'd let close, Boss included.

With the meal finished up and the few leftovers divided out amongst every one—I snagged the remaining new potatoes to add to eggs scrambled up with some of the lean brisket I'd also claimed for dinner in the next few days—Sadie and I escorted our silent new tenant over to the little trailer style RV just on the other side of the footbridge and made up the beds while Inna watched us with those big dark eyes all but glowing in between the vicious cuts across her face. They looked somewhat less terrifying with Sadie's goo smeared all over them. I showed Inna the amenities as they were, explaining the bathroom and the shower which occasionally confused folk, and gave my normal warning to keep it relatively calm in the trailer itself. We had the trailer hitch propped up and the wheels secured with blocks, but it didn't mean a body couldn't still manage to tip the small thing over if they were doing cartwheels inside or what not.

Sadie tried to leave with me, but Inna showed her first sign of fear and dragged her back in the door with her. Sadie sighed and gave me a look that said "I will be charging your boss double for this one" and then let herself be led back inside.

Better her than me, I thought tiredly, forcing myself not to lean back against the trailer as I knew I'd end up falling asleep where I stood, the exhaustion of the day finally sinking over me like a blow.

"You OK?" The words weren't enough to truly startle me as such, but they had my eyes opening. I'd expected someone to come find me, though I'd figured it would be Iris or the boss. Instead, it was Harvey, peering up at me from under that damn ugly ass trucker hat which he'd reclaimed after it was done being the collection plate. I made another vague mental note to burn it if I could. I'd replace it with another less neon one – I wasn't gonna be so cruel as to get rid of his hats entirely – but I wasn't awake enough to deal with how bright the damn thing was. Though his hat was keeping off the damp unlike my hoodie which I'd forgotten to lift back up after I'd left the trailer. He shuffled closer and asked again, "You sure you're OK? You look pretty out of it."

"Just tired, Harvey. It's been a much longer day than I thought it would," I said, finally forcing myself to walk back towards my place, nodding for him to join me when he hesitated as we passed his place.

He kept pace with me easily, reaching out carefully to place a hand under my elbow when it looked like I was starting to sway. "Long day and you didn't get much sleep last night, either, huh?"

"Yeah well, shit happens," I managed, ignoring the guilt on his face. "It would have been an exhausting day even if I had managed a solid nine hours. Not your fault today went to hell."

We made it to my trailer and trudged up the porch stairs, both of us cringing at the awful creak of the door I'd forgotten to WD40 during the day like I'd planned. Harvey toed off his boots inside the door without me asking and helped steady me while I dragged mine off, too. I let him, too past the point of give a shit to fight against someone helping me. "Fuck, I feel like I want a drink, but I know I have emails I need to get to since this afternoon screwed my work schedule."

"Get yourself the beer, Mel. The boss knows what you were up to all day. Doubt he's expecting you to finish anything up tonight."

I debated, then decided he was right. To hell with responsibility, I wanted a damn drink. "Yeah, yeah. Makes sense. Grab us something will you? I think I've got Strongbow in there maybe? Ray, the RV guy —you know who I mean?" Harvey nodded. "He always brings me over a couple six packs when he's trying to convince Boss to consign a couple new RVs. 'S like he thinks I can talk Boss into agreeing with him even though it hasn't worked yet."

"That or he's hitting on you," Harvey said, cracking open one of the cans like an exclamation point to his statement.

I took the cider gratefully but scowled at him. "Bullshit. I'd know if he was hitting on me. He's a smarmy sales guy, that's all."

"Mel, you're the last person to know if someone was hitting on you. Hell, half the trailer park has tried to get the 'property manager's panties perk' but you never notice." He huffed out a laugh at my wide-eyed shock.

I scoffed and shook my head, trying to make some sense out of what he'd said but finding nothing. "You're full of shit. And a perk? I'm a perk? You're out of your damn mind, Harvey."

"Whatever you say," he laughed, ignoring my scowl at him. He quieted for a moment, sipping the Strongbow and visibly weighing his words. "Thanks, by the way."

"For what?" I asked, tired mind trying to keep up but failing miserably.

"For trying to stick up for me. You didn't have to. Hell, you had reason not to, considering last night and all." He fiddled with the tab of the can, refusing to look at me. "So, thanks. I mean it."

I reached over and tapped my can to his, then lifted it in a salute. "I won't lie. I was pissed as hell at you earlier. Probably, more pissed about having to shoot at you than I was about you being off leash and stalking trash cans." I shrugged again, not sure how to explain myself. "But you made sense with what you were saying, and you were right there willing to help. Made it easier to keep myself calm about every-thing when we found the girl."

He mulled over that, scratching his forehead under the brim of his hat. "I guess. Didn't seem like many folks thought so, but I had to try, you know?" I nodded, and he took another long drink. "It fucks with you having to shoot at me?"

I had the feeling he hadn't meant it as a question until it came out that way.

"I... I don't like hurting people, Harvey. I'll do it if I have to because it's not likely anyone else can do it. And at least usually I'm doing it to protect somebody else, but it doesn't mean I like it." This time I was the one hiding in my beer can. "It's worse when it's people I know... when it's friends. It—it makes me feel even less human than I am. Like I'm worse than the monsters. They play by the rules of their nature for the most part. Me, I should be a bitty human, but I break all the rules of what I human should be capable of." I leaned my head back against the couch cushions. "I don't hate the boon. I don't. There's no point for one thing. Hating it won't make it go away. But it doesn't mean I'm comfortable being whatever the hell my family is. We're neither fish nor fowl, and I'm reminded every single time I have to use the boon against a resident."

He nodded slowly, green eyes fixed on me from under the mess of his hat hair. I wasn't remotely comfortable under that kind of scrutiny, but I'd been the one to invite him in and start pouring out my damn soul to him. I couldn't blame him trying to understand me and what I was saying. After a beat, he returned the gesture I'd made of clinking his can against mine. "For what it's worth, I'm sorry I've been an asshole about the collar lately. You were right, I do know better, and being an asshole got me in this fix with the girl showing up and folks thinking I must 'a done it since I was wandering last night." He scrubbed at his face again before going on. "This time of year is tough for me. My old pack—we celebrated the old holy days, Samhain especially. A couple of the senior pack members mated with witch types, so that was what you did. I guess I miss it this time of year. Gets me all restless and doing stupid shit."

"You can't go back, can you?" I asked quietly.

He didn't answer, but then I didn't really expect him to. We finished our drinks in silence, and then he headed on home for the night.

I checked the time and realized it was too late to call Mama. I texted her instead since she'd likely have her phone silenced, letting her know she could call me whenever she felt awake enough to do so in the morning. I wanted her take on the mess we'd had fall into our laps. She had contacts even the boss didn't; she might know of a rogue werewolf in the area or if the nearest pack out by Houston had lost someone or recognized the girl. I'd snapped Inna's picture, too. I didn't know if she'd have a clue, but it was a better chance than nothing.

Iris should still be up, but I honestly didn't know if I had the energy for rehashing the day's events, and she still had work in the morning and had gotten as little sleep as I had, probably less now that I thought about it.

No, I'd tell her in the morning too, I decided. Better to get some rest and hope the morning would be less stressful.

7

For the second morning in a row, I woke to knocking on my front door, this time at a bare 7:30AM, though as I saw when I sleepily opened the door, this knocker didn't come bearing gifts of sugary caffeine goodness. Miss Ginger waited for me, hands on her hips, and a stern expression on her face.

Her face wasn't always stern, but when it was, it was the kind of face that had a body sitting up straight and wondering what they'd done wrong. My first-grade teacher had a similar look and terrorized half the school with it, her students or not. Miss Ginger, though, you wanted to love, not fear. She was a middle-aged black woman, and how middle-aged or even if it was more Medieval Aged, I couldn't tell you because I certainly wasn't going to be fool enough to ask. She passed as human, except for the fact that she hadn't aged in the many years I'd known her, long before I'd signed on at Asphodel Estates. Hell, she'd been a friend of my mama's since before I was born. Mama'd even worked at Miss Ginger's beauty parlor while she was in high school and swore Miss Ginger looked the same age even back then.

Miss Ginger still owned the beauty parlor and worked there four days a week. Two of the remaining three days, she worked out of her trailer here at the Estates, offering her prodigious skills in beautifying hair, skin, scales, and feathers to those of our community who had a harder time showing their faces in public. She didn't charge her neighbors near as much here as the beauty parlor did either, something we all did our best to repay in plenty of tips and covering her share of the Rudy's trips every other time or so. Amusingly in my mind, she never changed her own hairstyle—what looked to be thick braids always wrapped up tightly under scarves—as long as I'd known her. It made me wonder if there was more to her hair than I'd been told, but again, I wasn't about to ask.

"We never got our meeting yesterday," she began, and I was unable to smother a groan at her words. "Excuse me?" Her eyebrows raised, and I cringed at the implied disapproval.

"Sorry, Miss Ginger. Sorry," I managed. "Not awake yet. You're right; we didn't. You want the boss, too? He may not be up yet, but I can call and see if he can come have his coffee here. I need to start the coffee maker anyway."

She eyed me, then blinked, her expression unexpectedly softening. "You are all done in, aren't you? You get any sleep at all last night?"

"A lot more than I did the night before," I answered wryly, then internally cringed as I realized that would feed right into her ire. I waved her in, leaving the main door open inside the screen as I knew the residents would be dropping by now that someone had been admitted to my office. Following her over to my kitchen, I scrambled to attempt to make up for my conversational fumble. "Harvey was by until about 10 p.m. last night to check on our guest and apologize for being an ass the past few months. He's promised to get his act together starting next full moon and explained a little of his behavior to me."

"And what was his explanation? He gonna pay for the damage to my trailer?" She accepted a seat at the bar, echoing Harvey's pick of stool yesterday morning though I wasn't about to bring up the similarity. She waited until I'd gone through the familiar motions of setting the coffee going, then pressed me again. "Well? What did he have to say for himself?"

I leaned on the counter. "Honestly, Miss Ginger, that's between me and him. It's private, and I take the privacy of my residents seriously, you know that."

"So, I'm supposed to trust that he's repentant and won't do this again? Without any explanation?" She looked incensed, and I was about to try to get my sleep brain wrapped around the right words to talk her down when there came another tap on the doorframe of the screen door.

Harvey stood framed against the dim light of the sun attempting to rise behind the clouds that still hovered low in the sky. His timing could have been worse, I thought, but not by much. He'd definitely heard Miss Ginger's ranting. Even if he'd been walking this way and not right on the porch, his hearing was enhanced like every other werewolf's.

Miss Ginger snorted and muttered. "Like a bad penny, always turns up when you least expect or least want them to."

Harvey shuffled his feet in that familiar movement but squared his shoulders. "Mel, can I come in? I was looking for Miss Ginger, but seems she's already here."

What the hell, things probably couldn't get any worse between them, right? I ignored Miss Ginger's thinned lips, and waved him on in. In yet another déjà vu moment, he pulled a hand carefully from behind his back, this time with a drink carrier from Starbucks, instead of the one drink. On it was another of the caramel fraps, along with an insulated cup for something hot. I couldn't smell it from where I stood, but from the way Miss Ginger's eyes narrowed in suspicion, I'd guess she could. He handed off the frap to me, and then turned hesitantly to his adversary. "I thought I remembered you liked the—the peppermint mochas, right?"

Miss Ginger put her hands on her hips. "Is this a bribe, young man?"

I tried not to choke on my frap at the amusing picture of Harvey being a "young man" to much of anybody, but she and Harvey didn't seem to notice my amusement.

"I thought more a peace offering?" he offered tentatively. "That, and these." With his free hand, he pulled out a pack of those paint swatches Home Depot handed out from his back pocket. "I can fill and epoxy the holes no problem, and I can paint your place, too. Thought I'd see though if you maybe wanted a new color or something or if you could remember the original color on it so I can try to match it right."

Miss Ginger didn't move her hands away from her hips, and her eyes narrowed further. "You came over here before eight in the morning to offer me fancy coffee and paint samples?"

"Yes, ma'am?" he asked, clearly wary about where the conversation was about to go. I couldn't blame him after yesterday, though I had to personally give him points for interrupting Miss Ginger and I to try to smooth things over. I hoped for the sake of the shyly hopeful expression on his face that she'd see it as the olive branch it was, that he meant the gesture to be more than just a gesture—to be the start of a true apology. "I thought—I mean I know that..." He trailed off and took a slow breath, settling himself before going on. "I know I've been messing up. I do. I told Mel as much last night. Gave her an apology since she got the brunt of it. Cleaned up the trash yesterday too, but I didn't see you until the creek and that was—pardon my language but that was a clusterfuck of a day."

He shrugged and offered her the coffee again. "Didn't seem right diving into my bullshit when there was somebody hurt. So, I figured I'd try to catch you before work this morning, but you were already here. If you want a professional or something to repair the damage, I'll pay for it, but I thought I could get it done quicker. I'd do it real nice, I promise."

"Give me the damn coffee," Miss Ginger almost snapped, her hard stance deflating as she gave in to either the smell of peppermint goodness or to Harvey's impressive puppy dog eyes. I'd guessed he would be good at them, but damn had I underestimated their power. The fact that he was clearly sincere in his guilt and desire to make it right only upped the wattage of said eyes. I didn't blame Miss Ginger for giving in. "Now, I'm still not best pleased with you. Don't mistake me."

"No, ma'am. I wouldn't."

She sighed and took a sip of the drink, closing her eyes blissfully. "Now that's the good stuff. Show me what colors you got. I wouldn't mind freshening up the place—the blue's been there since Mel was in diapers. I want something with some pop to it."

She ushered Harvey out ahead of her, still talking about paint colors and did Harvey think he could maybe do window boxes and she'd always wanted a deck like mine instead of the tiny little doorstep she had currently.

"Bye," I called after them quietly, shaking my head with wry amusement, but hoping not to recapture Miss Ginger's attention now that Harvey had offered me the save. I was already up, so as much as I wanted to go back to bed, instead I headed for the fridge and a package of potstickers that totally counted as breakfast food. I warmed and crisped them up in a skillet while blissfully drinking down my own Starbucks concoction. It was a Venti this time, and I saluted Harvey's wise decisions with regards to beverages and peace offerings.

Potstickers done, I shut off the stove and put some soy and teriyaki sauce into the microwave to warm up, then stuffed my face standing there in the kitchen. There, I thought. I was fed, caffeinated, and ready to face the day and the drama that I had a deep suspicion would be a' coming.

I sighed. Now, I needed a bra.

With the caffeine to clear the wool out of my ears and the haze from my eyes, I realized I'd missed messages on my phone after I silenced it for the night. Mama returned my text and suggested we postpone lunch and have a conference call instead—leaving me on site at the estates in case anything went more wrong than it already had. I momentarily mourned the glorious Elysian Fields $3.00 lunch special and hoped I wasn't missing mac & cheese but texted her back in agreement. The more I could multi-task today the better.

The plumber had gotten back to me as well yesterday afternoon, and I gave him a call as soon as the clock hit 8 a.m. to make sure I got my tenants on his schedule for the rest of the week. Tom did damn good work—his Yelp reviews were the highest I'd ever seen for a maintenance company—and his schedule filled up quick. I had gotten good at being pretty proactive about scheduling if I could manage it. Emergency calls were a crap shoot, but normal maintenance or things that weren't panic inducing—those I did my best to get on Tom's calendar sooner rather than later.

Next, while I was calling repair people, I called the boss's regular HVAC company for the heater checks we'd talked about. I hadn't turned mine on last night like I'd planned, and with the front door open, I was already feeling the need for socks even in the comfort of my trailer. I didn't think the AC had kicked on at all yesterday, either. I turned on the overhead fan in my office to try to keep the fresh air from my screen door moving throughout the trailer as best I could. Then I bundled up in an old hoodie I was fairly certain I'd stolen from one of Iris's college boyfriends on a visit out to Tulane, but couldn't remember which. With an HVAC tech on the way, I figured I could deal with the cold for another day or two until the system was guaranteed not to light my duct work on fire or abuse my already tired brain with the inevitable awful "first use of the heater" smell-induced migraine. I hadn't thought about it last year and ended up losing a workday hiding from light and sound over at Mama's place hating my life until the smell dissipated.

I texted the boss once I had confirmation that we'd have a small army of HVAC techs—well more like three, all of whom I was assured were in the know—on site by tomorrow morning. The text was as much to give him an update on the business we were running, as it was to toot my own horn for remembering what he'd asked me to do despite everything that happened immediately afterward—remember those 'above and beyond the call of duty bonuses?' I sure did! What can I say? A girl's gotta look out for her own finances once in a while.

Shit, that reminded me that I wanted to call and bitch out my cable provider for raising the rates on me again. Asphodel Estates had a very clear, very iron clad service package with the provider in question; our tenants could get a very reasonable rate through them as long as we kept above a certain number of folks signing on. I was, in fact, included in that deal, but for some reason I was the only person who had to deal with customer service over my personal charges. Every. Single. Year.

I was beginning to think it was some sort of prank on the boss's part, but even if it was, I still had to call customer service to get the charges credited back so I stayed within my budget. I supposed I shouldn't be too bitchy about it considering I had it pretty well made. The cable package—with HBO because who could say no to reruns of the Mother of Dragons?—was the one "house" bill I was responsible for in my employment contract. Rent (including rental insurance as insisted upon by my mama), utilities, natural gas, internet, and my cell phone were all paid for or waived since I used them as part of my employment. I couldn't deduct them on my taxes, sadly, but it was worth it with what I got in return.

Didn't make my annual 'bitch at the cable guy' call any less obnoxious, but at least it was the only one I had to make on a regular basis.

Instead, I made lots of calls for other people. I hadn't quite figured out if I came out better in the trade off or not. Though, most of my list of repair folks tended to be kinder to someone in the know, as it were.

I'd finished up an email and taken a quick "break" to finally throw a load of laundry in the wash when my phone rang, rocking the Janelle Monae song I'd picked out for Iris's ringtone. I shoved the last armload in and splashed in some detergent, then grabbed for my phone, holding it between my shoulder and my ear as I closed the washer's lid and pressed start. Hopefully the settings were on the right one. If not, it wouldn't be the first time I headed to a thrift store to re-up my wardrobe, nor would it likely be the last.

"Hey hon, what's up?" I finally managed to say, ignoring the sound of the washer kicking on and heading back to the office. "You don't usually call during the day job."

"And you don't usually 'forget' to give me the heads-up about a mess in our home territory. I get up this morning and hear from Bessie and Marvin that we've got a body tucked away in the guest RV?

What the hell, Mel?" Iris didn't bother with small talk and jumped straight into the drama.

"It's not a body—she isn't dead, only injured and apparently unable to speak. It looked like an attack from something supernatural, so Boss convinced her to stay here while she healed. It was a shit show for sure, but I didn't want to blow your workday. And then last night I was dealing with Harvey apologizing and...blah. Lots of blah."

"Yeah, it sounds like. But..." Here she hesitated, and I felt the first twinge of foreboding, "I saw something yesterday. Didn't think much of it, but after hearing the rumors going through the park, I think it might have been right around when y'all found her."

"Shit."

"Yeah."

I sat down heavily in my desk chair, not wanting to ask what she'd seen but knowing I needed to. That was the other thing that made Iris belong here in Asphodel, above and beyond merely being my best friend. The thing honestly that had drawn us together, the two kids in the redneck elementary school who were a bit 'other,' who Saw more than they should.

Iris saw omens, and always had.

Generally, those kinds of gifts ran in families, but neither of her parents knew of any of their relatives who saw omens, or no one who'd admit to it. In any case, Iris's world was awash with omens, signs of things to come that nature would reveal to her in a blink, leaving her sometimes certain of their meaning and sometimes only guessing. I figured yesterday had been the latter or else she would have called me in a panic. Either way, an omen wasn't *necessarily* a bad sign with regards to Inna's discovery... On the other hand, it wasn't necessarily a *good* one either. And if she was bothering to call and tell me about it, that definitely leaned the scales more in one direction than the other.

"You still there, Mel?" she asked, worry in her voice, as well as a little bit of guilt that she'd added to the drama of my day.

"Yeah, I'm here," I covered. "What did you see?"

"Snakes in the grass." I could all but hear her shudder over the phone. "A pair of them slithering right up to the center's doorstep. They looked like regular garden snakes, but I knew, Mel, I *knew* they both were poisonous as hell. I ran around the back to the garden shed to get a hoe or something to kill the damn things but came back out and they were gone like they'd never been there. I thought they were real, Mel. I almost never see an omen that clear, but they vanished like they'd never been there."

"Well shit," I managed, trying to come up with something more profound but stuck at what I'd said out loud. "Any way of knowing who or what our snakes are gonna turn out to be?"

"Hell, Mel, I don't even know if they're supposed to represent an individual or... I don't know. Secrets and betrayal? It's weird." She sighed, and I imagined her pacing around the perimeter of her tiny office around the battered desk we'd had to thrift shop for her since the budget at the LGBTQ+ youth center where she worked was limited to say the least. "You'd think with as clearly as I saw it, I'd have an equally clear sense of the meaning of them, but it's slipping out of reach the more I think about it. I should have called right after. I knew I should have called, but..."

I tangled my hand in my hair and yanked, wanting to soothe her but not sure how. Iris was always better at that sort of thing than I was. Maybe if I thought about what she'd be saying to me in the same situation, assuming I was the omen reader and not her? "You couldn't have known whether speaking the words to a listener would clarify them or not. Your gift is inconsistent, Iris; you know it and I know it. It's not for any lack of trying on your part. It comes and goes as it pleases and either it makes sense, or it doesn't."

"I feel like I should know more—be able to help *more*."

"Now we have a warning that something might be shadier than we thought. That's more than I had yesterday or this morning, and this I can take to Mama and to Boss and see if we can make something of it."

"But not to Sadie?" Iris asked softly.

I huffed out a curse under my breath. I should have known she'd go there. Iris knew more than anyone about my little unrequited beyond the physical *thing* with Sadie. "Sadie's already lording it over me that I had to call for her help yesterday in the first place. If I go to her with a request to help read an omen's meaning, I'm gonna pay for it. Don't know if it'll be financially or emotionally, but I'll pay for it."

"If the meaning's important though?"

I sighed heavily and closed my eyes, wishing I could hang up on the conversation I really didn't want to have but knowing Iris would neither appreciate being hung up on nor would she let the topic go. "Iris, I don't have the energy for dealing with whatever cost she'd charge me. I really, *really* don't. She had a damn minion carry her bag yesterday. Knowing I was the one who said we needed her, she still brought her latest bed warmer to the show. I just can't."

"Have I mentioned I hate the bitch and wish I could hex her for you?" Iris said, humor almost in her voice despite the gravity of the reason she'd called.

It was enough to make me smile slightly. She had that effect on me. "Not this week, so it's worth saying." I heard someone outside the trailer and boots heading up the stairs to my deck. "Much as I hate it, she's an asset and I can't avoid her all the time. But some of the time. Like today."

"Fair enough."

"Look, hon, someone's at my door—you want to do dinner here later?"

"I'll bring groceries on my way out of town. Stay safe."

"You too." I disconnected the call and pushed myself out of the chair to answer the first of the promised HVAC techs who wonder of wonders was already knocking on my door due to a cancelation in her regular schedule.

Back to the daily grind. I'd think about omens and snakes in the grass of the Estates later.

8

B efore my new favorite repair person Kacey had to leave to get back to her scheduled appointments, we managed to finish preventative maintenance checks at a total of four trailers. Those included mine and a few with residents that were home or answered my texts giving me permission to enter. That basic property manager courtesy was even more vital in a community where homes might be warded and/or contain seriously dangerous house pets. With the joy of my heater actually up and running, I faced the rest of the day with a slightly more positive, or at least warmer, outlook. Mama's conference call went about the same way the one with Iris went with the addition of a promise to put out some feelers to her personal contacts about the possibility of a rogue werewolf or other predatory species, as I'd hoped she'd be able to. I emailed the boss again with a summary of both calls plus the more mundane property management updates, then clocked out officially for the day at around 5:30 p.m. As per usual, my door still stayed open in case a resident needed to stop by after hours. They all had my cell and my email, but many were more comfortable with face-to-face communication.

It probably had something to do with how many of them had been born in times or places other than the modern one we lived on the periphery of. I didn't much mind it. If I desperately needed a night off, I'd close the front door and lower the blinds to block out the light from inside. It worked much the same way with slightly annoyed residents as it did with Trick or Treaters—which as it happened, was where I'd gotten the idea. I also made a point of going away for a weekend every six months or so to completely detach from the feel of being on the job basically twenty-four-seven despite technically only officially working from eight to five-ish. Honestly the idea of "normal" hours with as non-normal as half the people living here were, was pretty much ridiculous. I couldn't tell my nocturnal tenants they were shit out of luck when it came to contacting me for an emergency, now could I?

Well, I supposed I could, but I'd be a crappy property manager if I did, and I tried to do good work. Even if I didn't like what I was doing now, which I did, there was no telling if another similar job offer somewhere else might happen one of these days. It wasn't like the boss was the only supernatural landlord with supernatural tenants who needed a mostly human property manager to liaison with the rest of the human world.

It was a niche position for sure, but that didn't make it impossible to find a new one. Iris and I still talked about moving to, or back to in her case, New Orleans one of these days, and gods knew there were plenty of supernatural folk who loved to live the stereotype of gathering in "N'awlins." Mama kept hinting too that she wouldn't mind a beach house eventually if we could find one properly accessible for her retirement home. And if Mama moved, you could be damned sure I would, too, good working situation and bonuses here or not. Mama and Iris were it as far as family for me— I wasn't going to give them up for any amount of money or cushy job.

Realizing I'd put it off, I ran by to check on Inna and found Miss Ginger cutting her long dark hair into an artful shaggy bob to better hide the wounds that marred her hairline. They'd already eaten since Harvey had brought by take-out or so Miss Ginger told me with a satisfied nod that said it was more of his attempts at earning her good opinion again. Trusting Inna was in good hands, I didn't linger.

Iris showed up a little after 6 p.m., reusable grocery bags in hand and a tired smile on her face that told me she hadn't been blindsided by any additional omens during the rest of her workday. She also had a change of clothes with her, and I figured she planned to stay the night, if only to attempt to keep me out of any more trouble. I debated on whining that I hadn't gone looking for any of the recent drama, but I knew better than to argue with her when she decided a thing. Besides, if she left to go home thanks to me whining, I'd miss out on whatever she'd decided to cook. That turned out to be spaghetti thanks to an HEB meal deal and a sale on the red wine she liked to add to the store brand jarred sauce. Her spaghetti always took longer than mine what with her browning meat and simmering with the wine and whatever other kitchen witchery she was doing in there.

I wasn't proud to admit it, but when left to my own devices, spaghetti was noodles and discount generic tomato sauce straight out of the jar. Maybe with some pre-grated parmesan cheese on top if I was feeling fancy.

Iris feeling fancy meant we had salad while the sauce simmered, and the parmesan *she* added to the finished product came in a block and was freshly grated on top. Hell, I'd never seen parmesan that wasn't already grated before Iris moved back.

I wasn't terribly surprised when the smell of food brought Harvey sniffing his way to my door and peeking in. Iris invited him and shoved a plate at him before he could apologize for barging in or say he'd already eaten with Miss Ginger and Inna or take himself off on his own out of shyness. I almost wanted to hoard the food all for me, but she'd made enough to feed an army.

Even with a werewolf at my tiny "dining room" table in the corner of the living room, all three of us would have leftovers to pack into our fridges. I figured I might be able to take some over for Inna in the morning, assuming she wasn't a vegetarian. No, I remembered, she'd put in a good showing on the Rudy's the day before—ground beef shouldn't be a problem. Sadie, on the other hand, would have bitched... And I was *not* thinking about Sadie tonight, I sternly reminded myself.

It didn't help that I had the terrible suspicion that Iris might be very, *very* delicately flirting with Harvey or at least teasing him out of his shell.

She had that effect on more than me after all. I ducked my head and tried to focus on the food which certainly deserved my attention rather than the thought that Iris might be ready to date again after the terribly civil break up with her last boyfriend almost a year ago. Granted, Harvey would not have been who I'd guess she'd be into, but Iris didn't have a type so much when it came to the guys she dated, beyond the fact that they were always friends first. She was demi-sexual that way. Not surprisingly, most of her men tended to be openly liberal sorts, but then I knew her tentative dating was complicated even more by her gender itself.

I idly wondered again when and if she was going to try to bother with surgical transition, but I wouldn't push the issue. Not when it was so very expensive, and for now, she seemed content with the hormone treatment. That could change, I imagined, but if it did, I'd be there to help her out and maybe get the other residents to help crowd fund it if her insurance gave her shit about the process.

It was more than a little ironic considering I knew for a fact she'd helped several of the folks she'd counselled at the center to navigate the horrendous red tape of insurance and travel and doctors and psych approval and all that shit to help them get their surgical transition done, but she still hesitated with herself. I knew her well enough to know that it was hard for her to go to an extra effort for herself—always had been.

I could relate to a point—the fates knew it was far harder for me to access the boon to defend myself as opposed to flying into battle to save someone else. Thus, my awkward dance with Harvey on bad full moons. I didn't really feel like protecting myself was worth hurting someone else, I guess, though I tried to be better about it considering I knew Iris and Mama would lose it if I was ever majorly hurt beyond what the boon could handle.

I didn't want to do that to them, not ever, if I could help it.

Harvey finally made his awkward goodbyes about the time Iris mentioned watching an episode of some show or another. I started to hit food coma by then and frankly wouldn't care what she put on, but apparently whatever she suggested was this side of too girly for Harvey to handle. That or it was possibly too stereotypical of a super-natural creature show for him. The CW was, I knew, the bane of more than a few paranormal folks' existence.

Gabby, one of our traveling vampire tenants, in particular, had ranted about the false promises of a "sexy vampire lover" that shows offered impressionable idiots one too many times.

"If I wanted to date someone with a pulse, I wouldn't have accepted the bite in the first place!" she'd snapped the last time a baby goth apparently figured out her secret and hit on her at a goth/alter-native club up in Austin, which I had to admit had some cool themed nights. Iris and I had gotten all decked out with Gabby's help for the last steampunk shindig there. But the club definitely had more than its fair share of regulars who would do damn near anything to become a Real Vampire™ sparkly or otherwise. Which I think was half her problem. Siring a baby vamp was too much responsibility.

The depiction of werewolves was rarely any better in my experi-ence, but I couldn't resist some of the shows for the sheer giggle factor. Plus, bless them, most actors given artificial fangs and fur were hot as hell. I still wasn't over Alexander Skarsgaard's version and his tight tank tops even years after the show aired.

While Iris ogled improbable vampires in some sort of war over New Orleans—it's *always* New Orleans, which was half the reason we hadn't moved there yet, I cleaned up the kitchen, packing up the left-overs and leaving a note to myself on the fridge's dry erase board to take some to both Inna and Harvey. Then I tackled setting the pans Iris had destroyed in her cooking efforts to soak overnight—dishes were the only downside to Iris cooking for me, and one I was more than willing to put up with for better-than-my home-cooked meals.

I could grill, sort of, though breakfast would remain my one true culinary talent, if you could call it that.

But dishes? Those most folks could do, even if they weren't the most fun. It was like laundry. I was capable of doing it whether I didn't particularly want to or not.

And that reminded me, I'd forgotten to switch out my own laundry earlier. Damn it all to washateria hell. Iris laughed as I rushed by her to try to get my sheets done before I was ready to head to bed, something that wouldn't take too long with as tired as I'd been the past few days.

"You good if I take a bath?" I asked Iris, sticking my head back down the hall to yell at her in the living room.

She waved at me haphazardly, sitting with her elbows on her knees and staring dreamily at the screen. Ten bucks what's his name with the suit was on. I much preferred the villainy brother, though I didn't like what that said about me considering how often he ended up covered in blood. "Go ahead, hon. I'll take door duty."

"Sweet—bath bomb time it is!" I grabbed a beverage from the fridge and padded back to fill up my scarred old bathtub, ready to indulge as I rarely felt like I could with the way my tenants could come by at random. There was nothing worse than feeling all warm and relaxed in a bath only to have someone knock in a panic. Checking to make sure the water was at the perfect temp of barely below scalding, I stripped and grabbed one of my stash of bath bombs underneath the tiny sink, then stepped into the bath, hissing at the perfect bite of heat against my skin. I sank down and let the bath bomb sink gently into the water to start fizzing away, releasing a mimosa-esque scent into the air.

As I'd expected, I heard a knock out at my front door, barely muted by the thin walls. Instead of panicking for my towel as usual, I grinned and sank down in the water as far as the not terribly deep tub would let me, sighing in contentment as I watched the bath bomb continue to disintegrate. There was a faint sound of conversation, slightly panicked, though I didn't bother trying to make out exactly what was said.

Iris could handle it.

Iris would handle it, right? I forced myself to ignore the nagging worry that always hit when I let someone else take over for me, even temporarily.

Iris. Could. Handle. It.

I took a long drink of my hard cider and leaned back again, closing my eyes, and tuning out the conversation that was getting ever shriller in nature. I'd almost pushed it out of my mind when another knock came. This time on the door to the bathroom.

"Son of a bitch," I muttered.

9

"Mel, honey, I'm sorry, but Marvin's gone missing again. Bessie's insisting that she needs him found as soon as possible and I mean, it's not like I can look for you..." Iris trailed off, the regret in her voice and the sheer love I felt for her the only things that kept me from cursing a blue streak. She already felt guilty I hadn't gotten my bath after all.

I stared mournfully as the bath bomb finally disappeared in one last burst of fizzy color, leaving the water a sparkly blue. So much for that.

"Mel?" Iris called again.

I sighed and reached for the plug, then hesitated. "I'm coming. You want the bath instead? I sacrificed a bath bomb—someone ought to get to enjoy it."

"Yeah, why not. Sorry again, hon."

"Not your fault. Let Bessie know I'll be out as soon as I'm dressed."

I normally preferred to rinse off the residue from a bath bomb, but figured I hadn't been long enough for it to bother me too much. Sighing with regret, I stood and dried off, wrapping the towel around me and scooting out the door as quick as I could to keep the steamy heat from escaping before Iris could get in there. Getting dressed didn't take long, and I thanked my stars I'd pulled my hair up into a knot so I wouldn't be going out into the chill with wet hair.

"Hey Bessie," I said, pulling on my jacket as I headed down the hall to the front door. "Marvin went walk about again, huh?"

Asphodel's resident hedge witch and gardener extraordinaire—the gardener who'd taught Mama all she knew as it happened and the one who supplied Sadie with most of her potion ingredients, though she decidedly did *not* approve of Sadie as anything other than a practitioner—wrung her wrinkled hands together, her bouffant of silvery white hair drooping as if in response to her worrying. "I'm so sorry, Melanie. I know it's late, but you know how Marvin is. He gets lost if he wanders too far and—"

"I'll find him," I promised. I felt bad about interrupting her—Mama had taught me to respect my elders and Bessie was near enough to an adopted great aunt for me to feel the instinctual shame of cutting off someone impolitely. But bless her, Bessie could and would ramble on about how frantic she was about finding Marvin immediately for the next hour. And she was right: he'd wander off quick-like if we weren't careful. I didn't have the time to let her keep talking. "Do you want to wait here in my living room or back at y'all's trailer in case he comes back on his own for once?"

"I'll—I'll go on back home, if you think that will be best," she managed to answer, still wringing her hands and furrowing her wrinkled brow.

I nodded gently. "I honestly do. You'll be more comfortable that way." And Iris wouldn't be guilted into waiting here with her and thus miss out on the bath I was missing out on instead. "I'll be back in a while, Iris!"

"I'll be here 'til you get back. Good luck finding him."

I ushered Bessie out ahead of me, grabbing my mini flashlight from the shelf by the door. I escorted her back to her cozy vine wrapped trailer first, enduring her continued babble of concern as we went. I didn't go past the white picketed fence that made up the edge of her garden—Bessie's plants were territorial, and the fence had been erected as much as a warning to intruders as to keep Bessie's garden contained only to her rented plot in the trailer park. I'd been dumb enough to enter without explicit invitation from both Bessie *and* her prize roses only once, and while luckily the boon apparently considered the resulting blood caused by Bessie-grown rose thorns a magical wound as opposed to those of the mundane version of the plant and endeavored to heal my scratches, they still stung like a bitch.

I was only ever that stupid the first time I tried something. Say what you will about me, but I did learn from my mistakes. Usually. One specific redhead notwithstanding.

Bessie waved from inside the gate, and I stressed again that she needed to make sure to stay home until I got back, with or without Marvin. The last thing I needed was her wandering off in the damp cold to look for him, too. She might have magic to boost her immune system, but she was still elderly and more susceptible to colds than I was.

With her safely stowed away, I turned back to look toward the rest of the trailer park and closed my eyes for a moment, doing the odd mental *click* I'd discovered through trial and error that would help adjust my Sight to the specific task at hand.

Marvin was Bessie's husband.

Her *late* husband. As in he'd died four years ago but wasn't anything like ready to "move on" or whatever mediums called it when ghosts stopped being ghosts.

Chasing down a wayward ghost who'd gotten it in his head to go for a walk in the rainy moonlight was just one of the services I provided as property manager, and, like dealing with Harvey knocking over trash cans, mostly merely annoying instead of dangerous. Marvin usually stayed within the trailer park's boundaries, especially during the day, but occasionally his age showed in his memory going a little more fuzzy than usual. He was as old as a ghost as he had been the day he died, stereotypical beautiful Hollywood ghosts be damned. And sadly, like many older folks, he'd get distracted somewhere between his and Bessie's trailer and the edge of the property and try to go looking for his old office in the joint law firm and accounting space in town.

That wasn't a problem for *him* considering the whole ghost thing meant he couldn't be harmed, but he was remarkably bad about hiding from the human and solely mortal townsfolk, particularly drivers and had thus caused a couple traffic accidents when he went wandering off the last few times. Bessie could normally keep a decent watch on him, faithful after his death, though I guess it hadn't parted them, now, had it? But I figured she'd been working in her garden nonstop since Inna was found—Sadie could get demanding when working a local case like this one, especially when Boss was footing the bill since it was Asphodel Estates business and not an individual resident's issue. When she got the chance to hose Boss and get reimbursed for the *really* good spell ingredients in the back half of Bessie's garden, she jumped at it.

Regardless, Marvin did need some looking after on his bad days, and apparently this was one of his bad nights.

I hoped I wouldn't have to Look too hard for him. For whatever reason, Seeing ghosts wore me out more than my normal ability to See the other paranormal parts of folks that were trying to look normal. Even the occasional fae or nature spirit showed up pretty easily if I focused but searching for the dead required taking my Sight to a whole 'nother level. One that always gave me a nasty headache if I was searching for more than an hour or so.

The one good thing was that ghosts, well Marvin, as he was the only ghost I had repeat contact with, left the faintest of trails as they traveled, something like the ghost—pun absolutely intended—of a footprint against the ground, even in spots where an alive person wouldn't be able to leave any traces like on asphalt or over the top of water.

Damn it, I hoped he hadn't gone crossing the creek. I did *not* want to deal with backtracking to cross the footbridge in the dark.

I switched on my little flashlight and shined it off to my left, leaving enough light that I could see where I was going, but not enough to completely blow my night vision—the ghost trails showed up better in the dark. Unfortunate, but not the least inconvenient thing about ghost chasing.

After all, it wasn't like I could physically drag Marvin back when I found him. Oh no, mortal hands went straight through him like he wasn't there. No, I'd have to *convince* him he needed to come back with me.

Did I mention he could be a stubborn old man?

The trail led me off through the middle of the community, weaving in between the mobile homes and then RVs as though Marvin didn't remember he could go straight through them if he wanted. That wasn't a good sign for his cognition. I sighed and kept going, following the meandering path he'd taken through to the far boundary and then around in a circle, skirting back toward the creek and all the way down past his and Bessie's trailer again. I'd tracked him nearly to the county road and had almost given up on any chance of him having stayed on the property when I caught a flicker of something over toward the massive bank of community mailboxes by the main entrance.

There Marvin stood, trying to open his mailbox without a key or physical fingers.

It was going about as well as you would expect.

I hurried over, hoping to catch him before his frustration transitioned from cursing under his nonexistent breath to shouting and trying to kick at the boxes with his nonexistent feet.

"Marvin, there you are!" I called softly, trying to keep my voice down while at the same time peppy so he didn't immediately get his back up. "Bessie was wondering where you were. She's holding dessert for you back at your trailer. Don't want to keep her waiting, do you?"

He didn't respond and kept reaching through the door of his mailbox, the movement growing jerkier and angrier each time he tried it. I came up right next to him, then hesitated. His face looked...*wrong* somehow. Blanker than I expected it to be with his dander getting up judging by his body language. But there was no expression on his face, no scowl or squinting at the box.

Nothing but blank.

I tried again. "Marvin, you want to head back to your place now? I can bring the mail by in the morning as a favor. How's that sound?"

He still didn't respond, so I reached out and waved my hand in front of his face, trying to get his attention. Only then did he seem to notice me, but I didn't think that was a good thing. His head turned toward me slowly with that same blank expression, only now I could see his eyes clearly.

Those friendly affable eyes I remembered seeing for so many years were jet black, as if the pupil had swallowed the iris and white.

I pulled my hand away from him and took a step back, then another as he turned the rest of his ghostly body to face me, hands growing more solid as they slowly clenched into fists.

"Marvin, you in there? You're freaking me out right about now. You know Bessie wouldn't approve of a—oh shit." I yelped and ducked as Marvin shot toward me, blank expression giving way to a snarl that twisted his lips until they seemed to stretch wider and wider baring a dark chasm between them, one that looked to swallow me whole. As I leapt to the side, he surged past me with a roar like a predatory freight train missing its prey at the tracks. The force of him pushing away bent and twisted the front of the mailbox, and when he 'landed' if you could call it that without a body, he set the gravel of the road spiraling into the air around him like a nasty halo that shot outwards to clatter against the front half of the bathhouse building with the force of one of my shotgun blasts.

So, less Casper, more poltergeist now, I thought, wishing I had stopped for the shotgun and my handy salt pellets after. Oh good. Contain the threat, Mel, contain the threat. Got it.

"Everyone stay inside!" I shouted, trying to warn the undoubtedly awake residents nearby not to come out bitching about the noise. This was going to suck enough. Better to keep bystanders out of the way. "I repeat, stay inside and out of my way. Angry ghost on the premises. Do not come outside!"

My voice already strained from the volume I was trying to force out of it and the yelp I'd made on his first attack pass, it wasn't a surprise that I barely made a peep when Marvin doubled back quicker than I expected and somehow flung me back into the now extremely abused mailboxes with a slam that jarred every single bone in my body. I wheezed through the pain of what prior experience told me were broken ribs and struggled to my feet. I needed every bit of distance between me and the ghost, but knew I also needed to keep the ghost focused on me and contained within the trailer park's boundaries.

I didn't want to think about the damage a deliberately destructive ghost would cause out on the highway.

Still reeling and seeing double which was odd enough with normal sight and considerably more dizzying with the Sight, I stumbled away from the mailbox and toward the empty pair of mobile homes at the front of the first row, hoping he'd be drawn to me without me having to resort to the clichéd "Over here asshole" yell. Loud would make my headache worse, I figured.

Luckily he still focused on me with that same chilling stare, and as if he'd been waiting for me to move and continue the game, he barreled toward me again. This time I tucked and rolled to the right behind the fence separating the mailbox and entrance "courtyard" from the rest of the community, shrieking as the fence exploded into splinters in front of me. Behind me, I could hear doors opening and shouts of alarm as my residents did exactly what I'd warned them not to. "Stay—ow—the fuck inside!"

As I'd expected, shouting hurt like a bitch, and I gagged, trying to keep myself from vomiting as I got to my feet again and tried to run. But where was I running to? He could follow damn near anywhere I went. I needed a plan. I needed a weapon and back up too, but who was I going to risk?

Who could even deal with this shit? We didn't have any trained exorcists lying around—they didn't tend to get along with most of our residents.

I kept up my half stumble half jog, ducking as best I could any time Marvin made another violent pass at me. I frantically waved my residents back to their homes as we passed them. Luckily—again...luckily??—he seemed focused solely on me and not anyone else we passed.

I was glad Bessie hopefully remained inside her place at the far edge of the property. She'd be less likely to come investigate the ruckus and attract her husband's attention away from me. I could run a hell of a lot faster than she could. And damned if seeing her honey gone full horror film might strain her sweet old heart.

"Mel!" I turned my head at the shout to see Harvey running full out toward me carrying my shot gun. I could have kissed him, I swore to all the well-armed gods of the ammo store. He tossed the weapon to me as I felt Marvin coming in for another shove at me. I caught it and turned to face the ghost, raising the shotgun to my shoulder in a move all muscle memory and no conscious thought, then fired sending a spray of rock salt and rosemary and clove and sage and rue and half a dozen other things I couldn't remember off hand but that Bessie had sworn would be a proper defense against any kind of malevolent spirit.

The irony of her providing the herbs to defend against her husband was not lost on me.

The ghost shot took Marvin straight in the face and torso, blurring the edges of his spirit form in a glitching pattern that made my concussed Sight force another wave of dizziness through me. So, good —that worked, I managed to think. Then he seemed to draw himself back together all at once, and he let out a silent roar of pain and rage that set the windows in the closest trailers shattering. My residents screamed. Never a good sign when preternatural creatures freaked out.

"Either the boss or Sadie should be able to deal with him—you need to get him to them, Mel!" Harvey shouted again, drawing my attention long enough to sling a fanny pack of shells to me. He tried to reach me but kept sliding backwards, the force of the wind Marvin was generating keeping him away from Marvin's target—me.

I nodded, winced, and fired again. Then I turned and tried to run again as another silent concussive scream sounded behind me. Boss or Sadie? Boss or Sadie?

Harvey was right—they'd be the two on site most able to handle a spirit, something that should have occurred to me sooner. I blamed the concussion. But which to head to? I had to decide quickly—it wasn't like they lived anywhere near each other, and I didn't have enough time to run to both.

Time. Distance. I fumbled a pair of shells out of the fanny pack, reloaded, and spun to fire again, barely managing to pause Marvin in another wicked attack upon my person. More glass flew in the wake of his rage, and I leapt to the side as a two by four from someone's deck soared by me like a redneck's javelin.

Sadie, I decided, had to be Sadie. She was only maybe two minutes closer at my current speed, but two minutes might keep my ass alive. "I'm going for Sadie," I called back to Harvey over my shoulder. "Warn her I'm coming!"

He set off at a sprint back the way he came, his heightened speed in human form the guarantee I needed that he'd make it there in time for Sadie to hopefully be prepared for the ghostly hurricane I brought with me. I kept running—or stumbling—as fast as I was able, falling to my knees to vomit once, then twice, despite my resolution not to puke.

I had to keep moving. Just keep moving, Mel.

Easier said than done. I made it to the center of the community, skirting around the pool and trying to avoid the deck chairs that went flying at me in Marvin's wake. I caught a glimpse of Khoi's wide eyes peeking over the edge of the pool but couldn't spare the energy to do more than wave him away as frantically as I had the others. I was all out of breath to yell to him. It was only after I passed the end of the pool's chain link fence that I realized an ancient Vietnamese water whatever-he-was might not have been a bad bet for dealing with a poltergeist, but it was too late to turn around. There was no chance in hell I'd make it past Marvin to head back to him at this point.

No, better to stick to my plan and try to reach Sadie's RV before I got sent flying further than the boon could keep me breathing.

As if the thought jinxed me, I stumbled the next time I tried to dodge. Marvin slammed into me like a freight train made of ice, sending me slamming face first into the side of someone's airstream with a sickening thud, fanny pack and shotgun sent gods knew where.

I slid painfully down the trailer's metal, siding to the ground, feeling every one of the rivets against my abused face as I went. I hit the grass—thank nature there was grass—hard and moaned, unable to keep from making a sound at the pain in my stomach and hips, let alone my poor face.

That would leave a mark—probably several marks.

I tried to push myself up to a crouch to face Marvin, but swallowed a shriek as one of my shoulders revealed it was likely dislocated and entirely unwilling to support my weight. I rolled instead, determined to die facing him.

He slowed to a stop, watching me try to sit up with the same blank expression and hate-filled eyes. Everything was so cold, I realized, the thought accompanied with full body shivers. The night was chilly enough but the full body contact with the ghost had added an arctic edge to the air around me, and some of my bare skin almost felt frostbitten from his touch.

I thought the cold would have numbed some of the pain of my injuries, but no such luck. If anything, it made it all worse, like the cold amplified the agony of the bruises and broken bones I had in abundance.

I wondered if the boon had limits on what it could and could not heal. If Marvin didn't kill me, I might find out.

"Shit, he's gonna kill me," I breathed out incredulously. Really? This was the way I was going to die? I once fought a traffic-gods-be-damned bridge troll with a minivan as my weapon of choice, and *this* was what was gonna kill me? Fuck my life.

I tried again to find the energy to sit the rest of the way up, but every muscle in my body protested the move and I flopped back again. I barely managed to lift my head enough to track the ghost that had started moving once more, pacing his slow way toward me.

My voice was too weak to make much in the way of noise. So much for any final words. I closed my eyes and waited for the dead to come for me.

"Get away from her!"

My eyes popped open, and I turned my head as much as I could to see what looked like an avenging angel stalking toward the ghost in front of me. Sadie, in pants for possibly the first time I'd seen her, angry and carrying two enormous jugs in each hand. "I said, get away from her!"

Her voice struck me as more aggravated than anything, but I chalked that up to her sheer arrogance in the face of a poltergeist, even one this blatantly murderous. Marvin didn't move away, but he stopped in his stalk toward me, and I considered that a check in the plus column.

"Move away now, Marvin, or I swear upon my Lady's name, I will be forced to end you." Sadie sounded almost gleeful at the prospect of an exorcism, but I couldn't blame her too much for that. Sadie and Bessie rarely got along at the best of times, and she'd always made it clear she thought Marvin to be an abomination even as a friendly ghost.

He was no longer remotely friendly, and well, I figured that gave Sadie all the excuse she needed to deal with him. That he was hurting me might have registered as a boost to her reasoning, but I didn't know if I believed it.

She gave him one last chance. "Move away as I command or be banished. This is your last warning."

I only saw the edge of Marvin's face, but I could almost swear the anger in his eyes shifted to mild confusion, but I couldn't be sure. Then as Sadie raised the jugs up, the rage returned, and the moment of confusion vanished as he gathered the cold of his strength and flew straight at her.

Sadie never moved, didn't retreat a single inch, only waited resolutely. Once he was within reach, she swung both jugs forward, splashing whatever they held directly into Marvin's ghostly face. I half expected the liquid to simply fly through him like other physical objects, but instead the glowing white fluid clung to him. He roared in pain and fury, this time with the sound that had been missing from his other screams of rage. His outline started to smoke instead of blurring at the edges like it did when I hit him with the salt pellets, and I wondered what had been in there.

The witch who'd come to my rescue distracted me before I could wonder long. She darted forward as Marvin flailed, pulling a bag from her pocket and running in a circle around her opponent, the fine powder in the bag falling to ring around him in midair. Sadie began to chant, a vicious edge to her voice that had me trying to crawl backwards despite knowing I wasn't her intended target.

Marvin spasmed wildly, trying to claw the potion from his nonexistent skin and failing as it continued to eat away at his ghostly form. Sadie's chanting increased in volume and pitch, the unfamiliar words falling harshly on my ears. I tried to lift my hands to cover them, to block out the horrible sound of the words and Marvin's screaming. I only screamed weakly myself as the movement jarred my dislocated shoulder. I fell still again, panting desperately and unable to anything but watch. The ghost, once a sweet little old man, continued to flail about in terrible agony, and I wished with everything in me for it to end.

It didn't. Not for another long few minutes.

With one last gut churning cry, the wraith of Marvin burned out into nothing. Those awful eyes vanished last, still filled with fury and pain.

10

In the jarring silence left as Marvin's screams cut off, Sadie sagged, the fierce energy leaving her all at once. She stumbled, then stood firm. With a quick swipe of her hand, she broke the line of powder still floating in midair, and it vanished without a trace. Only then did she turn to look at me still laying pitifully on the ground. "Well, that was fun, wasn't it? I haven't gotten to do an exorcism in ages!"

"Glad...you enjoyed...yourself," I managed, more than a little put out by her glee at what she'd done to Marvin. Vicious killer though he might have been there at the end, he'd been my friend and Bessie's husband.

Oh fuck, who was going to tell Bessie?

"I will," Boss's voice preceded him around the corner, and I realized I must have spoken out loud though I didn't mean to. Concussions, I swear. He stepped past Sadie with one unreadable look in her direction, then sank down at my side. "Are you all right?"

"Um no idea...to be...honest. Probably...not?" I wheezed, ribs reminding me of their abuse with every word I tried to speak. On the upside, for the first time ever I didn't feel the slightest hint of his allure. Probably due to the excruciating pain, but I'd take whatever win I could get. "Someone's...going to need to...pop my shoulder back in."

And wouldn't that be fun?

"Understood. Sadie, you can head on back to your trailer. We've got her."

"She's bleeding. I should—"

"Not enough for her to need your kit. You know that. And in any case, you've done enough tonight." Sadie looked surprisingly reluctant and almost angry to be dismissed, but Boss's odd stare refused to waver. She finally tossed her head and stalked off, barely having the decency to look tired as she went. She didn't look back at me, either. I tried not to let that fact add to the pain.

Boss looked apologetic. "You'll have to ride it out after that. I'm sorry, Mel. Can you walk?"

I laughed weakly. "Pretty sure that...walking...requires me standing. And I don't think...that I can do that...right this second."

"I can get her back to her place to rest," Harvey's rough voice broke into our conversation like a blow, but I didn't flinch at the surprise of his arrival. I hurt too much to risk flinching. He knelt down next to me and helped me sit up slowly, then ran a careful hand along my shoulder. "I think I can pop this back, but it'll hurt like a bitch."

"Already does, but it'll hurt less after you do. I can...handle it." I tried to support my own weight as he braced me.

"We'll go on three. One...Three!" He pushed and pulled on either side of my shoulder hard, and I bit back a shriek at the near blinding spike of pain that accompanied the audible 'pop' of the joint realigning the way it was supposed to.

"You *asshole*," I panted, wishing I had the strength to hit him. "What happened...to two?"

He shrugged. "You'd have tensed up for it, and it woulda hurt worse. Better to get it done fast."

"Oh, you are so not my favorite right now." It was only partially true—my shoulder did hurt less already, so bitchy move or not, he'd earned a low-ranking place on my good side. I glanced back at Boss to see him watching us with that same inscrutable look he'd tossed

Sadie. "Do...do you need me for anything else?" Please don't, I begged silently. Please let me cry in pain in private.

He slowly shook his head. "No, I don't. Or not anything you're up for yet. We'll deal with your report and the—" he gestured vaguely to the debris scattered about the community back in the direction I'd run from, "the mess tomorrow once you're feeling stronger."

"K." I intended to say more but couldn't find the energy and gave up with a shrug. I turned back to Harvey, still crouched by my side. "How we gonna do this?"

"Just hold on. I'll get ya there." With one smooth motion I probably wouldn't have been able to follow even if I'd been at full strength and watching him closely, he slipped his arms around my shoulders and under my knees and rose with me in his arms as if I weighed nothing at all. It hurt—any pressure against the bruises and cracked ribs hurt —but it was less than I expected and far less than had I tried to stand and walk on my own.

"You all right there?" he asked, and I nodded tentatively.

"I think so."

"Good. I'll get her back to her trailer, Boss. Do you want...?" Harvey trailed off, and I looked up to follow his gaze over to see Bessie's frail form standing past our little group. Harvey sighed softly. "Damn."

"Marvin?" Bessie called out, looking everywhere, barely seeming to notice us standing around, me like so much luggage in Harvey's strong arms. "Marvin, honey, where are you?"

I opened my mouth to try to speak, to tell her where her husband's ghost had gone and maybe what he'd done to deserve it, but my throat closed up around a sob at the lost look on her face.

"Marvin?" she called again, coming closer with tiny, terrified steps.

Though nothing remained of Marvin or the circle to normal eyes or my Sight, Bessie stepped right to the edge of where the circle had been as if drawn there like a magnet. Her worn hands fluttered up to rest against her heart.

"Oh Marvin, no. My darling, no."

Then she began to cry quietly, so painfully quietly, but desperately like a tap had switched on behind her eyes.

My heart broke for her, but there wasn't anything I could do. I didn't know if I had the strength to hug her, or if she'd accept it from me.

I'd been the reason Sadie banished him.

Harvey hitched me up tighter in his arms, apologizing softly at my wince. "Come on. Nothing we can do here. Boss has her."

He turned away, but I looked back over his shoulder to see that he was right. My boss slowly folded the old woman, now somehow tinier than she normally was, into his arms.

Harvey walked as carefully as he could—which as a werewolf was pretty damned careful—but every step still jarred me. I clenched my teeth against the pain as we went, which unfortunately only added to the bitch of a headache from the concussion. I knew from past experience the boon tended to work almost at random when it came to healing. A broken bone might knit here, a bruised internal organ there but not the one next to it, a minor bruise on a hand... It was just luck of the draw which injuries would start to feel better first, and I'd have to suck it up until they all did.

In the meantime, I tried to ignore the residents we passed on our way to my trailer. With the conflict ended, most ventured out of their homes to see what all the fuss had been about.

I hated seeing them stare. I was supposed to be capable and stronger than a normal human in their eyes—not carted around like an injured puppy. I hated it, but I was helpless to walk on my own so carted about I would be after all.

Iris met us at my front door, holding it open for Harvey and directing him back to my bedroom which was already prepped with the bed turned down and ice packs and the first aid kit at the ready. Harvey set me gently on my feet, holding me steady until Iris got an arm under my shoulder to help me bear my own weight.

"I'll—I'll track down your gun and the ammo," Harvey said, then took off, looking embarrassed he'd been in my bedroom at all.

I turned to Iris as she gingerly worked me out of my now ragged clothes. "So did you get to enjoy the bath, or did I ruin it?"

"You didn't ruin anything," she said sharply, then gentled her tone. "I had a good hour in there before all the commotion. Harvey wouldn't let me leave. Said I wouldn't be much help." She paused, but I didn't contradict her. Harvey had been right. Better to keep her out of harm's way. "He did let me find the shotgun and Bessie's spirit warding salt mix for you though."

With me in just my sports bra and panties, she eased me down to lay flat out on top of my covers, then started applying bruise balm and ice packs with a will. "Least I can do this much for you."

"It helps. It really does." I said, trying to soothe her. In reality though, I hurt worse, I realized. I couldn't get warm with the ice packs, couldn't shake that vicious chill I'd taken on when Marvin managed to hit me that last time. I shivered but tried to suppress it as much as I could before Iris noticed. It wasn't like I didn't need the cold on the bruises—I could deal with it. I could, I told myself fiercely.

She kept spreading the paste, then switched to antibiotic ointment for the wounds that on a normal person would need stitches, but on me merely needed to be kept clean until they closed on their own. "What happened to Marvin?" Iris asked quietly. "I heard him scream, but then nothing else."

"Sadie exorcised him. He's gone," I managed. I found myself crying, though nowhere near as quietly as Bessie had. I tried to stop sobbing, broken ribs telling me it really would be for the best if I could quit, but I couldn't. The adrenaline crash plus the memory of that sweet old man gone so terribly wrong combined for a crying jag I should have seen coming.

Iris tutted and climbed half into bed, letting me curl up as best I could to put my pounding head in her lap. "It's not your fault, Mel. I know it feels like it right about now, but it's really not. I swear."

I didn't answer, just kept crying until the cold had me shivering so much that I began to hiccup. Iris sat up straighter, helping me sit up and rubbing my back as I tried to stop hiccupping. If I'd thought sobbing hurt my ribs, this was definitely worse. "Mel, you all right?"

"So so collldd," I chattered. "Ccccan't gggettt warmmm."

"Shit." Iris grabbed the icepacks and tossed them on the floor dragging the quilt over my lap and rubbing briskly at my arms. "How long have you been cold, hon? Since the ice packs?"

"Sssincce M-Marvin."

"OK. OK lay back now. I'm gonna bundle you up, then call your mama and see if she's got any idea how to help."

I did as she ordered, wrapping my arms as best I could around myself under the thick quilt and extra blanket she added, unable to curl up into a ball the way I wanted to. I didn't think any of my bruises would agree to that, anyway. I wanted to be warm and stop hurting. That's all I wanted—why couldn't I get warm?

Iris hurried back into the room, iPhone pressed against her ear as she hummed her agreement with whoever was on the phone. "Yeah, he's gone. I know. It's horrible. I—I have to focus on Mel. I can't think about that now." She shifted the phone to the other ear and helped me sit up again, wrapping my hands around a steaming mug of tea. "I'm getting the tea in her now, and I'll get her in the bath once that's done. There's really nothing else I can do for her? Yeah, OK. Thanks, Shelby. Yeah, I'll keep you posted. Bye."

She helped me drink the tea, wrapping her own hands around mine as the shivering made it hard for me to hold on. "Sip it slowly, honey. Don't want to burn your tongue, but we have to get your body temp up. Your hands feel like ice even around the damn mug."

I didn't bother to answer and drank as ordered. Harvey came stomping in while I tried to finish it, shotgun and now torn fanny pack in his hands. He pulled up short at the sight of me wrapped up in Iris's arms and the quilt, but still not wearing anything more than the bra. "Shit sorry—I should, I should go right?"

In any other mood, I might have found his flush and averted eyes funny, but I wanted to get warm. Iris answered instead. "It's fine. Can you get a bath running? Marvin got her colder than expected somehow. Her mama said the boon might need help getting her body temp back up."

"Yeah, yeah I can do that." He backed out of the room, still looking flustered under the trucker hat, and a moment later I heard the water start running through the pipes.

"There you go," Iris praised as I finally tipped the last few drops of tea back. I vaguely resented being treated like a child, but damned if I wasn't weaker than a two-year-old right about now anyway, so I really couldn't blame her. I leaned back, letting her broad shoulders take the weight of me and closed my eyes, knowing she'd take care of getting me into the bath as soon as it was ready. Sure enough, Harvey knocked back on the bedroom doorframe only a few minutes later.

"It's getting close to full. I didn't put any of that frilly bath stuff in. Wasn't sure it'd be good for the cuts." He rubbed at his scruffy jaw, still looking away.

This time it was Iris's turn to pick me up like her personal damsel in distress, reminding me again of how strong her six-foot frame actually was. "That's fine. I might add some Epsom salts for the bruising. Most of the cuts are almost healed except for her scalp wound. It'll still sting some if she gets it wet, but not for long, and we can try to keep her head out of the water 'til it closes."

"Gotcha. You got her there? I can take her if you need me to." The admittedly impressive sight of Iris hefting me up full in her arms was apparently enough to shake off his embarrassment at my lack of dress, but Iris shook her head.

"I've got her. You could get the door for me though," she replied, nodding toward the bathroom door that he'd closed behind him when he came back.

He nodded and hurried over, ducking in to shut off the water then stepping back out to give Iris room to carry me into the tiny bathroom. "I'm gonna leave your undies and all on you, hon. I doubt you'll be able to get back up by yourself."

"Thanks," I managed, not that I cared much either way. I might not be technically nude, but my panties and bra would soak through, and the thin comfy cotton wouldn't hide much of anything. I'd let Iris feel like she was protecting my dignity, though. She was always more body shy than me, and with reason considering the nasty reality of body dysphoria. I, on the other hand, had no qualms about her or Harvey seeing me naked, especially not at the moment. Maybe once the concussion faded, I'd get embarrassed, but that was a concern for later after the boon decided to get its ass in gear.

Now, however, I only wanted warmth. Iris lowered me straight into the tub, and then I was embarrassed by the sheer volume of the moan I let out as the heat hit my frigid limbs. It was just on this side of way too hot to the touch. Iris didn't seem to notice, and I wondered if it was cooler than I actually thought it was. She helped me lay back against the wall of the tub so I could sink a little farther into the water, then stepped out to the hall closet to get the bag of Epsom salt I kept out there with the extra towels since neither would fit under the tiny sink. Iris poured a liberal amount into the water, and I hissed as it stung the few open cuts I had left. The pain faded after only a moment. It could have been worse; at least I was warm. I'd be willing to take on a lot more annoying pain in return for that.

Slowly the heat began to ease some of the aching soreness, and I could feel bruises and strains fading away as the combined bath and Epsom salt treatment seemed to remind the boon about what its duties were.

So much better, I thought.

Then all at once I shifted in what was apparently the wrong way. A blinding stab of pain ripped through my chest, and I coughed and coughed and coughed up what I could taste was blood. Iris scrambled forward, trying to support my shoulders as I tried to keep my face above water but not drown myself with my own blood.

Then I felt and heard a sharp 'pop' in my torso. After a few more coughs, no more blood filled my throat or mouth. I gingerly reached to prod at the site of the pain and there was another pop. I let out a low sigh of relief.

"Mel? Mel, are you all right? Answer me!" Iris's frantic words finally broke through my hazy mind, and I looked up and nodded weakly.

"I'm all right," I said, surprised at how less rough my voice sounded. Thank you boon, better late than never. "Rib. Think it was broken. Pierced a lung. Fixed now. But..." I shook my head, exhausted by basically everything happening and so, so ready to fall asleep right where I was. Could the boon keep me from drowning? Probably better not to risk it, I decided. "But hurt like a bitch," I finally finished, realizing Iris still waited for me to speak.

"Christ, Mel, don't scare me like that again." Iris leaned her head down to the top of mine, thankfully avoiding the still tender spot where I'd been bleeding not terribly long ago. That was better; that was *much* better.

A faint shuffle of sound pulled my gaze to the door to where Harvey stood there, leaning against the door frame with his arms crossed protectively across his chest. He looked down when he realized I was watching him. "What she said. Could you try not to get the crap kicked out of you for one whole day? Shit."

I resisted the urge to remind him that he'd been the reason I'd injured myself on the collar not two days prior. He was right anyway; this shit was getting old. An injury-free day sounded pretty good right now.

"I think...I think I've cooked enough. Shivers are all gone," I said, awkwardly nuzzling Iris where she still leaned against me. I thought I'd felt a tear or two slide down her chin to my cheek, but I was nice enough not to mention it, and it didn't seem like Harvey was going to either. "Can you help me stand up so I can rinse off?"

"I brought by a space heater for your bedroom to make sure you don't get too cold again. I think you've got a draft in there—central air's not doing shit. I'll get it checked out for you," Harvey said. He turned on his heel to leave, probably as much to avoid watching me come out of the water in my see-through undies as to set up a space heater. Thoughtful of him either way.

Iris helped me stand and pulled the drain plug, letting a good half of the water leave the tub before turning the faucet back on and pressing the button to engage the shower head. I gently nudged her away to keep her out of the spray and gingerly reached up to tilt the shower head away from the open room since she hadn't closed the shower curtain. I then leaned heavily on the wall, letting the spray fall over my skin and wash away the worst of the Epsom salt residue which I knew from past experience was guaranteed to make my skin itch something fierce. My hair got wet unsurprisingly, so I said screw it and leaned forward enough to soak it completely and rinse away the blood from the scalp wound that a gentle prod told me was finally closed.

As a bonus, I could tell my legs were working better than they had an hour prior, but they weren't quite up to snuff yet. I'd probably be able to walk down the hall with Iris's help without needing to be carried, but doing so completely on my own didn't seem possible yet. To prove to myself that I could manage it, I leaned over and switched off the faucet, reeling a little as I forced myself up straight again. Still dizzy even with the head wound closed; hopefully the less visible effects of the concussion would fade next in time for me to sleep instead of staying awake due to pain and that awful spinning sensation the dizziness caused.

Iris stepped forward again to wrap a towel around me and gently dry off the worst of the wet. Only then did she help me over the lip of the tub and down the hallway, taking most of my weight, though as I'd hoped, she did let me pretend to be walking somewhat under my own power. I hated feeling helpless. I was glad she and Harvey were the only ones who'd see it—though damned if I could figure out when *he'd* joined the list of those I was OK with seeing me weak. Sometime around his showing up with Starbucks the first and second time, I thought wryly. Who knew the way to a girl's trust was icy caffeine, honest self-repentance, and paint colors?

It should have come far sooner, considering what I'd known of him before: his care with the cars of his fellow residents, the little repair projects I discovered people hadn't had to call me for, his oddly sweet friendship with the harpy sisters who made a point of disliking damn near anyone on principle.

And now, averted eyes and a space heater, complete with a humidifier rigged from a bowl of ice water in front of it to make sure my skin didn't get too dried out—or so he told me in an almost inaudible mumble before retreating from the room again in the face of Iris removing my towel and finding me panties and a t-shirt to sleep in.

It wasn't the first time Iris had seen me changing. We'd ended up in the same oatmeal bathtub back in grade school with the chicken pox since Mama'd had it as a kid but somehow neither of Iris's parents had. From then on it honestly seemed silly to be body shy around her, though there were a few tense moments in high school when her folks thought me a slut for casually changing clothes in her presence.

Admittedly they weren't wrong about me having a thing for Iris, but the nakedness really wasn't as much of a factor as the fact that she was *Iris.*

Not that she ever seemed to return the regard, and why would she? She'd never dated girls that I remembered, and gender was the one thing about myself I was pretty sure of. Besides, she was family and me, I guess, a sister to her. And that was enough, I reminded myself firmly. That would always be enough.

Dressing again was less of a hassle with her help, but only slightly less. Iris tucked me into bed like the little sister I knew would be all she ever thought of me as, then brushed my hair to the side, checking the head wound had closed. "You need anything else, Mel?"

I shook my head, tired and ready to pass out. "I'm good."

"OK then. I'll stay the night—sing out if you need me. I hope you sleep well," she said and ran a hand over my hair softly again. Then she stood and turned out the light, closing the door behind her.

11

I don't remember falling asleep or what I dreamed. Since I woke with every inch of me still plenty sore, much more so than after any previous injury, I figured that was probably a blessing. If I'd dreamed too much, I knew I'd have flailed in my sleep and hurt myself worse than I already was. And it would be just my luck if the boon decided *those* injuries didn't count toward its requirements, despite being layered on top of wounds that clearly did.

A fumble for my phone told me I'd slept through the rest of the night and well into the next morning nearly to lunch. My phone also revealed multiple texts: from my mama checking in and promising to get someone to bring her by for the aforementioned lunch, from Iris letting me know she'd had to leave for her every other Saturday shift, but that I could call her if I needed her, and, shockingly, from Boss, ordering me off work for the day possibly for the first time in the course of my employment.

Either Mama had called him and badgered him into it, or I looked worse after the fight last night than I'd realized. He had an odd sense of the mortal capacity for harm, and I suppose mine and Mama's gifts didn't make it any clearer for him.

I'd take the time he offered though, for damn sure. It would be the first true time off that I could remember in months, aside from vacations out of town. Even weekends were open door for me, and thus normally, I'd need to be up and at 'em regardless of the world's view on weekends versus "work weeks." Today though, I would leave the damn thing shut and locked.

I managed to stand on my own, glad I wouldn't need to call anyone to help for the humiliation of getting me to the bathroom. That would only happen once in twenty-four hours. Hell, once in the next year if I could help it.

Food took more effort, not the least of which included simply walking across my living room since leaning on the wall as I did in the hallway would cause me to trip on the couch. As it was, I had to rest on one of the bar stools before I could gather myself enough to make a couple pieces of peanut butter toast—all I felt up to making which at least had a little bit of protein in it. Better than toast and butter or a single cup of coffee which I'd almost been tempted to stick with since Mama would be around in an hour or so. I ate on the couch, one exhausting bite at a time, washing the peanut butter down with a glass of almond milk in hopes of getting a few more calories in me.

I'd burned through a lot of energy healing last night or so I gathered from my sheer exhaustion. I wouldn't be surprised if I'd lost a couple pounds too, though I wasn't in the mood to see the scale agree with me.

I barely finished swallowing my last bite of toast when someone knocked on the locked door, then let themselves in before I could get up. Sadie winked at me as she came in, and I tried to ignore the momentary rush of heat in my cheeks. She'd winked at me like that before, usually before she maneuvered me into another one-night stand that inevitably led to a weekend luxuriating naked with her in my bed before she calmly got up and sauntered off again for who knew how long. I had to nip this in the bud, I decided, and tried to play it cool. "You know, I am aware that door was locked."

"Mm, yeah, but that could hardly stop me, now could it?" She shrugged, tossing all that red hair over her shoulder like a shining wave in a practiced, calculated move that always, *always* set my mouth watering. She strode across the room and sat herself down at the other end of the couch without an invitation, toeing her shoes off and stretching out to press her feet with their emerald green painted toenails against my thigh. Damned if that didn't work for me, too. "Besides, if I waited for you to unlock it, you'd have to get up, and you do look awfully comfortable there."

She bit her bottom lip, and I sighed. "Sadie, why are you here?" She opened her mouth to speak, but I held my hand up. "Seriously. I'm beat all to hell, and it's not like you've spoken to me in weeks except for business like with Inna or last night." I shrugged at her affronted look. "Tell me I'm wrong. You're not here for my sake. We both know it."

I tried to pretend my voice didn't quiver a little. A pitying look hit her face, one that made me want to order her out, but we both knew I wouldn't. "Mel, sweetie. You know I'm not ready to settle down. We've talked about that. Doesn't mean I don't enjoy you though, does it? And I know you enjoy me, too."

"Still doesn't explain why you're here today when I'm not up enough for you to enjoy me," I said, looking away to stare at my glass tiredly.

I heard her shift and then her hand was pressing against my thigh instead of her toes. One long perfectly manicured finger pressed against my chin turning it to face her, and she smiled slowly. "Maybe I wanted you to enjoy me this time instead." Before I could protest, not that I honestly wanted to, Sadie leaned in and kissed me deep and slow, sending me spinning even more than the concussion had. She pulled back and stared at me, an odd possessive light in her eyes I'd never seen before. "I thought I was watching you die, Melanie. Maybe I'm not in this for the long haul, but don't think that didn't affect me."

She shifted back, a hand on my hip encouraging me to slide with her and then lay back against the couch cushions. I felt terribly exposed in my shirt and panties, not that she hadn't seen me in far less on more than one occasion. Those long fingers traced up the side of my thighs to my waist and she looked up at me through dark lashes, almost coy if not for the lust in her eyes. "Let me pamper you a little. Please?"

Sadie breathed out the last word like she was begging, and just like that, I was helpless to say no despite my better judgement. She must have seen it in my eyes, because she grinned wickedly and hooked her fingers in the waistband of my panties to drag them down my legs and off me. "Now, I know you probably have a lunch date, so I'll do my best to make this quick, hmm?"

Then her mouth lowered down on to me, and I let my head fall back with a gasp, reaching down with my less sore arm to tangle my hand in her hair. I closed my eyes and let myself go, lost in her like every time she came to me, no matter what I tried to decide in between times. I writhed on the couch, the pain in my still-healing body adding an edge to the sensation. I bit my lip to add to that sharpness, swallowing back my moans like letting them escape would mean I lost some battle with her.

As if hearing my thoughts, she redoubled her efforts, and all but forced me up and up and up and—

I came all at once, bowing back and sobbing out her name like I knew she wanted.

It tasted like shame in my mouth.

Sadie sat up and daintily wiped her lips before kissing me, knowing I wasn't a fan of my own flavor. Knowing exactly what I liked and didn't was how she managed to weasel her way back here time and time again after all.

"Well, that was fun—I better dash. Gotta go check on Inna. Poor thing has to be feeling all alone in the world, don't you think?" She stood up before I could say anything, running her hands through her hair to straighten it from 'just fucked' to merely 'tousled.' "Talk to you later, darling. Don't miss me too much."

With one last wink, she let herself out again, and I saw the dead bolt turn on its own to lock back up.

"Abrupt, much?" I muttered, pissed with myself that I'd somehow expected more down in the pit of my stomach where I wouldn't admit it out loud. I shook my head at my idiocy for giving in yet again, though at least this time I hadn't fallen all over myself to return her favor. The only good thing about being injured, I guess. I checked the time and grimaced—Mama'd show up before too long. Even dependent on someone else to drive her, she made a point to be punctual at all costs. I should be able to get a shower in, I thought. I wanted Sadie washed off me, especially with Mama coming over.

I creeped down the hallway like an old lady, my soreness almost worse now after Sadie's attentions, and I barely made it into the bathroom without weeping. I practically crawled into the shower and lathered up, leaning against the wall again and washing one handed. Thankfully, my soap smelled like me, or more accurately, smelled like Iris since she was the one who bought it. She preferred that if she was bathing over here, she'd have the expensive shit she used regularly, whereas I'd be fine with whatever was on sale at HEB. She was also the source of my new bath bomb addiction; as a dealer she was generous and kept me stocked up without often asking for me to pay her back. If she super spoiled me some month, I lowered her rent and paid the difference. She gave me the side eye for it, but she never argued. She knew the deal.

With thoughts of Iris putting me in a better mood as always, I shut off the water and crawled back out of the tub, drying off halfheartedly and easing my way into a change of clothes in my bedroom. I didn't bother with anything tight and slipped on an oversized long-sleeved t-shirt and a pair of scrub pants I'd found at Good Will, both items comfy as hell for a day lounging around the house in pain. I'd barely finished getting dressed when I heard the knock on the front door.

Mama was right on time. I hollered that I'd be right there, then eased my way back down the hallway to unlock and let her in. She rolled herself up the slight door ramp from the deck the boss had paid for me to install for her, then waved someone in behind her. To my surprise it was Harvey, and he carried the large bag of takeout boxes from the assisted living center's excellent dining room. I knew Mama had finagled a chauffeur, but I hadn't figured it'd be him for some reason.

He paused as he entered, nostrils flaring and eyes wide before he blinked and turned a disappointed look at me. Damn werewolf senses, I thought, but ignored him as if I hadn't noticed anything odd.

Mama rolled up to my tiny square dining table, her spot lacking a chair as always, and ordered Harvey to set out the boxes and me to get some drinks. I complied, grabbing a bottle of iced tea and bringing it with me to the table. "Harvey, are you joining us?"

"He certainly is," Mama said in the kind of tone that told me Harvey had already tried to argue with her once about it and wasn't getting the opportunity to argue again. I ducked my head to hide my smile and went gingerly back to the kitchen to grab three glasses.

"Mama, did you get the plastic silverware sets with the meals or do I need to get some?"

Harvey checked the bag as he pulled out three Styrofoam cartons. "Nah, Mel, there's some in here. Maybe extra napkins? Doesn't look like there's any but those thin crappy kind in with the silverware."

I nodded and snagged some of those as well, then finally lowered myself into the chair at the table, Harvey nervously sitting across from me as if unsure of his welcome. Though why after he'd been such a help to me yesterday, I didn't know.

"How you feeling, honey?" Mama asked after we'd all started eating the lasagna, garlic bread, and salads the boxes had contained. "Iris was awful worried last night."

"We all were," Harvey added, then ducked his head as if embarrassed that he'd spoken up.

I smiled gently at him, trying to calm down whatever had set him off, but he wouldn't meet my eyes. Maybe he was still stressing about seeing me practically naked last night. Oh well, he'd get over it. "I'm still sore, really sore, and my energy level is crap. But it's much better than I expected it to be."

"Iris said you were hurt pretty bad last night," Mama agreed, giving me the look that said she wanted an accounting of my injuries and quick like. I didn't want to spoil the meal though, and I told her so.

"Not sure a listing of the damage will be lunch worthy, Mama, not if I want to keep my food down."

"That bad, huh?" She looked at me, clearly more worried now than she had been. I nodded reluctantly. "Fair enough. Don't think you'll manage to weasel out of it after lunch though."

"Wouldn't dream of it."

She let me eat a good chunk of my meal before breaking the comfortable silence again, her topic of conversation making me decidedly less than comfortable. "So according to Sadie, Marvin was bespelled. She give you any details when she stopped by? Harvey said she told him she'd check on you since he'd be at work this morning."

"I—no, no she didn't give me any details. Mostly just poked her head in," –in *between my thighs*–"checked I was breathing and left. Didn't tell me shit about it." I let myself sound as aggravated as I was, though maybe not for the reasons Mama would know. Harvey clearly did, judging by his frown, but screw him. It had been a while since I'd gotten laid and I deserved an orgasm after such a shitty night, right?

I ignored the fact that I had judged myself less than half an hour earlier. That was me; I was allowed. He didn't get to make judgements about my problematic sex life. I shook my head and the annoyance away, not wanting to dwell on it right then. "Makes sense about Marvin though. He didn't seem to recognize me at all except as a target, you know? And the trailer park itself—it's his home, has been for decades. But it might as well have been an obstacle course for all the care he had about damaging things. Not that I've met a lot of ghosts, but I wouldn't have thought one could change that suddenly so drastically on their own." I took a bite of garlic bread to soothe myself with carbs. "Poor Bessie. She loved him so damn much."

"Hard to risk loving like that knowing you can lose the person," Harvey offered quietly.

Mama nodded. "Ain't that the truth?" I flushed, realizing this was probably hitting too close to home for her after losing her own husband, but she went on without seeming to notice. "And sad as hell that if someone hadn't deliberately done that to him, Bessie might never have had to lose him at all. Not as he was."

"I honestly thought she'd turn into a ghost with him when she passed," I admitted. "Boss and I already had a plan for how we'd 'charge rent' to them after so they wouldn't have to give up haunting the trailer. That or we'd see if we could find a hedge witch who'd be willing to apprentice to a ghost if it meant getting to learn from someone with Bessie's knowledge and expertise, and then we'd charge *them* rent instead."

Harvey and Mama both chuckled in response, though the sound was sadder than it should have been. Harvey swallowed an enormous mouthful of lasagna, then sighed heavily. "Felt like both of them would always be here. Comforting to know it, too. Now this shit happened."

"Seems like things are going too wrong right about now. First Inna, then Marvin. Doesn't make sense. We've never had trouble like this. Never." I shook my head, appetite leaving as I considered it.

Mama nodded thoughtfully. "You're not wrong, honey. We've had issues crop up. Turf wars spilling onto the property, rogues killing human prey and trying to hide out here, that sort of thing. But even then, it was maybe once every few years we'd get a single incident of that kind. But back-to-back like this—and back-to-back with different *kinds* of wrong happening—that seems too strange to believe almost."

"Can you see if anyone's mentioned someone or something that could successfully curse a ghost like that? I know spirits are supposed to be harder to spell, aren't they?" I asked.

Harvey shrugged when Mama looked from me to him. "Don't look at me. I'd only dealt with packs before—before coming here. Knew a bit about the others, but still had a learning curve when I got here. I wouldn't know where to begin looking for people to ask."

"Even about the assault on that girl, Inna's her name?" Mama asked, voice carefully casual around the verbal landmine.

Harvey tensed, then visibly forced his shoulders to relax. "I can put feelers out about that, yeah, but there ain't many folks who'd be willing to talk to me about it. A packless wolf doesn't have much clout with pack wolves." Mama's face went sympathetic, and he looked away. "I'll try though. Do my best."

"That's all we can ask. Thank you, Harvey." She squeezed his hand gently, and he looked simultaneously like he wanted to escape and like he wanted to let her pull him into a long hard hug. Mama didn't mention that and answered me directly now. "I'll definitely start working my phone tree; you can be sure about that. If someone's pushing the rules this way, there's plenty of people who will want to know and help, if only to limit the chance that person will come back and interfere in their home territories. I bet I can find someone who knows something, even if it's only rumors and gossip."

"I swear Mama, if there's anyone who could weaponize gossip, it'd be you. I almost feel sorry for whoever did this knowing you and your phone tree is after them," I said, only partly joking.

Harvey finally cracked a smile. "I think the military calls those 'civilian intelligence agents,' and they pay them the big bucks for it, too."

"Well, I'm sure Big Brother knows where I am and what my bank account number is if they ever want to hire me."

That time we all laughed. If there was one thing the government deliberately *didn't* want to know about, it was folks like us and places like this trailer park. That 'plausible deniability' thing again, or so I guessed. It meant fewer speeding tickets for me. The local sheriff's department kindly turned a blind eye to me and any of the other Asphodel Estates residents that might be out and about the mortal neighborhood. As long as our people weren't causing imminent danger to the townsfolk, and if they were, the deputies knew to call me. At any time and for any odd reason they might not want to have to explain over the phone.

The system worked for us.

"I bet if they were ever going to hire on a paranormal intelligence gatherer, you'd be right at the top of their list, Mama," I said, grinning like a loon for the first time today.

"Damn right." She took the last few bites of her meal, then leaned back in her chair. "Harvey, do you need to be getting back to the shop soon or do we still have time?"

"I took the rest of the afternoon off. Seemed easier." He shrugged off Mama's thanks. "I worked plenty of overtime last week in case of a hangover or shit going wrong on the full moon. Still got plenty of hours in for this week's paycheck. Plus, I still need to finish up painting across the way. I can take you back whenever you're ready."

Mama nodded her satisfaction. "Well in that case, I think I'll spend some more time with my daughter, if she doesn't mind."

"Course not, Mama."

"Good," Harvey said, finishing up his own meal. "That's good. Thank you for lunch, Shelby—I'll get outta y'all's way so you can chat."

"Oh, before I forget," Mama said, grabbing hold of Harvey's sleeve as he started to rise from the table. "We know if anyone's getting a deer this year? Archery season's wrapping up, and Maria was asking if I knew if anyone would have whitetail meat this year."

I deliberately did *not* look at Harvey. It wasn't a secret he hunted, nor that he hunted without a license. In his defense, considering how he hunted, he could almost get away without a license since the game wardens rather unsurprisingly never liked to question any of our residents any more than the sheriff's office did. And sure, technically selling venison wasn't strictly legal in Texas either, but the few extra pounds of doe he might sell weren't doing anybody any harm. Well, aside from the deer. Besides, there was more important news in Mama's tidbit of conversation.

"Maria looking to make her whitetail chili already?" I asked, stomach almost rumbling at the thought despite the meal we'd eaten.

"It is getting to be that time of the year," Mama replied, looking smug at my ridiculous glee at the thought. "She's down to her last few pounds of ground from last year, though."

Maria's whitetail chili won awards all over the state. She cooked it for hours on end and served it with homemade corn bread that damn near melted in your mouth like the butter I always slathered it in. She did catering on the side as well as being the head chef at Elysian Fields, and aside from her pork tamales (always a big winner around here at Christmas) and tres leches cake (star at every birthday party ever in this town), her chili was easily her most requested item.

You had to catch her when she had the supplies to make it, which, with deer season being as short as it was and her not being a hunter herself, wasn't often. She occasionally experimented with other deer meat like fallow and axis since they counted as 'exotic' game and could be hunted year-round. They made decent chili. They just somehow weren't the same as her 'famous' whitetail chili, and her exacting standards didn't allow for merely 'decent.'

As I usually got to help sample her experiments, I was on board no matter what, though the whitetail was damned amazing.

The thought of her not being able to cook any time soon was tragic to say the least.

"I probably will get a deer or two," Harvey offered, carefully refraining from saying when or where. Some of our residents did have arrangements with local ranchers and the like to hunt legally. Some, like Harvey, waited out by the road at night.

Whitetail in the Texas Hill Country were vastly overpopulated and consequently dangerous as hell for motorists. It usually wasn't a question of 'if' you'd hit a deer once in your life down some backroad somewhere, it was 'when.' Really, with that in mind, Harvey was doing a public service nabbing the animals before they got out onto the asphalt. I reminded myself that whenever the deer did suddenly appear—no one ever saw him carry it in, plausible deniability and all—hanging by the harpy sisters' cabin, I'd make sure I put in an order for some of the ground meat and his special handmade smoked sausage both for me and Mama.

"I'll let Maria know you'll reach out when you have something for her then," Mama said, mildly.

He scrubbed the back of his neck and attempted to look less intimidating, not that anyone intimidated Mama as long as I'd known her. "Sounds good. I'll do that." He glanced at me and then back at Mama as if to see if we were going to ask him anything else. "I'm gonna go get another coat of paint on Miss Ginger's trailer. Just holler when you need me to take you back into town, Shelby."

"Of course. You have fun painting, now," Mama said, waving him off.

With one last look, as if trying to figure out if she was joking about painting being fun or not, Harvey headed out, waving awkwardly as he left.

12

That left me and Mama sitting at the table, and her with a decidedly knowing look on her face. I swallowed and tried to look innocent, knowing she'd see right through me with that "Mom" telepathy I swear people got as soon as they had a kiddo.

She waited long enough to be sure Harvey closed the door, though it wasn't like he couldn't listen through it easily enough if he concentrated, and then she then pinned me with a stern look. "What exactly is going on between you and Sadie this time? And don't try to tell me nothing is—there's no way you would have forgotten to ask her about Marvin if you weren't otherwise distracted." I closed my mouth around the denials she was right to expect. She waited a beat. "Plus, you've got that damn look on your face. Same one you get every time she messes with your head and gets you all tied up. You're fooling around with her again, aren't you?"

"Mama…" I trailed off, not knowing what to say, and all together more than a little uncomfortable having a conversation about my one-night stand partner to begin with. "She showed up again, yeah, and I guess got emotional after seeing me get hurt. If she feels emotions, which, who knows?" I debated on hiding my head in my arms on the table but figured it might pull too hard on my shoulders, so I leaned back in my chair instead. "It's just physical for her when it comes to me. Always has been, always will be. It's not a big deal, Mama."

I shrugged and got up to clear away the trash as much for something to do as because I was worried about the mess. Mama sighed and grabbed her glass, then wheeled herself over to the couch and gingerly transferred herself from her wheelchair. I realized Harvey hadn't taken his drink with him and detoured for a moment to grab it, refill it, and set it out on the picnic table outside. He'd smell it and know I meant for him to make sure he stayed hydrated while he worked, not that hydration seemed to be an issue for him in all the time I'd known him. Must have been another werewolf thing, though I didn't think I ever saw him pant in two-legged form like canines did.

Out of ways to procrastinate, I hobbled back inside, legs stiff again after sitting in the hard kitchen table chair. Though the flea market dining set was relatively pretty after I'd tackled it with reams of sandpaper and cherry-wood colored stain, it wasn't terribly comfortable, especially not on the butt and hips. Thus, the reason Mama didn't bother trying to move from her wheelchair to one of the dining chairs. It would be even crueler to her hips than it was to my bruises to say the least. Sometimes Mama wondered aloud if it would have been less painful to have lost feeling completely below the waist given how sore her hips could get, but privately I doubted she'd prefer the lack of control over bodily functions that would have caused. Either way, I didn't feel it my place to comment when she said things like that. I just did my best to make things as comfortable for her as I could and jumped on it any time she asked for help. Which, given the Smithson stubbornness, wasn't near as often as I'd like.

"Honey, sit down. I won't ask you about her again," Mama finally said, tired of my procrastination attempts. I sat as she bid, curling up my feet with a groan that turned into a moan as I finally got comfortable up against the back cushions. "I hate that she makes you unhappy every time. That's all."

I closed my eyes and shook my head. "Not much to be done about it, Mama. If I'd tell her 'No I'm not doing this again,' it wouldn't be a thing. But I...don't."

"I know, honey. Doesn't make her any less shitty for jerking my baby around, but I know." She reached out and rubbed a hand up and down my arm soothingly. "Let's talk about something else. You did promise me an injury run down."

"Ugh, I did, didn't I?" I leaned my head against the couch, almost wishing I could burrow into the softness and not come out for a while. But I had promised. I turned her way and obediently recited the long list of body parts I thought I'd managed to break or bruise in the course of my retreat from Marvin's rampage. Mama's face grew paler the longer I talked, but she knew what we were both capable of, so she didn't fuss.

"There probably were other internal injuries too, considering the lung, but no telling what specifically," I added once I'd run out of certainties.

"And it's not like the boon makes it any easier to tell, haphazard in the healing as it is," she agreed ruefully.

"Ain't that the truth?" I closed my eyes, feeling a prickle of tears sneaking up on me though I wasn't sure why I was crying now of all times. We weren't talking about Sadie anymore or even Marvin and Bessie's loss. Yet I cried, all at once.

"Oh, honey." Mama reached over and pulled me into a hug. I huddled there, practically in her lap, breathing in the smell of the soap she'd used most of my life, made by Bessie especially for her and no one else. I felt safe there, and I let the tears fall freely, no longer bothering to try to hold them back. "Oh, honey," Mama said again, stroking my hair in calming strokes. "Little overwhelmed today, huh?"

I chuckled wetly. Trust her to narrow in on what was bothering me before I could. I was overwhelmed, painfully, utterly overwhelmed and out of my depth. One tragedy or another—and I was counting my "whatever the hell I had with Sadie" in that list—I could have handled. But this back-to-back-to-back round of injuries and mysteries was one too many blows after another.

"It's good you're off today, I think," Mama continued. "You need a day to breathe and get your equilibrium back, on top of your physical health." She paused, her hand stilling on my hair, then offered, "I can stay for the night if you want? I can send someone for my toiletries and sleep in the guest bed."

"Mama, you said my mattress hurts. I won't ask you to do that," I finally said, sitting up slowly, though I stay curled against her.

She shrugged. "It'd only be for one night. I'm not going to leave you if you need me. So let me know if I should stay or not. It's your choice, Mel. I won't be disappointed either way, I promise."

I took a deep breath and made myself seriously consider her offer. My gut reaction was not only no, but hell no. Bad enough she'd had to come out here when I knew it still made her uncomfortable to be seen by our residents in a wheelchair—we shared our distaste for any public appearance of injury or weakness; adding a night of poor sleep for her seemed shitty.

But, on the other hand, Mama never offered to do something she didn't think she could handle. If she was willing to stay the night on my guest bed with its discount minimally back-supportive, ten plus year old mattress, then who was I to tell her no?

And a sleep over with my mama there to make sure I slept undisturbed sounded pretty damned amazing honestly. I knew Iris would likely offer to stay the night, too, but after a round with Sadie, I almost felt guilty at the thought of letting her, even without any kind of real claim between Iris and me.

"I—I'd love it if you could stay, Mama," I finally answered. "That—that sounds really nice."

"Then that's what I'll do. Can you call Harvey in so I can let him know I'll need him to run by my place? I'll give Donna Rae a call to ask her to put a bag together for me for him to pick up."

"Can do."

Saying was doing. I got up with a groan to go out front and give Harvey the message, then returned to the couch to curl up with Mama and watch some mindless television. I napped later, retreating to my bedroom while Mama pulled a book off my tiny office bookshelf and reclined on the couch without me. We didn't need to talk much;

having her there helped steady me, like her presence was the foundation I'd been missing too much the past few days. Off and on over the course of the day, part of me wished she'd agree to move in after all, but I knew better than to ask again. She wanted her little apartment at the assisted living place, wanted the community and her best friend Donna Rae in the apartment next to hers. Most of all, she wanted the surety that if something went wrong, there'd be people there who both knew how to help her and wouldn't judge her for not being the strong Smithson woman who had stood in my role for so many years with the supernatural community in Tartarus.

I knew all that, I did. It was harder to make myself care about all I knew when I was so worn out. That would pass though. Surely things couldn't get any worse, right?

For about a week, the thought proved to be true, thank all the mostly benevolent scheduling deities. With the exception of the memorial for Marvin—the second one we'd held now in four years and the last time I wanted to ever see Bessie cry that hard again—most things continued on as normally scheduled at Asphodel Estates.

Inna settled in fairly well, managing to share via pen and paper that she was used to working freelance from home and could do so in her trailer if we helped her get her things. Prior to her attack, she'd apparently been staying a couple small towns away in a tiny efficiency apartment over the garage of a family who traveled a lot. They were gone when the boss and I took her to get her things and leave a note about a "family emergency" causing her to move out suddenly. It was unfortunate—we'd hoped her prior landlords could help give us some insight into who or what might have stalked her and attacked her, and why said creature had ended up taking her all the way to Tartarus. She didn't have any idea, and we had no physical evidence to track thanks to the rain washing everything away in the days after we'd found her.

So, she signed a contract with Boss like everyone else did, though in her case it was only on a short-term basis to start. In under a month, we'd know if she was going to be one of the norms in our collection of supernatural residents or not. She might stay if she was human, but it was less likely. Even if she was handling the trauma remarkably well—aside from the not talking thing—living around folks completely alien to mortal beings wasn't easy on a long-term basis. I didn't know if Iris would have felt comfortable in the trailer park if she hadn't been an omen seer. It was just shy of "normal" enough for her to be "other."

Like all the rest of us.

Either way, Inna was settling in and cautiously forming friend-ships or at least neighborly acquaintances with a decent number of the other tenants. Sadie continued to be a common guest at her trailer, ostensibly to keep 'checking her wounds.' I tried not to think about what else she was likely checking out.

Iris and Harvey made a point of looking in on me almost as often as folks were checking on Inna and Bessie, and I tried not to feel penned in by the attention. I was all healed up, and I wasn't going to break or lose my mind or anything. Things were stressful, sure, but I'd gotten my crying jag over and done with while Mama was here, and that was it. No more tears for me. Well, except for Marvin's memorial, but that was expected and indeed justified.

Otherwise, I kept on doing my job. Checking in on late rent payments, helping a prospective tenant decide on which of our avail-able furnished rentals she'd like to move into: a brownie who might or might not stay long without an actual house and foundations to sink her magic into. I worked up the contract with Mama and Boss's contributions on what exactly we did and did not want the new tenant, who was one of those older butch lesbians that just oozed charm with every inch of her barely four and a half feet of height, to feel comfortable doing on our property. There was far more of the former than the latter. Brownies were consummate hearth mages and considered it their honor to clean and care for their 'hosts' as they once called the owners of the places they inhabited back when it was harder for fae kind to move about safely in our world without being beaten to death with cold iron. Now that places like the Estates had become more common in the U.S., there were brownie homeowners, something Mama told me would have been damn near unthinkable as recent as some fifty years prior.

Technology still wasn't terribly comfortable for them to be around, however, and I had to hire Harvey to help me remove or insulate all the steel and iron in the unit she finally decided on. Some brownies were more sensitive than others, to the point of being incapable of tolerating iron-containing alloys like steel, but Mrs. Hudson —as she'd introduced herself and signed the contract with no first name and no Mr. to be seen—swore she wasn't near as worried about it as I was. Instead, she'd seemed thrilled to be 'allowed' to help with tidying up the community as much as we'd let her, cleaning the bathhouse and attached game room/community library (which I normally had to contract out and which was always a little dicey as there were somehow fewer housekeepers in the know than there were repair people), keeping the gravel swept nicely, and making sure the picnic and barbecue area was clear of trash and too many weeds.

I felt a little bad putting it into the contract, but like with Khoi and the pool cleaning, having something 'hers' to do made the place feel more like home, or so she patiently explained to me. She also mentioned helping cook during any and all potlucks and barbecues. That *wasn't* included in the contract, but I had to admit I was excited to try her cooking whenever we did have one. Brownie cooking was supposed to be top notch comfort food, but I'd never known one personally well enough to get to share a meal with them. Mrs. Hudson promised she'd make just the thing, winking at me with a grin that had me blushing.

I didn't see her move her things in. Instead, I only noticed as I was walking by the next morning that her small deck had been transformed into a lovely outdoor living room and curtains I knew were higher quality than we could furnish hung in the windows. Well played, Mrs. Hudson. Well played.

It was only a couple days after Mrs. Hudson settled in, that the peace shattered right to bits.

13

The trouble started as a simple argument from my point of view. I got a call from Ellaria, the youngest of the harpy flock sisters, warning me Muriel and Nataline were having a spat. A big one from the sound of it on the other end of the line, and one that might end up damaging property if someone didn't come by to distract them and break it up. I fought back a groan and promised I'd be by immediately.

The thing about harpies was they liked to fight, and frankly they didn't much like people, including other harpies. The trio of sisters didn't have many friends in the community, though Ellaria came the closest, still young enough to not hate everything with a proper adult harpy furor. I thought Harvey might be the only resident they'd ever willingly invited over to hang out, though that usually meant they had some kind of kill to share if he was open to the idea of cleaning and skinning it for them. That kind of friendship worked for them. But they weren't really keen on anyone else, even each other most of the time. Harpies didn't really do family love: not if love meant being *kind*.

Let's just say they rocked the "I'm a bitch to my sister because she's *my* sister but if you so much as look at her the wrong way, I'll peck your eyes out" sort of sibling relationship.

Still, they were usually better about keeping the squabbles to a minimum around Asphodel Estates property as opposed to the modified extra tall doublewide they'd settled onto one of the rental slabs behind the pool. If they were outside and brawling—that didn't bode well for anyone getting in the middle of it.

Shame "getting in the middle of it" was part of my job description.

I grabbed a couple of large bird nets we kept on hand for just such an occasion, then hurried out to head the couple rows over to the harpy nest. As soon as I left my door, I could hear the fight, which had turned into a hell of a commotion. A pair of voices shrieked and hissed in turn, and serious clatters and crashes warned me there would be a mess when I got there.

Sure enough, the two eldest harpies were going at it like winged alley cats, ripping and tearing at each other with claws and sharp hooked beaks, rising to the air for a few beats only to descend again to roll about the grass like angry kids on the playground. Decorative pots of succulents and cactus were strewn across their concrete patio slab, and both sisters had cacti spines sticking out of various body parts—mostly wherever feathers gave way enough to bare vulnerable skin. Those body parts also sported more than a few cuts and bruises.

Harpy folk did *not* fight fair on the best of days.

Behind them, Ellaria huddled against their trailer, wings mantled protectively in front of herself and bruises on her face showing she'd already made the mistake of trying to either calm them down or, more likely considering harpy predisposition, to get involved in the fight herself. She was too young to have made a dent though, I guessed. Harpies grew larger and stronger as they aged. Ellaria had barely grown to the size of a ten-year-old human child so far, while both her older sisters stood closer to average human female height with wing spans to match.

She nodded when she saw me but didn't make a move to either help or hinder my task. I knew she likely wouldn't no matter how bad the fight got between the sisters or between me *and* the sisters.

I groaned, already feeling less enthusiastic the longer the fight continued. I squared my shoulders and walked as close as I dared to the brawling pair, readying the nets and hoping I'd get one of them on the first try. One I could probably hold back from the other, but keeping both apart? That was a good way to lose fingers and a lot of blood. I waited a beat, gauging the distance and haphazard rhythm of the fight, trying to find the right moment. I didn't know if they'd pull apart long enough for me to net one of them, but I decided if they did, I'd aim for Nataline as the oldest, and thus strongest. I'd rather wrestle Muriel to the ground if I had a choice.

I took up the first net in both hands and bit my lip. I counted off silently in my head. *One...two...three!*

I hurled the heavy weighted net like my daddy taught me down at the Galveston coast on a rare fishing trip. It spun into the air like a spider web in flight and collided with Nataline as she tried to gain height for another diving charge at her sister. She shrieked as the thick weighted rope wrapped around her outstretched wings, forcing her to fall back the few feet to the ground. She struggled against it, cursing me with every other breath, but I ignored her. For the moment, I still had to deal with Muriel.

I looked to see her picking herself up from where Nataline had thrown her into a picnic table, one with a definite lean due to the newly broken leg and bench seat. I hurried and stepped between her and her fallen opponent, not sure Muriel wouldn't attack despite Nataline's helplessness. One never knew when it came to harpies with their bloodlust up. Behind me, I heard something dragging across the ground and risked a glance to see Ellaria was in motion, pulling her sister out of the way to give me as much room to fight as I needed. Wisely, she'd left Nataline still safely wrapped in the netting, cursing her youngest sister and I all the while.

I pulled the other net off my shoulder and set myself to face Muriel. Only, when she lifted her head, I wondered if I faced her after all.

Instead of the vocally angry harpy I'd expected, Muriel'd gone utterly silent in a way so sinister after the shrieks and curses she'd thrown with such glee only moments before. No, now she stood quiet and voiceless, with her forehead—the only part of a harpy's beaked face mobile enough for expression of emotion—perfectly smooth.

And her eyes. Fuck me, her eyes looked like Marvin's. Empty and black as night, pupil swallowing everything else until I looked at empty shadows where a person had been in her usually angry gaze.

"Shit!" I cursed. "Ellaria, I need you to get Boss or Sadie right now!"

Behind me, Ellaria all but audibly rolled her eyes. "Little busy here, you know. Get them your—"

"Get them *now!* She's spelled like Marvin was!"

"Oh shit. Oh *shit*." She breathed.

I gritted my teeth and didn't respond, determined to save my breath for the fight ahead.

Muriel cocked her head, dark eyes locked on my form as I took several careful steps toward her, trying to keep her away from her sister, now helpless on the ground thanks to my interference. Muriel looked only at me though, which told me whatever or whoever had spelled her had once again set me as their target. If not, she'd still be trying to get at her sister. It was the harpy way; a fight wasn't over until one of them yielded, even if someone interfered.

Muriel didn't seem to realize her sister existed. Just me, my net in my hands. Weighted and sturdy though it might be, it would *not* hold up against a harpy truly out for my blood.

Behind me, Nataline shrieked for someone to let her out, and Ellaria muttered desperately into her phone, hopefully calling for help. Please, fluffy feathered lords, let her be calling for help, I thought.

Then there wasn't time for thinking, only reacting as Muriel charged, leaping across the space between us with a crash of wings opening to send her into flight. She spun towards me with the speed of her take off. I held steady until the last minute, then whirled to the side, flinging out the net but keeping hold of it. I hoped to drag her clear of the harpy trailer and into the tighter space between trailers to try to keep her on the ground. I only caught the edge of one wing, but it sent her to the ground in a crash of gravel and a rush of air from beneath feathers.

She still made no sound, not even an attempt at the silent roars Marvin had been capable of, and I hoped that wasn't a worse sign for me. I yanked at the net, trying to drag her close enough for me to engulf her in the net completely. Instead, she twisted her head and bit straight through the ropes snagged against her wing joint, freeing herself as her sister, more tightly wrapped, had been unable to. I back pedaled and tried to gather the net up again for another throw, but Muriel lashed out with her clawed hands to deliberately tangle her fingers with the strands.

This time she pulled me off my feet when she gave a vicious yank, towing me toward her feet's claws which were aimed directly at my face. All at once I let go of the net and tucked and rolled. As I'd hoped, the sudden lack of resistance sent her stumbling back, still tangled in the net, though now it was for my benefit and not hers.

I didn't dare hesitate while she was subdued if for only an instant. I darted forward and kicked out hard against her left knee to knock her half to the ground, glad as always for the sturdy heels of my work boots. I spun to kick again, this time with my steel toes against her torso, aiming to break a rib if I could.

I'd do more damage if I aimed for her precious flight-awarding keel bone, but I didn't want to go that far. Not yet. Not when there was a chance of help arriving to free her from the spell before one or the other of us died screaming in my case or silent in hers.

I felt bone give beneath my boots, but Muriel still gave no sign she noticed the pain. She finally shook off the net and lunged at me, clawed hands trying to tear through my jacket to the skin beneath. I ducked again, striking out with my elbow to her face, immediately regretting it as I felt her wicked beak slice through the thin skin there. I hissed with pain and turned enough to send a fist striking out, this time careful to make sure I hit her eye, saving my hand, though the heavy occipital ridge might leave a nasty bruise on my knuckles. I followed up with a quick jab to hit her again, then lunged down to my knees under another slash of her claws.

She was moving too slow, I realized.

Not to be ungrateful, but I knew harpies; I'd watched them fight on more than one occasion, and Muriel moved slower than she should, each blow slow with hesitation as if fighting on a delay.

It had to be the spell, I realized. Whatever had her was only controlling her—Muriel was still in there. Had to still be in there.

I didn't know if the knowledge would do either of us any good. If I couldn't hold her off, I would have to choose between her life and mine.

"Come on Boss, Sadie, get your asses over here," I muttered, ducking again, this time from a kick Muriel's controller had decided to try, echoing my aim for the knee but falling barely short.

Only barely, though—that move had been quicker, and who knew what the learning curve on 'deadly possession' was. I kept fighting, ducking and dodging and kicking and screaming my frustration as I was yet again forced to attack one of our residents. This one might not have been my friend but was still a living thinking being who didn't deserve to be used as a weapon.

I kept up the pace, staying ahead of her attacks.

Murphy's law sent me sprawling, as I tripped over a piece of the pots destroyed in the early stages of their scuffle. I fell flat on my back, the force of it knocking the wind out of me long enough for Muriel to leap down over me, legs on either side. Both clawed hands raised over her head, ready to tear my heart out of my chest.

I tried to move, but still could barely breathe. Her hands began to fall—

Then she choked, blood bubbling up between the sharp edges of her beak. She took a step backwards, then two. She toppled sideways to reveal Nataline behind her, her claws holding the still beating heart of her sister.

Now I could move. I rolled and crawled to Muriel, somehow wanting her to be alive though I knew how impossible it had to be with her heart literally torn out between her wings through her back.

Her eyes opened to the sky above her, but golden again.

Whoever controlled her was gone. Her body no longer of use.

Nataline stepped toward us gingerly, then lay the bloody heart down on Muriel's chest. I had to force myself not to vomit at the gruesome sign of respect.

"She was going to kill you," Nataline said softly, her beak clicking around her words. "I had no choice."

"I know," I managed to say. "I know."

"Do *not* thank me for it," she said, eyes hard and filled with the first tears I'd ever seen from a harpy. "Don't you dare."

"I won't," I said. It was a debt neither one of us wanted to acknowledge the weight of. "I wouldn't. I am sorry for the loss of her wings from your flock."

"The flock is sorry to lose her," Nataline replied, completing the ritual phrase for the death of a harpy family member. "I am sorry she was lost."

"So am I."

Boss came running around the corner then, Ellaria trailing after him in half leaping half flying bounds to keep up with his inhuman speed. They both slammed to a halt at the sight of the three of us...or more accurately the two of us and Muriel's body.

I spoke before either of them could apologize for being too late. This was no one's fault but whoever forced Muriel to try to kill us and thus forced Nataline to kill her own flock sister. "It was just like Marvin, Boss. Same eyes, same hyper focus on me. Same...same fucked up ending to it."

"There was no way to save her?" Boss asked, looking from the disembodied heart to me to Nataline, then back again. The harpy elder hissed, hearing the implications and liking none of them.

"We could have left her alive, sure—but you'd be finding another property manager." She eyed me disdainfully, wrapping her grief up tight in a blanket of anger and disgust like a proper harpy bitch. "I doubt even her boon could save her from bleeding out from an open throat."

"No, I suppose it probably couldn't," Boss mused, looking back down at Muriel and keeping his face carefully blank. "Though it would be an interesting experiment either way."

114

I blinked at the careless tone as he spoke about the possibility of my throat torn open but shook it off. I knew our boss wasn't heartless; demonic sure, but not heartless as such. This would be a shock to him, almost as much as a shock to Muriel's flock sisters. Now two of his tenants, those under his protection—and mine, of course, but it was his not-a-name on the contracts—had been lost to this unknown magic user. It was more death in our trailer park in a few days than we normally had in years, including both violent ones and those of natural causes.

This wouldn't be an easy thing for anyone to brush off. Not now. Not ever.

"We need to find this asshole," I said, finally able to look down at Muriel without the urge to scream. "We need to find them and kill them, once and for all."

No one argued with me.

14

Later than night, we built a pyre for Muriel in the center of the community memorial grounds, with all the residents carrying what branches and sticks they could find across the footbridge in a quiet procession to build a round nest for her to be burned in like a phoenix, only one who'd never rise again. Fire was the harpy way of honoring the dead, of releasing their bodies back into the sky and stars as ash and embers. Normally, it was a dangerous task as feathers and fire were a terrible mix, but Nataline asked me to do the honors. I wasn't sure if it was to keep her and the surviving sister singe-free or simply as an offering of respect for the fact I'd tried to save her sister as best I could. Nataline had told me so, though it was hard for me to believe. But she was right—I hadn't killed Muriel, and I could have. Flighted fates save me, I could have. Harpies had the same hollow brittle bones as their less sentient avian cousins. I could have ended our fight with one swift kick to the keel bone or the pelvis...or to her throat. Any of those would have injured Muriel far beyond repair—harpies being truly mortal if supernatural in nature. They healed slowly, same as all other mortal creatures, no matter their gifts.

Unless they were my gifts, of course. And wasn't that a bitch sometimes.

Regardless of Nataline's reasoning, I would honor Muriel with the flame as she'd asked. I owed her that.

"May the sky reclaim its child," Nataline, as the eldest surviving harpy in the flock, shouted the ritual words, and all who watched echoed them. "May her flight now be unending." *May her flight now be unending.* "May her wings hold her for always." *May her wings hold her for always.* "May fire light her way." *May fire light her way.*

That was my cue. I took a deep breath, then threw the flaming branch as hard as I could toward the rickety pyre, part of me hating it was the best we could do for her. The branch whipped through the dark night like something from the dancers at the Texas Renn Faire campgrounds, spinning poi around themselves like a whirlwind of light. The makeshift torch landed perfectly on the lighter fluid-soaked pallets and bracken, and the entire pile went up in a circle like a roman candle. Fire whooshed up to consume it all with a kind of physical press of sound sending me swaying backwards.

The flames quickly reached the sheet wrapped bundle at the top of the pyre nest, and the scent of burning flesh began to fill the air. Iris retched under her breath but managed to keep a straight face out of respect for the dead. Of the rest of those watching, only a few would have the same kind of visceral reaction to the smell of a body burning. This wasn't the first pyrrhic burial I'd attended since taking on the job of property manager. Luckily, there wasn't a burn ban on—the last death had come right around midsummer and hiding the smoke from the fire marshals had taken some creative combined magics. We could burn Muriel without any panic about the law. Even if it seemed odd to avoid the law for the investigation of what was clearly a murder.

I shook with barely contained rage at the thought of murder coming into our odd little mix of a community. Sure, most of us registered as monsters on a 'normal' person's register, including me and Iris with her omen chasing eyes and a body some closed-minded religious types would 'fear' on principle, but we took care of our own. We did our best to keep the out-of-the-know in the local town safe from others like us, and by all that was holy, *we took care of our own.*

But now Muriel lay dead and torn to pieces. Forced to become a monster without any chance to save herself. Killed by her own sister to save my sorry life.

It looked more and more likely she and Marvin had been bespelled by the same person who'd left Inna's battered self on our proverbial doorstep. How they'd managed to injure Inna, I couldn't be sure—but the timing of her being found and the possession of the others was too close to ignore. I worried Inna was at the heart of the mess, but Sadie had examined her and was certain Inna wasn't a spell caster. She wasn't *normal* exactly, but not a magic worker. We still wouldn't know for sure if Inna had been bitten by a werewolf until the next full moon —whatever the bite looked like—but we knew for sure one *hadn't* killed Muriel or Marvin.

The strange magic user might have possessed a werewolf to do their bidding, though, and that opened up the possibility Harvey could have been used for the attack. Even if he had and somehow couldn't remember, he'd be innocent of the intent of the act.

I might not know much, but I knew damned well neither Muriel nor Marvin had been themselves. If they were innocent, then Harvey would be innocent of the possibility of a possessed attack, too.

No, Harvey was in the clear, but there were always those who doubted someone's words on their own behalf. I hadn't believed him guilty anyway. I'd seen Harvey lie more often than most, usually when he was trying to get out of trouble for knocking over trashcans after slipping his leash. The rest of the time though, Harvey was almost unflinchingly honest. If your vehicle was fucked, he'd tell you when you brought it in for repairs. If you'd compounded the issue by avoiding regular maintenance, he'd pull no punches in his lecture and then he'd charge you exactly what his time would be worth to bring the battered truck or car back from the brink of vehicular death. If you pissed him off, you knew it.

If he trusted you, you knew it.

No, Harvey hadn't lied when he'd said he had nothing to do with biting the young woman, but I hadn't been the one he had to convince. Even Miss Ginger's forgiveness hadn't swayed some of the doubters, but Muriel's death finally seemed to have done so. Some of the other residents were standing closer to him now than they had since the full moon. It was a silent show of semi-support, but one I imagined Harvey would cling to with both hands.

Iris gave me a quiet look, then tilted her head in his direction. I eyed her, then nodded. She'd know how to comfort someone in this hell of a situation. She took the few steps to his side, then slid her hand over one of his clenched fists, easing her fingers in to hold his hand. His shoulders tensed, then slowly shook at the contact, but I knew he'd refuse to cry until later. Muriel would have denied it if asked, but to Harvey, she had been one of his friends, the vicious tongued harpy matching his own, often argumentative attitude. He'd helped build the screened-in porch they'd added on to the doublewide, complete with massive wooden perches Harvey helped them muscle in despite the flock's cracks about the "ground pounding mongrel dog."

Muriel had been the only one to thank him after, though she'd laughed all the way through the collective vitriol. But then, Harvey laughed, too.

He'd lost a friend today, and I'd been part of the reason why, if not the person who *was* the reason. That thin line separated me from true responsibility, and my psyche kept tiptoeing over it again and again until my logic pulled me back.

I watched him and Iris for another moment, knowing Iris might have known I did so, but Harvey likely wouldn't. She'd stay with him tonight, I guessed, to offer companionship while he mourned since the harpies would likely close ranks on their own and probably wouldn't have welcomed Harvey there anyway.

It hurt a little, knowing I would head back to my trailer alone to deal with my guilt and the lingering ache from the fight we'd had. But there was nothing for it really. The harpy sisters would hold their private vigil until the fire died down, so I had no excuse to stick around. I debated on a brief patrol around the community, but doubted we needed it. The mystery asshole hadn't stuck around or left any traces of their presence after Marvin; they gave me no reason to believe they would now, either.

With that in mind and knowing my mood would drag the solemn event down even further, I edged my way through the small crowd of tenants to head back home alone.

When I got there, Sadie was waiting, leaning against my front door like she had all the time in the world to wait for me.

As if she ever waited for anyone. The top three buttons on her blouse were undone, and I could barely glimpse the top of her bra at the bottom of the line of skin those buttons revealed.

"You want company?" It wasn't actually a question, though part of me was grateful she pretended it was.

I thought about sending her on, of refusing to play her game tonight, but all I kept thinking of was Iris's hand in Harvey's and how lonely I was. I didn't want to brood alone tonight, didn't want to be alone period, even if the only other option was utterly stupid on my part.

I opened the door. "After you."

To our credit, if you could call it that, we made it to my bed this time.

She left before I woke up.

15

I tried to avoid Sadie after that night, I swear I did. Instead of keeping her at bay, my feeble attempts to not see her backfired and seemed to draw her back to me more often in the next few days than the entire time we'd done this bullshit, not even "friends with occasional benefits" thing.

It didn't help that Iris spent more and more time with Harvey.

I couldn't blame her. He was a surprisingly decent guy underneath the trucker hat and they seemed to enjoy each other's friendship, or whatever the hell they were building to. I didn't want to guess they were dating yet—yet being the key word—as Iris would have told me if she planned on dating another tenant, or hell, dating anyone.

It wasn't my right to get jealous, not when I couldn't get the courage to tell her I wanted more than the damn near codependent friendship we'd had for so long.

Didn't mean I wasn't jealous. Didn't mean Sadie wasn't more than willing to let me work out my jealousy between her thighs until her hyper-controlled self was wrung out with one orgasm after another after another. Until, of course, she decided she was done with me for the day and went off to enjoy another one of her 'friends,' usually starting off with a kiss in my line of sight to make sure I knew where she was headed.

And yet, I still welcomed her back to my place the next time she showed up.

Let's just say, I wasn't proud of my behavior the week after Muriel's death. Poor life choices were definitely a thing.

I hated to admit it, but my downward spiral of wrapping myself around Sadie's little finger like her more pathetic admirers might have continued if not for a conversation I would have sworn would make things worse.

The day after Thanksgiving which the community basically ignored, Mama and Iris had their standing shopping date of that capitalistic mob frenzy 'celebration' known as Black Friday. I stayed at the Estates to work, having managed to duck the shopping this year, bless the thrifty misers everywhere. I would say *fortunately* managed to duck the trip, but the excuse to avoid screaming credit-card waving crowds centered around a particularly nasty tenant mediation over on the RV side of the community. I'd spent three frustrating hours straight explaining to our resident half-troll, Tully, that Bessie's familiar was *not* a stray tabby cat anyone could claim for dinner, and in any case, part of his contract explicitly stated domesticated animals in general and cats in particular were *not* a menu item on our property, damn it. The intervention was eventually concluded successfully...until the next time it came up yet again as I'd feared it would when Boss agreed against my recommendation to take Tully on as a tenant in the first place.

Almost wishing I'd braved the crowds after all, I exhaustedly returned to my trailer to find deck once again occupied. This time, Sadie wasn't the one waiting on my doorstep trailer. Instead, there stood Harvey, still wearing his engine grease splattered coveralls from the shop and twisting his hands together like he dreaded whatever he had to tell me.

I stepped up to the deck and waited for him to speak. Harvey looked down, the brim of that terrible trucker hat hiding his face, and honest to gods shuffled his feet like an anxious little boy. I choked back the tired laugh that wanted to escape at the sight, and I wondered again when and how I'd started seeing him as a friend instead of an occasional annoyance. "Mel, I gotta ask you..."

He trailed off, and I nudged him with my elbow, raising my eyebrows in question when he peeked out from under the brim of the hat. I shook my head. "I had a long day, man. I'm not up for dancing around shit. Gotta ask me *what*, Harvey?"

"Are uh... Are you and Iris like... *you and Iris?*"

I blinked, not unfamiliar with the question—I'd had similar conversations every time I visited Iris at Tulane, but I hadn't expected it from *Harvey* of all people. Honestly, I had seen the possible pairing coming, but I thought it would surely be Iris who told me. How had he not had this conversation with her already? "Harvey, are you asking me if Iris is single?"

"Well not exactly. I mean, I thought she spends a lot of time at your place, you know, and everyone says she moved in because you already lived here and I'm wondering if maybe... Aw...hell if I know what I'm trying to ask." He sat down on my picnic table as abruptly as a puppet with its strings cut. I shoved down a shiver at the thought. Puppets freaked me the hell out, right up there with rooms full of porcelain dolls—you knew something creepy would go down when you stepped into a room like that. And considering the whole possession thing, puppets hit closer to home right about now.

"You want a beer?" I asked, trying to cover my discomfort at both the minor mental creep out and the subject at hand. He nodded, and I stepped inside to grab him one of the Heinekens I kept stocked for Iris and a Jack Daniels Pink Lemonade for myself out of the fridge. He scoffed at the sight of the bright pink bottle in my hand, but I rolled my eyes. "These are delicious. Asshole."

He chuckled and cracked open the beer, taking a long sip and then leaning forward with his elbows on his knees. I twisted the top off with a wince as my palm decided to protest the abuse, then took a sip to soothe myself with the sweet alcoholic bliss. We sat in silence for a moment drinking while I tried to figure out how to say what I feared I needed to say. I hated the thought of outing Iris to anyone, but if he didn't know... I cleared my throat and decided to be blunt about it. "Harvey, you do know Iris is..."

I trailed off, my courage failing against the threat of betraying my friend if somehow Harvey'd missed the memo on her gender. Iris didn't hide who she was, but people could be surprisingly unobservant—men interested in dating her, in particular.

He coughed, nearly spitting out the beer he'd just drank. He wiped his mouth and scowled at me, then carefully took another drink. When I didn't go on, he sat up a little straighter and looked me dead in the eye. "Yes, I know Iris is trans. I know half the park thinks I'm a dumb redneck, but I'm not stupid. I mean it's not a secret what with where she works and her trans symbol bracelet and all." He shrugged, and I felt my shoulders relax all at once in the face of his nonchalance. "I know what you're worried about, and I don't blame you, but I'm not that kind of an asshole. I... Iris is 'bout the prettiest woman I think I've ever seen in real life. Probably the nicest I've ever met, too."

"She's probably the prettiest woman most folks have met, let's be real."

"Sure prettier than you," Harvey cracked, and I leveled an amused glare at him. He caught the humor in my eyes and laughed. "I never said I wasn't an asshole. Just not about that. I mean, it's not like our landlord ain't gay as hell. If I was a queerphobic piece of shit, I'd hardly have picked this place to move into, even with the lack of werewolf friendly places to rent."

I nodded and tapped my bottle against his can. Fair enough, I figured.

He rubbed a hand against the scruff on his jaw. "So y'all together or not? I ain't trying to come between a couple or anything. We've been spending some time together lately, and I didn't want a make a move 'til I was sure and all."

I fiddled with the bottle in my hands, picking at the label and beginning to roll it off as I always did when I was anxious. This was a conversation I had deliberately avoided with Iris and her attraction to dudes, but we'd danced around it often enough. "We've never dated, no. But." I cleared my throat. "She's my person, you know? It's not like she isn't gorgeous or I'm not into women or anything. More that I don't want to risk fucking it up, assuming she wasn't straight, which she is. Never wanted a girl as far as I know. But she's *Iris*. Prolly the most important person in my life next to Mama." I shook my head, angry at myself for dancing around it. "No, we're not together, Harvey. You—you should ask her out, if you're interested."

"But *you* are interested." His voice was quiet and a little resigned. "Shit, Mel, 's not like I've got a chance if you're the competition. You're her person, too, you know."

"But I'm not her *girlfriend*, and I won't ever be, much as I might want to. She's straight, Harvey. I know she's straight, and even if she wasn't, I don't have any right to scare off someone who isn't too chicken shit to actually ask her out. She's single, and that's what you were asking."

I took another drink, then turned my head to look him over, really looking for the first time maybe. He'd been the asshole werewolf who'd gotten cocky with me right off the bat while filling out the contract giving him a home. And dear sartorial deities help him, he dressed terribly, which coming from me said a lot. Aside from all that, though he was not unattractive under the trucker hat, far from it if I was honest with myself. Which might explain some of my rough edges around him, now that I thought about it. I did *not* flirt particularly well, thus my dismal love life. I laughed a little and looked away. It would be my luck to figure out I had a thing for him when he came to ask if my bestie was single. Too late to do anything about it now.

Disaster bi-ness strikes again. Fuck my life.

"Look Harvey, you're a better man than you pretend to be. You and I both know it. You'd be good for her, I think." I narrowed my eyes at him. "Screw her over though and you best believe there will be more than salt in my shotgun when I hear about it."

"Fair enough," he said, chuckling though I didn't think it was because he thought I was joking. Good, we understood each other then. He worried at his lip for a moment, fiddling with the bottle in his hand. "If you're interested in Iris, why're you screwing around with Sadie for, anyway?"

I choked. *Motherfucking werewolves,* I swear to every damn furry power that might be.

He waited a moment for me to speak, then shook his head. "Ain't like you're obvious or nothing but it's not a secret. Ain't like you the only one she's got twisted up, neither. Half the women in the park have likely shown up when she crooked her little finger."

"Harvey, I didn't need to know that."

He pushed back the truck hat and raised his eyebrows at me point-edly and waited.

"OK yes, I fucking knew. I don't like to think about it. So sue me." I almost wished I didn't have my drink in my hand; I would have had the option of crossing my arms over my chest to do something anything with my hands but all I could do was take another sip. I debated on draining it and decided what the hell. If we were going there, I definitely could use another. "Be right back. You want a re-up?"

"It's your booze. I'm just drinking it."

"We'll call that a yes then."

It seemed fair, though he wasn't liable to get drunk off the bitty alcohol percentage in what I had available. I really needed to invest in some hard liquor if he made a habit of heart-to-hearts. Because I could, I grabbed two of the pink lemonades this time, shoving it into his hand with an 'I dare you' glare on my face. He scoffed and shook his head, but opened in and took a swig all the same. He blinked. "Well shit, that *is* good. Damn it, there goes my street cred."

"As if you had any in the first place. Bailey's and hot cocoa is not exactly the manliest of drinks. It's delicious, sure, but certainly not whiskey straight or some James Bond 'shaken not stirred' shit." He nodded, allowing me the point, and kept drinking, deliberately quiet as if forcing me to break the silence. I tossed back some of my drink, then finally spoke. "Iris was in a serious relationship when Sadie moved in. Like talking about moving him in from Louisiana serious. Wasn't anything I had a right to say about it, but it hurt, you know? And then Sadie gave me a wink and damned if I wasn't naked in under five minutes and not totally sure how it happened." I shrugged tiredly.

"And then I got the 'you know I can't settle down with just anyone, right? Oh, darling you didn't know did you? I'm so sorry...' bullshit from her. So, I thought I'd shake it off and put it behind me."

"But?" he prodded, though he looked like he couldn't believe he was doing so.

"But she's so hot," I whined, hanging my head. "And the sex is *so* good. It sucks 'cause I'm not built for casual. But that's all anybody's interested in with me apparently."

"Bullshit," Harvey snapped, then softened when I looked up at him, shocked at the tone. "Mel, you sell yourself way too damn short. And I swear you don't look around. Too focused on taking care of other people but not on what they're actually thinking 'bout you." He blew out a breath and knocked his shoulder into mine. "Maybe you and Iris can't ever be *you and Iris.* But you can do a hell of a lot better than the witch bitch, Mel. Don't let her make you think otherwise."

I stared at him but couldn't think of a damn thing to say. Sure, Mama and Iris thought the absolute worst of Sadie, but mostly anyone else I heard talking about her always seemed like they'd be thrilled with whatever they could get. If I ever got up the guts to ask, I'd been sure they'd say *she* was out of *my* league.

But here was Harvey saying different.

And damned if I knew what to think about it. I was so used to Sadie existing as this unattainable gorgeous thing, one who would always get away because she refused to let anyone catch her. Especially not someone like me whose bi-ness meant I 'straddled the fence and wouldn't commit to the pussy already' as she so delicately put it. I never felt good enough for her, and she didn't help with the way she played games avoiding anything resembling commitment like the plague. I'd almost thought she was aro except for how nasty she was about aces and aros not belonging in the queer community any more than bi folks did.

Which again, she really was *such* a bitch, wasn't she? Why had I put up with it for so long?

I deserved better. I tested it out in my brain, all but tasting it. It didn't sound right, sounded damn near the opposite of right, but Harvey didn't bullshit. Not ever except for when he was ashamed of himself after a full moon. Other than that, though—if he said something, he meant it.

"I deserve better," I tried, barely managing to make the words out. At Harvey's slow nod and serious eyes, I felt something settle in my stomach, and I said it again. "I deserve better."

"Damn right." He clinked his bottle against mine in a toast. "Here's to deserving better."

"Damn right," I echoed.

We drank the rest of our frilly drinks in silence and then he headed out, back to his trailer or Iris's though I didn't want to ask which. Either he'd ask her out or he wouldn't. Either way, I felt more settled than I had in a long, long time.

I slept hard, and through the night without waking. Odd how restful it can be not to dream.

16

The next few days were an exercise in sticking to my guns regarding the "deserve better than Sadie" issue. I did my best to actually avoid her this time instead of 'trying' to avoid her only to fall face first into her lap like the week prior.

Luckily the universe seemed to be working with me. My period hit which, considering her profession, I could guarantee Sadie knew, and since that wasn't her particular kink, she usually avoided me those few days a month anyway. Oddly, she made one extremely reluctant offer but seemed painfully relieved when I put her off with a vague excuse.

Work kept me busy with a couple of new prospective tenants coming by to check out the property and meet with the boss and me to see if their particular brand of other would work well with the rest of our renters and the spaces we had available. I had my doubts about one of the two: she was a kitsune, a Japanese fox spirit thing I'd never personally encountered before. I liked her—she seemed funny and neat and tidy which were all things I preferred in tenants I'd have to clean up after—but as soon as we'd reached the pool part of our tour, the fur on her ears stood straight up when Khoi came into view, splashing despite the chill to the water at this time of year.

Khoi was cagey about his own species, and I couldn't remember at all if they were supposed to be friendly or antagonistic with other Asian supernaturals—we currently didn't have any other Vietnamese residents besides him to ask. Boss couldn't remember either when I asked him, so I shrugged and kept Ms. Tenko's (like Mrs. Hudson, she didn't offer a first name in person or on paper) application filed in case she came back the next week or a year from now. I had a stack of "maybe someday" apps stuffed in drawers in my office. She wouldn't be the first to show up suddenly months after her original interview.

However, the other tenant signed up and moved in almost on the spot, though I wasn't sure how I felt about him. Mr. Joe "call me Bubba" O'Malley was a swamp ogre relocating after some kind of clan dispute out in Mississippi. He wasn't the boss's first ogre client, but he was mine. I won't lie: the sheer number of "you may not eat this sentient species while a tenant or while living near to Boss's territory whether said sentient species is a tenant here or otherwise" line items added to the contract had me twitching for my shotgun more than once while we filled out the paperwork and handed over keys.

Bubba seemed polite enough, but something about teeth looking like broken hunks of really sharp rocks reflecting against so much pale gray leathery skin made me nervous and far too aware of my possible prey identity. That happened to me sometimes with some of the more visibly predatory tenants. One of the downsides of being mostly human, I guess. We were *way* farther down the supernatural food chain than I like to think about, and sometimes a tenant's physicality reminded me of that fact and then some.

Anyway, once he'd left my office to get his furniture unpacked from the back of his beat-up old pickup, I made a casual note in my phone to see if Mama knew how to take down an ogre. Never hurts to be prepared, right?

Sadie seemed wary around Bubba and Ms. Tenko, as she'd kept her distance almost as carefully as I had those few days. The petty part of me didn't doubt she figured I'd be in the "absence makes the heart grow fonder" or more accurately "the libido grow more desperate" mood by the time she showed back up. But honestly, it made things easier on me.

I had time to really work on convincing myself I didn't need her without being distracted by her glorious hair or her hands. Granted, my strength had built over only a few days, and I couldn't be sure I wouldn't cave again like the Sadie sex addict of the past me. But I felt a little more confident I'd be able to say "no" instead of "come on in" the next time showed up on my doorstep.

When she did finally show up, I wasn't actually expecting it. I wasn't sure how, but according to my trusty moon tracker app, a solid twenty-eight days had passed since my run in with a drunk ass werewolf. A full moon was due to rise again that night. I had lunch with Mama at Elysian Fields in an attempt to regain our normal routine after the month's upheaval. She gave me a sadly lackluster report about her contacts regarding our unknown enemy. No matter how many rocks we'd all turned over, no one could seem to figure out who the asshole was. It was frustrating to say the least, but there wasn't much we could do about it. And without an enemy to fight, my gift was damn near useless.

It was in that frustrated mood that I arrived back to my place and found Sadie sitting on my deck, all bundled up against the cold and looking irritated that she had to wait for me.

I stopped at the bottom of my deck stairs and looked up at her, girding my loins for the argument to come.

"Bout time you showed up. Thought I'd freeze out here," she said. She stood and stretched deliberately, sending her soft looking sweater hitching up to reveal a pale strip of her tummy above her flannel leggings.

I pulled my eyes away from the bared skin and shrugged. "I'm scheduled to go to lunch at the same time every day. Not like that's new." I kept my voice as cool and casual as I could, and wished I could keep my pulse casual too instead of thumping with adrenaline. I *hated* emotional confrontations like this. "And you didn't make any kind of appointment that would have me coming back early, now did you?"

"Aww, don't be like that, Mel," Sadie said with a smirk designed to be as come hither as possible. "We both know you missed me." She took the few steps down off the deck to stand beside me and stroked a hand toward my chin.

I ducked out of the way before her fingers could reach my lips and stepped around her and up to my deck in two long strides, desperate to get out of reach. "It's not like there's any kind of promise there to miss, is there?"

"Honey, you know I don't make promises," she said, perfect lips pouting at my retreat. "It's not like I want to hurt you though, right? How 'bout I make it up to you?" Sadie started to climb up the stairs again after me, but I shook my head once and then again. I straightened my shoulders as she stared at me, clearly taken aback at my refusal.

"Look Sadie, it's the full moon. I've got shit to do that's more important than being your toy for the afternoon," I said softly, trying to keep from causing a scene and attracting the attention of the neighbors to my telling Sadie to take a hike. She pissed me off and treated me like dirt, but that didn't mean I wanted to embarrass her.

Unfortunately, she didn't seem to have gotten the memo. "What did you say to me?" she snapped, voice plenty loud enough for Mrs. Hudson to hear all the way inside her trailer across the way. I tried to lift a hand to signal to keep her voice down, but Sadie didn't pay any attention to what I wanted. She never did. "What the hell is that supposed to mean: 'shit to do that's more important' huh?"

"Exactly what it sounded like," I snapped back, ignoring the sick feeling in my stomach from the confrontation I'd hoped to avoid. "You're not that into me, Sadie. We both know it. And frankly, I deserve better than to be another one of the bitches you fuck when you're bored. Now, I have a day job I need to pay the bills. I have a responsibility to Boss and to the other residents. Which, yes, is more important than letting you talk me into bed again." I threw up my hands. "I'm not doing this with you anymore. That's it. That's where we stand."

Her pretty mouth scowled in a way that was entirely unattractive, the venom in her voice ugly. "*You* are breaking up with *me*. Is that what you're saying? Seriously?"

"Well, considering you never wanted a relationship with me, it's technically impossible for me to break up with you," I replied. "But otherwise, yeah. That's exactly what I'm saying. I deserve better, and I'm done."

"Maybe I'm not done with you, did you ever think of that?" she snarled back at me.

If anything, it made it easier for me to stand my ground. I'd had enough of her calling the shots. Harvey'd been right. She didn't get to treat me this way. "I don't care if you're done with me, Sadie. Consent is a thing, and I decide who I'm sleeping with and who I'm not. And I say, I'm not sleeping with you any more or ever again. So go run along and play with whoever is next on the list. It won't be me."

I deliberately turned my back on her and headed to the front door, pulling out my keys and considering the conversation done.

Sadie, apparently, still thought there were things to say. "Who else do you think is going to want you? There's a *reason* I never wanted a relationship with *you*. No one with sense would trust you to stay faithful, little bisexual slut that you are. When was your last serious relationship again? Oh wait, you suck at them. Any lesbian with a brain won't bother with you, and if you lower yourself back to men, they'll just want a threesome." She tapped her chin, venom dripping in her words. "You'll never get with a real woman like me again." Her lovely eyes narrowed to slits. "So, what are you going to do, huh? Throw yourself at that asshole Johnson. Disgusting."

Rage swept through me, accompanied by a strange heady sense of relief and gratitude. She'd finally done it; finally said the one thing that would make this easy. The one thing she'd never dared say to me before, either out or calculation or who knew what. It didn't matter. My shitty self-confidence might have let her get away with the biphobic comments directed my way for far too long. But no one, absolutely no one, got to say shit about Iris to me. Or about any other trans darlings, for that matter.

"Thank you," I said, shaking my head, "for finally informing me that not only are you a biphobic bitch, you're also a transphobe. And thus are the absolute last type of person I would ever sleep with. Of any gender. Fuck that noise."

Sadie's eyes widened in something like confusion at my words, and I scoffed at how utterly wrapped up in herself she must have been to miss that about me. But then, she always was the center of her own universe.

"You'll regret this, you know," Sadie said, her voice petulant now, disbelief still threaded through her words. "You'll miss me, and you and I both know it."

I snorted and gave her one last look. "Miss you or not, it's still not worth it. It's not." I unlocked my door and opened it. "I hope you figure out how to be happy, Sadie. I honestly do, if only because you're going to keep hurting so many people until then. But I'm not going to put up with your shit anymore in some pathetic hope you finally figure it out with me. Because you won't, and you and I both know it," I finished, deliberately echoing the words she'd said. "I have to get back to work now. See you around."

I really hoped I wouldn't.

17

It only took me attempting to answer two emails to figure out the conversation with Sadie had left me too wound up to concentrate on anything requiring sitting still. I tried to answer one more, then said screw it and allowed myself up out of my chair to escape the office. There were other things I could be doing, luckily. I finally remembered to WD40 the hinges on my front door and screen. Look at me go remembering a personal home improvement task after only a month without a reminder! Also, look at me forgetting to set a reminder for a month for that particular task. Anyway, it was finally done.

No judging yourself, I sternly told myself. Sadie would be doing enough of that for both of us. And, oof. Talk about being emotionally unable to cope with confrontation after the fact. Get it together, Mel.

I wandered back into the office to put the can away and read through my remaining to-do list items, still standing, as sitting down again suddenly felt like the very worst thing in the world. There, that would work perfectly, I thought. I'd hit the full moon with my silver salt rounds running low. Reloading it was.

There was something strangely soothing about loading or reloading shotgun shells. Or, well, it's soothing so long as I don't think about the reasons I usually need said shells on hand. But the act itself, sliding in empty shells to the equipment, pulling the handle, mixing up the shell fillings, lather, rinse, and repeat, over and over again for however many empty shells I felt like filling. That was the kind of mindless low effort manual labor that let my brain go utterly quiet. Repetition can be comforting, or so I've found. I got to know for sure I did things properly. I did something right, so all the unknowable powers help me.

I did something right as I loaded up my particular brand of supernatural specific weaponry, and I'd done something else right calling things off with Sadie once and for all. Just as I'd done during my talk with Harvey, I made myself say the words outload. "I did the right thing walking away from Sadie. I did."

It was as hard this time as it had been the night before, but that was fine. I'd make it be fine.

I could have gone on reloading all afternoon if I let myself, but the bag of empty shells ran out about an hour and a half later. I finished putting my equipment away in time to field a call from Boss reminding me a couple residents still worried Inna might go furry after all tonight, despite all evidence that it wasn't, in fact, a werewolf threatening the community.

"Or not only a werewolf *that we know of*," Boss reminded me, ignoring my obvious need to narrow down our list of problems. "We can agree it wasn't Harvey who attacked her, but there's no way to be sure our mystery foe didn't possess a strange werewolf to attack her."

"But that still doesn't make sense," I tried to argue. "So far it seems pretty clear this asshole is after me with the way Marvin and Muriel both targeted me. Why would they have gone after someone I didn't even know? And more than that, why would they have left her alive?"

I could hear the boss's quiet frustration on the other end of the line. "I don't know why, Mel. I have no idea. That's what worries me, and what is worrying our residents. We can*not* rule out the chance Inna will be a danger tonight."

"All right," I said, letting my head drop forward in tired submission though he couldn't see me. "I'll go hang out with her through the moon rise, OK? If she doesn't shift then, we can mark off that as a possible issue." I couldn't exactly blame my boss for wanting me to do my job, pointless though I personally felt this particular task to be.

"Acceptable compromise, Mel. I am proud of you." I stuck my tongue out at the phone at his patronizing tone, and he chuckled, knowing me well enough to know what I'd likely done. "I mean it, Mel. You're doing as well as anyone could expect with this mess. Get us through tonight, and we'll regroup as we must in the morning."

"All right. See you in the morning, then."

Hanging up was a relief to say the least. Awkwardly, the emotional impact of a full-on incubus giving honest praise made the occasionally sub side of me want to curl up in his approval like a blanket. I didn't have time for the odd lust and adoration mix it caused to lull me into a near contented nap mode like it usually did.

I hadn't told him he had that particular effect on me. The regular kind of lust he inspired was bad enough. This somehow seemed more personal.

I shook it off as best I could, doing a few jumping jacks right there in the office, feeling the loathed exercise sweeping through me to force away the good vibes.

I knew some people claimed to enjoy exercise of any kind, but I was not at all one of those people and honestly half the time I believed those people were full of shit. Going for a run and lifting weights and stretching and generally all the things I had to do to keep myself up to "wrangling non-human residents on a rampage" levels of fit might be required for my job, but it doesn't mean I liked them.

Mama did, or did before the accident. Even now, she did arm and core work regularly at her community's little gym. I would have used that kind of injury as an excuse to never lift another free weight in my life, if I was honest. Mama had more motivation than I, however.

Still standing, I wrapped up my last few admin tasks, finding the give-a-shit to answer another couple emails, one of which directly related to the fears about Inna, then packed it in for the day. I threw together a quick meal from leftovers and ate on the couch, not bothering to do more than leave the dishes in the sink afterward. The meal had taken enough of an edge off my hunger, but I didn't want to overeat—not when I'd likely have a long night ahead of me and couldn't afford to hit myself with a food coma.

I eyed the shotgun and shells where they stood ready, but decided they might give the wrong impression to the quiet young woman. I didn't need her terrified, not solely because on the off-chance she did shift, her fear would shift with her. Every single were I had ever known tended towards aggression when afraid. I would like to avoid that if at all possible, considering said aggression would inevitably be mine to deal with. New werewolf PMS (post moonrise syndrome) was a bitch on the bruises, and I had enough of those in the past month, thank you very damn much.

Inna seemed to be expecting me when I arrived, and I gathered that either Sadie (whose perfume nearly choked me when I walked through the door which I knew had been deliberate) or Boss had told her I'd be hanging out. She still wasn't talking, but she didn't seem terribly concerned by her own silence or by my presence in her temporary home. She waved me in and gestured to the couch for me to sit and relax for a while. She didn't have the best TV, or more accurately Boss didn't have the best TV included with the furnishings in this particular unit—I made a note on my phone to see if we needed to do a furniture audit again to see if anything needed to be replaced or upgraded. It only had the bunny ears installed to reach the local stations, and she channel surfed before settling on some cooking show I didn't recognize. It wasn't thrilling entertainment, but it did make my stomach try to convince me I needed to eat a second dinner. I ignored the urge to hobbit it up right then and there. I wouldn't be here terribly long, and I could eat if I really needed to when I got back to my place.

The winter sun set early as expected, and I felt myself tense as we sat there through the dusk hours and on into true night. I'd never quite figured out what determined a werewolf's sensitivity to the moon; some would shift almost immediately after sunset, barely making it past dusk, but others took hours to shift, losing half the night until they caught one glimpse of the moon through the clouds.

The latter sometimes wouldn't even hit a full shift if the moon stayed hidden behind heavy storms. I'd checked the weather, and I wouldn't have to deal with that kind of wait this evening—it was the clearest night we'd had in several weeks. I could see the moon past the clearance curtains I'd personally hung in the windows. A glance at Inna confirmed she hadn't twitched with the sun going down or as she looked out the window to follow my gaze.

Negative on the werewolf-ness, then. Finally, something had gone right this month.

I texted as much to the Boss, getting a thumbs-up emoji for my pains, but no other response. I wondered if I'd be responsible for telling the community that in the morning too, or if I could get away with assuming everyone guessed since we hadn't had a wolf wandering the neighborhood. To be on the safe side, I waited another hour with Inna. She only drifted off to sleep against the arm of the couch, her chest rising and falling serenely as if she didn't have a care in the world. I still didn't know why her wounds had closed slowly, then healed so quickly even taking into account Sadie's obvious and oh-so-tender ministrations, or why they hadn't scarred, but I could safely say they had *not* been made by a werewolf.

Once and for all, Harvey was in the clear, though damned if it didn't mean we might have a bigger problem on our hands with an unknown supernatural killing folks. Werewolves I could handle, possession, not so much.

I'd dive deeper into research in the morning, I decided. Maybe see if Boss could call in a few more favors and ask if any of my tenants might have access to off-site literature since our perusal of the resident occult library hadn't turned up anything connected to the murders.

Still, we knew now for sure none of the attacks were done by a werewolf. I supposed crossing off an entire species could be considered progress, even if I'd already essentially crossed it off. This just made more "official" in the eyes of our residents.

With one last look back at our newcomer, I stood and slipped through the front door, careful to ease it silently shut so as not to wake her. Then I made a quick patrol round the edge of the property, only pausing to see Harvey curled up in his shed, fast asleep himself with his fur to keep him warm and the collar to keep him contained.

He hadn't complained once this month, not with last month's horror to remind him. Hadn't had anything to drink, either, and bless him for that.

With all my charges tucked away and silent like good little mice, I returned to my own trailer and, after loading my shotgun with the normal rounds of silver and salt, fell face first into my bed, falling asleep before I could do more than kick my shoes off and not giving a shit that the lights were on.

18

For the second full moon in a row, Harvey's howls jolted me out of a dead sleep.

But these weren't the random 'hellos' of a drunk werewolf off their leash and amused at the world and all the goodies its trash-cans contained. There was a vicious danger to these strained angry howls, and that more than anything sent me scrambling for my shotgun and boots. I knew instinctively something was utterly, desperately wrong for Harvey to sound like that. I shot out my screen door at a dead run, ignoring the slap of it slamming back into my trailer as I full-on leapt off the side of my porch and sprinted down the rows toward my friend's shed. Was he all right? Was Inna? Was *Iris*? Had she, against all sense of sanity, stayed so near to a shifted werewolf?

Merciful graces, what if he'd hurt her?

I picked up my pace, desperate for answers only to slide to a halt in shock as his trailer and shed came into view. Harvey's front paws were bound before him with a thick rope of some flowered vine, leaving him unable to stand on all fours as would have been more comfortable for his shifted form. He strained against both the vines and the collar, trying to lunge away from the shed and past his place toward the RVs on the other side of the property. I ran to him, the danger inherent in a raging werewolf nowhere near as important as helping my friend against whatever or whoever had dared harm him this way. Before I could reach him though or call out, his head shot to face me. He roared, bringing up his bound forelegs to point off in the direction he'd been looking.

"Stooop her. You mmmmust...stop hhhhher!" The words almost had me falling on my ass in shock. Harvey never spoke when shifted. He could make himself understood, don't get me wrong, but a wolf— even a werewolf—didn't have the vocal cords to make speech come easy. Let alone to shout it clearly enough that I could understand him from several trailers away. That required effort and then some.

"Stttop herrr!" he growled again, still pointing. I shook my surprise away and nodded once, then hurried in the direction he'd pointed, giving up any pretense of stealth for the chance at speed and to stop whoever the 'her' he mentioned was.

Out of the immediate range of the sound of Harvey's continued howls, both a warning klaxon to the rest of our community, and an outlet of his helplessness, I guessed, I could hear the faint sick sound of blows against giving flesh. It was a wet, horrifying sound in my ears, and I strained to hear some kind of accompanying groan, some sign the injuries might be occurring to a living person. When I turned the corner, what I found didn't give me any hope.

Inna, the same Inna I'd tucked in back in her RV, the same young woman I'd done my best to comfort and protect after her attack, the one I *thought* was a victim, tore someone to pieces right before my eyes.

"What the hell?" The words fell from my lips all without me meaning to speak. The words were enough to stop the sound of tearing flesh as she paused, going still over her prey before lifting her head to meet my gaze. Her eyes showed no humanity, nothing but predatory hunger, and I raised the shotgun with hands gone unsteady. When I spoke again, my voice shook too, but I couldn't deal with that right this minute. "Inna, back away from them and keep your hands up."

With a movement almost too fluid for her human form, she tilted her head left, then right as she studied me, then with a smile, Inna smoothly to her feet. "All right, Mellll. Whatever you sayyy."

Once again, words struck me as a blow worth of surprise. We'd all thought her voice irrevocably damaged by the attack, or else chased away by the trauma, never or unlikely to return. Instead, here she spoke, though less clearly than I would have expected and carrying an accent I couldn't quite place. Her voice had a strange lilt to it, as if she didn't know how to end sentences and trailed off to run into the next one. Like the way a question would be spoken only somehow in reverse. I allowed myself a step closer, trying to get an eye on the person...no, the *body*... lying still in death on the ground. I gagged as I got a good look, even my familiarity with supernatural horrors giving way to bile at the sight.

There would be no identifying the victim by looks alone. Inna had so ravaged the body I couldn't tell who or hell what species it had been. It was now no more than a pile of blood and muscle and sinew, bones stripped and sticking out of the limbs they were torn from, glowing white in the moonlight.

"Whatcha whatcha think, Mellll. Isn't this nicccccce? Don't you want to plaaaaaaaaaay?" Her words took on the same cadence of her body, hips and shoulders moving in time as she spoke. I tried to look away, but something about the movement made it hard to focus. Her fingers dripped blood as she seemed to conduct some music I couldn't hear. I took another step forward, the shotgun drooping slightly in my grasp.

The howl continued in the distance, growing more panicked by the moment. The ferocity of the werewolf's fear and rage added ragged edges to the noise pounding in my ears, but I couldn't answer him. Didn't know if I had words to give him even if I could find the urge to speak.

Harvey had followed the rules for once, and ironically, that might be what killed me.

Before me, Inna swayed back and forth, almost dancing in the moonlight, her hands still slick with blood from the body tucked away at the base of what I finally recognized as Alex's RV. I silently prayed the shy little barrow wight was working tonight, stocking shelves at the Outlet Mall overnight like normal. I prayed that sweet soul wasn't the lump of meat whose face was far beyond recognition.

I didn't know who else to pray for, and that scared me more than anything else.

Inna's face began to shift in time with the movement of her body, flickering in my Sight over and over, leaving minute changes with each sway. The lines at the corners of her eyes and mouth faded away first, leaving flawless smooth skin where a faint hint of normal aging had been. Then her skin started changing color, turning a sickly gray like the rainy dreary weather that had dimmed everything around us the day we found her. Her already thin limbs grew even more twig-like, sinking into themselves to mere matchsticks attached to an equally painfully slender torso. Her hands curled into sharp four-inch-long claws she reached up to slide through scraggly iron gray strands of hair, leaving dripping blood in their wake.

Finally, her face twisted to something no longer recognizably human to my eyes. It was more a caricature of a human, a semblance of what one might think a time-ravaged woman might look like, one who never felt kindness even once in her long lifetime.

Within a body unable to shake with fear, my heart plummeted.

I didn't know what she was, couldn't name her. I had never, ever seen anything like the craggy visage in front of me whose wrinkled gray lips bared to show vicious teeth to rival any werewolf's dental additions for the title of "most predatory mouth ever." Whatever she was, I needed to fight her, had to get her away from my people, away from my *friends*, away from that ragged band of beings I lived with and worked with and loved in the way of community.

But, I realized, I couldn't. Couldn't fight her off; hell, couldn't move at all. The confusing sway of her body leeched over my mind until my body stood helpless and paralyzed by the strange hypnotic hold she'd placed over me.

I could feel the boon straining within me like a physical force, a caged bird fluttering desperately against the bars of its prison hoping to escape only to slam into a window and break its neck. Whatever she'd done to me, it wasn't a physical attack or a risk to my life, at least not yet, and thus the boon couldn't fight it, couldn't free me from the simple state of being unable to do anything except stand there.

My eyes widened. As the panicked look came over my face, Inna, if that was the creature's real name, smiled, a wicked thing all sharp teeth and hard, pitiless eyes. "You understanddddddddd now, Mellll? Youu know whatttt I've donnnnnnne? Do you like it, Mellll?" She was the reason I couldn't answer, but still, my silence seemed to anger her. She gnashed her teeth when I didn't respond. "Welllll? Do you like itttt? Don't you know it's rude not to answer, Mellll? Answeeeeeeeeeeeeeeeeer!"

Ironically, I wanted to. I wanted to answer her as badly as she wanted me to speak. I wanted to tell her exactly what I thought of her daring to take me prisoner, and worse, daring to harm one of my charges. I simply couldn't.

Her eyes narrowed as she studied me, and then her ire seemed to vanish all at once. This time, she bared her teeth in a cruel, hungry smile as she sauntered over. The sway of her body still moved in time with her long almost disjointed steps on legs which seemed to contain an extra pair of knees or hips or ankles. There was nothing human about her now, nothing more than humanoid at best, or worst more accurately.

She stopped directly in front of me, still swaying back and forth as she brought a hand up to my face so gently I barely felt it. "Is that better Mellllll? How do you feellllllllllllllll, hmmmmmmmmm?" Inna leaned in and then to my disgust, licked a long stripe up my cheek, moaning at the taste like something out of a bad porno. "Oh, you tassssssssssste so gooooooood, Mellll. She said you woulllllllld. I kneeeew you would. Better even than *I* tasssssssssssssssssted."

I tried to understand what she was talking about—how *she'd* tasted? Horror dawned as I realized it might have been *Inna* who'd torn apart her own face and throat, *Inna* who'd taking a bite out of her own arm with those vicious teeth. Why? Why had she done such a thing?

145

How would I stop her from doing the same thing to me?

I couldn't stop her.

And so I didn't. I stood there motionless save for the terrified and enraged tears slipping from my eyes as she lunged, burying her teeth in the flesh where my neck and shoulder met. My vision started to white out at the pain so terrible as to almost fade into numbness, but I still saw her pull back with a strip of flesh dangling from a mouth full of my blood. I saw what she did next, too, pulling a jam jar from a pocket of the jacket Miss Ginger had bought especially for her at Costco. Inna spit out the blood and skin into the jar and carefully tightened down the lid, her long clawed fingers more dexterous than I would have guessed. Then, I watched her walk away without a word, pausing only to tear one of the arms from the body she'd ravaged and toss it over her shoulder like a prize.

I saw her go, and could do nothing, still held up and standing motionless in her sway as I bled all over my shirt.

19

I didn't know how long I stood there, feeling my life pulsing out of the wound at my neck. The edges of the torn skin burned as the boon tried desperately to literally pull my battered body back together. My mind stumbled, failing to focus on anything but flashes of moments of this most recent attack and those that cost my tenants their lives over the past month. I couldn't begin to understand what she'd said to me or what she'd intended taking a jar of my blood and... And *meat*. Surely if she just meant to eat me, she'd have carted me off like whoever her poor victim had been.

Whoever it was I hadn't been in time to save.

I could dimly hear Harvey still howling, and then of the shock of silence as the howling cut off. Then the sound of running on both two legs and four made its way to my ears, and a furry form entered my view followed by the boss, I thought. Probably? My eyes watered fiercely, my inability to blink finally catching up with me, though that discomfort barely registered against the other pain. Boss skidded to a stop in front of me, stripping off his white t-shirt and balling it up to press firmly against the wound. Part of me wondered vaguely why he bothered, while the other part desperately wanted to cringe away from the new spike of pain at the pressure. His free hand came up to cup my face in a much kinder echo of Inna's action. "Harvey, get our witch. This is well beyond simple first aid."

The furry form, which I now barely recognized as a werewolf, bounded off toward the other side of the community. I still couldn't move myself, but it seemed others could move around me as Boss lifted my hand up to replace his before sweeping me up into his arms as carefully as he could. "My place is closer," he said to someone out of my frozen line of sight, "both to here and to Sadie's trailer."

He set off at a smooth run, the effortless motion not jarring me in his arms, and never slowed even to cross the bridge. Well, that explained why he never worried about handrails. Who knew incubi had superior balance? I blinked, realizing my thoughts were going off on a tangent likely due to shock, then blinked again as I realized I'd managed the movement in the first place. I tried to move my hands and arms, but only my fingers twitched yet. Still, it was something, anything besides the helpless paralysis and pain.

My body edged towards my own again, glacially slow though the improvement might be. I would take what I could get; I tried to pray that whatever spell Inna had cast wouldn't interfere with the boon, and that the paralysis itself wouldn't have any negative effects on my health, but it was hard to muster up the energy to care.

Damn everything all to Hell. I knew we needed to know what she was, *who* she was to have caused such terrible damage to our safety in such a few short weeks. And why, why, *why* had she done what she did? What had any of us done to draw a predator like that here?

"I've got the door, Papi," said a voice behind us. Terry rushed past us on the porch steps to reach the screen door before we did, the wood lurching under their feet to my eyes like a much greater weight had pounded up the risers. As if unaware of the porch's strange reaction, they simply held the screen and interior door open for Boss and his unwieldy armful. "Guest room or couch?"

"Guest room, though those sheets will be a loss. Sadie might have an easier time on the kitchen table, but I don't want to move her any more times than we have to."

I'd last seen the first-floor guest room when we'd let Inna rest in it a month ago. Bile rose at the thought, and I fought back the urge to vomit. That could only go poorly considering the blood loss and with my neck still as immobile as the rest of me. I didn't know how much Inna had injured me beyond the obvious with that bite; if she'd hit tendons, I'd be in for a world of hurt if they healed. The spasms needed to hurl would make it worse.

If they healed. I shook away the thought. Fatalism was not the Smithson way by all the gods and monsters, and I was not ready to die. Not until Inna was dealt with at the very earliest. I just had to convince myself of that. I had a purpose, I told myself, a reason to keep going.

Boss very gently laid me down on the surprisingly comfortable bed, careful to keep me off the pillows so my neck stayed as straight as possible. My eyes stared up at white painted shiplap and an antique light fixture, blessedly off as I doubted my eyes would adjust easily from the dark outside. A light was switched on to my left, on a bedside table probably. I thought about trying to see out of the corner of my eye, but that seemed like a lot more effort than blinking and I decided not to push it. I'd wait for Sadie to come work her literal magic, and then we'd see how I felt about moving my line of vision.

I vaguely felt one of the men remove the T-shirt plastered to my neck and replace it quickly with a fluffy towel. Whoever it was sat on the bed next to me to get the leverage to continue pressing firmly at the wound.

"What is taking them so long?" Boss snapped from beside me, his voice thick with more worry than I could ever remember hearing from him before. I heard footsteps in the hall stomp toward the door, and then come hurrying back.

"Looks like Harvey's coming now with Bessie, but she's having trouble with the footbridge."

"Why would he be bringing Bessie? She's a good hedge witch, but Sadie's better with triage work."

I barely caught a blur of movement in my peripheral vision that I guessed was a shrug from Terry though the hazy silhouette held too many limbs. "Maybe she was..." they paused, and I imagined they glanced my way, "occupied or out?"

Maybe, I thought. It wouldn't be the first time I'd been second or third or dead last on her list of priorities. I'd never been enough for her, never... I tried to force the thought away only for another even more terrible to tease at my mind. *Or...* What if I hadn't been the only target tonight? Every time, it had been me and one other of the residents. I'd thought it was whoever Inna had killed before I reached her tonight, but what if she'd gone after Sadie too? Or, what if the body *was* Sadie? The shit I'd said to her the last time we talked...

Maybe I didn't deserve her help to heal even if it *wasn't* her body.

I whimpered at the thought, and Terry joined us on the bed and stroked my hair. I knew they hoped to soothe me as best they could, but their hand seemed to loom above me, much larger than it should possibly be and sharper around the edges. I tried to stay calm, to remind myself that they were still the same gentle soul I'd known for months, but somehow that made my anxiety worse. Why would they bother trying to soothe me anyway? Maybe just for Boss's sake. Tears leaked out of my eyes, and Terry tried to shush me gently, which unfortunately, set off the same spiral in my head. What was wrong with my vision? Was I—was I going mad? Would anyone care if I was? Would they even notice?

Outside the room, I heard the screen door slam and the odd clicking footsteps of Harvey's other form headed our way, Bessie's tottering footsteps close behind and moving faster than I'd expect of a woman her age. "Out of the way, Terry, honey," she ordered. "And you, young man, keep pressure on that wound while I get my kit ready to go."

A hysterical part of me wanted to laugh at the thought of the Boss being a "young man," but it came out as only another whimper. I shivered, or tried to against the spell, then the bed bounced beneath me when a heavy bag landed beside me with a soft whomp as Harvey set it down at her direction. It only somewhat jarred to my neck with Boss's careful hands to steady me, but I couldn't fight a wince. At least,

I *could* wince; that too was progress against the paralysis if not against anything else.

The contents of the bag splayed out on the bed, placement too careful to be random, though from what I could see in my peripheral vision, it looked like a cluttered mess. Bessie mumbled under her breath as she sorted it, voice too low for me to hear.

After a moment, she nodded once sharply and gathered two jars and a small tub, all three with odd colored contents smelling strongly of flowers and herbs once she opened them. Bessie smeared the contents of the tub in a thick layer on one of the gauze pads she'd also unearthed from her bag and thrust it at Boss.

"Here, replace your poor towel with this. The yarrow in it should help slow the bleeding while I get the rest of this mess in her." Her voice lowered as if to keep her next words from me, but I heard her all the same. "We need a real witch, Boss. This... this is beyond my skill. I can feel a taint to the wound—and her boon trying to fight it, too—but I've only got my salves. They're strong, sure, but they ain't proper spell work." She threaded gnarled old fingers through my hair, much as Terry had done, though at least her hand matched what I thought it should look like. "And that's what she'll need if we want her to survive."

Did they want me to survive? I suddenly wondered. *Should* they want me to survive? I hadn't kept my people safe, had I? What was the point of them trying so hard to save me?

Something about those thoughts didn't feel right, but the pain took them away again before I could figure out why.

There was a deep sigh from Boss and a low moan from Harvey, and then Boss said, "Babe, get my phone and call Shelby—her number's in the contacts. She may have a witch contact or two I've never met that might be close enough to get here in time. And she needs to know what's happening with her daughter either way."

Terry jogged out of the room at his direction, taking a too large shadow with them. Bessie mixed a little of each of the other two jars into a mug with some hot water, making a concoction that smelled like something out of an east Texas swamp. She leaned over to me, bringing the mug to my lips. "I don't know how much movement you've got yet, child, but I need you to try to drink this. Let it trickle down your throat if you can't actually swallow now, you hear?" She tipped it between my lips, and I gagged at the thick slimy texture and rotten aftertaste. "Now none of that—trust me, you'll feel better if you just get it over with."

I shuddered, moving every part of my body finally, though the movement was admittedly slight. That was progress, I reminded myself, which was better than nothing. And if Bessie said that crap would help, it would. One never argued with a hedge witch if she gave you something to drink. I steeled myself and opened my mouth back to the mug and drank as quickly as my sluggish throat muscles would allow. On the upside, it seemed like my barf reflex was still somewhat paralyzed, and I managed to keep all of the concoction down. Blessedly, Terry returned with a cup of water and Bessie allowed me to drink it and wash away most of the swampy taste. "There now, dear. That should help you sleep."

Sleep? I didn't want to sleep, did I? I didn't deserve to sleep, not when... Not when I needed to—I felt my eyes drifting closed within moments despite my attempt to fight it. As I fell into blackness, I heard Bessie say "It's the only kindness I've got for her—to keep her out as long as possible. Once the spell wears out...she's going to hurt."

I wasn't sure how long I'd been out when I heard a familiar voice as if through the static of a cell phone fighting the Hill Country for signal. The voice was rough, more ragged than it should be, though I couldn't say why I knew considering I didn't recognize the voice yet. After listening a while longer, I recognized the sound.

The voice was singing a Garth Brooks song. "The River," specifically, and the recognition of the artist made me realize who was singing.

"Mama," I tried to say, the word coming out as more of a sigh than true speech. She'd always loved old country music, and Garth had long since been her fave. She'd even bought and claimed to love the odd alternative name single CD mess he'd come out with. He'd been one of the few concerts she and Daddy had been able to afford when I was growing up—they probably couldn't afford it honestly, but the three of us still went and watched one hell of a show.

Mama hadn't stopped singing, probably hadn't realized I was trying to wake up yet. Part of me wanted to let her keep singing, to let it soothe me back to the soft cushion of sleep I didn't feel I'd earned, but the pain had crept in around the edges of my grogginess. I wouldn't be able to crash out again without Bessie helping, or so I guessed. I might as well let Mama know I still lived, since it seemed like she cared, though damned if I knew why. I forced my eyes open, one painful crack at a time, then gave speaking another try. "Mama?"

This time she heard me, and I managed to turn my head enough to meet her shocked gaze before she lunged forward from the waist to hug me, surprisingly gently after the violence of that movement. "Oh, my baby, you're alive, you're alive, *you're alive.*" She pressed a kiss to my forehead, hands trembling as she brushed my hair out of my face. "There's those pretty brown eyes again. There's my baby."

I tried to hug her back, but only managed to lift my right hand far enough to rest it on her arms. My left—the side where I'd been bitten—seemed weaker and less willing to move.

"Mama," I managed to say again, then coughed at the cotton mouth feeling on my tongue. Then cringed and whined as the coughing sent shooting pains through the still torn flesh on the side of my throat.

"Shit," Mama muttered, reaching across me, and then pressing a glass of water to my mouth. "Drink it slow, honey. Small sips to keep it from hurting quite as much." I did my best to do as she bid, letting a tiny amount trickle between my lips and then down my throat.

It still was the most refreshing thing I'd ever tasted. So cool when I felt so hot I realized I wanted the damn blankets off me. "Mama –'s too hot. Off?"

"Shit, you are burning up again, aren't you? Bessie! The fever's back!" she called, the volume startling me into another cringe, though luckily this time I suppressed it.

Bessie bustled back into the room, all but chased in by Harvey right on her heels, the familiar trucker hat back on his human form. He came up short in the doorway, his hands fluttering at his sides desperate to do something, anything to help. I looked away from him, the sight of his helplessness more than I could bear right then. Instead, I tried to focus on Bessie as she rummaged through her bag again, now settled on a dining room chair on the far side of the bed. She made an 'aha' noise, and came back up with a jar, though I wasn't sure if it was one of the ones I'd been subjected to before. "Now, let's see what we got here. Oh, you're awake! That's—well, that's progress, ain't it?"

I might have believed her if I hadn't caught the worried looks she shot my Mama and Harvey. She laid her hand across my forehead and clucked her tongue. "Yup, fever's rising again, damn it. Harvey, can you get the fan going?" She turned back to me, busy shaking the jar in one hand like a can of spray paint. "Now, I want to keep that blanket on you, honey—just in case your temperature drops too low again. I want you shivering as little as possible."

"Bessie...?" Mama asked, and there was a wealth of meaning in that single word.

Bessie sighed and shook her head. "Honey, I can keep her breathing, keep the fever at bay best I can, but I can't fix this. I can't draw out whatever spell or poison or... *filth* is in the wound, keeping it open. We need a witch—a strong one, too."

"How soon?" Mama asked, brushing the back of her hand against my cheek. "I may know someone, but they don't come cheap and are often booked up months in advance even for emergency cases."

I squirmed under her hand, hating the thought of the expense for something like this, for something like *me*. Not when I'd failed so badly. I blinked as the weight of my failure pushed down on me again, then was all but gone in a breath, allowing me to focus on the conversation again.

"That good then?" I could hear the near disbelief in Bessie's voice, and with my mind somewhat cleared I could agree with it. For Mama to suggest someone that expensive was rather unlike her, even for a remedy for me.

"She's the current Greyhaus matriarch."

Bessie paused and stared across me to Mama, her eyes wide. "How in the Goddess's green earth did you meet the Greyhaus matriarch?"

"They've got a shop in Austin—most folks think it's just another New Age shop and cafe. But to the Sight, that place lit up like a Christmas tree." I felt Mama shrug against my shoulder. "I decided to risk a Tarot reading and ended up in an interesting three-hour conversation about raising daughters and fitting in with the non-supernatural world. I like her. But she's experienced enough to cost dear, and I don't know if she'll do favors, either."

Bessie shook her head, soft gray curls dancing across her face from where they'd fallen out of her bouffant. "You wouldn't want to ask her for a discount or a favor anyhow. Strong magic requires respect—requires recognition of its own worth, don't you know."

"I'll pay for it." Boss had appeared in the doorway without a sound; I had no idea how long he'd stood there either, watching over all of us with more benevolence than anyone would expect of him, especially for a lowly little peon like me. "Whatever she asks. If she's worried about working for an incubus or coming to one's home, I'll take myself off until it's done."

Mama leaned down to look me square in the face and touched my cheek again, then straightened and gave Boss a single nod. "I'll make the call."

Boss helped her back down from the cushy guest bed to her chair and followed her out of the room. Harvey slunk in to hover on the side of the bed Mama had originally claimed. Looking at him...*hurt* somehow, in some strange way deep inside me I couldn't explain. Something was wrong...something was *missing*, wasn't it? Or maybe someone? But then, it wasn't like I deserved even the folks gathered around taking care of me now. I'd let them down. Didn't they under-stand how badly I'd let them down? I wanted to shout it at Harvey and Boss and Mama and all of them, but I couldn't force the words out. I started to feel dizzier and dizzier, and the pain began to climb higher, but Bessie was right there with that jar she'd readied for me.

"Drink up, honey," she said, tipping this surprisingly tasty concoction into my mouth and rubbing the undamaged right side of my throat with a single gentle finger to help me swallow. "There now, rest."

I didn't have the strength to argue.

20

They told me later I lingered in that half healing state for another forty-eight hours before that old friend of Mama's came through. She'd apparently been dealing with a family emergency of her own, so no one seemed willing to blame her for taking that long; me, least of all. I was pathetically glad they'd bothered to find someone, and someone almost local if still more than an hour away thanks to central Texas Hill Country highway traffic being the shithole it was.

While we waited, Mama stayed close. I remembered that, though part of me I didn't recognize expected her to have left long ago. And though I wasn't always awake, I knew even while dreaming that either or both Boss and Harvey kept close, too, sleeping on a cot in the guestroom or on Boss's couch. I sweated and moaned in the bedroom, freezing cold and burning up by turns, clutching at my grandma's quilt which had been fetched from my place or tearing the sheets from the bed.

Everything felt too comfortable beneath me, more than I deserved, so much kinder than I should be treated. In my brief moments of wakefulness, I knew I'd failed them, failed them all. Marvin, Muriel, whoever Inna's last victim had been—they were all gone, gone, *gone*. They had been my responsibility, mine to protect, and...

I didn't. I didn't protect them. What was I good for with my boon if I couldn't protect them? Without it, I was nothing special. Not gifted like Sadie, or powerful like Boss, or compassionate like Iris.

Iris. Where was Iris? Shouldn't she be here? I wanted her with me, needed her with me as she so often was every time I went beyond the limits of my boon. I couldn't remember the last time I'd been injured and she hadn't been there.

Maybe she was finally tired of it, tired of how useless I was on my own, how weak. Maybe she was finally leaving me alone with my wounds the way I deserved.

Maybe they all should just leave me alone.

It surprised me that they didn't and instead kept trying to reassure me that help was on the way, that everything would be all right if I just held on a little longer.

I didn't believe them, but I was too weak to send them away, too selfish to let them leave me to find better things to do. I just lay there with my misery and waited to prove them wrong, to prove that no one would bother to come save me.

Then, a woman who I didn't recognize finally appeared in the bedroom doorway. She had to be in her sixties or seventies, I thought. She had a teenage girl behind her, probably her granddaughter or so I guessed, and both carried working bags not unlike the one Sadie carted about—or more often had flunkies cart about for her. The woman didn't look like the kind of person who'd give any mind to fools, much like Miss Ginger, now that I thought of it, but there was kindness about the edges of her face somehow, a faint promise of comfort if I could bear to trust her.

I wasn't sure I could. I still had that feeling in the pit of my stomach that they shouldn't have wasted their time or their money on me, that eventually they were going to realize just how wrong it was that they cared at all. Maybe this witch would finally tell them it was best to just...let me go. Maybe it'd be better that way.

"Honey, this is Ms. Greyhaus, the witch I told you about," Mama said, sitting in the chair Harvey had carried to my bedside for her.

I blinked, a stray thought winking in and out but leaving me worried for some reason. Oh, right. I croaked out the words, trying to make myself heard clear enough. "Not, not the witch from San Marcos you knew who got caught making curses...?"

It would serve me right if it was.

"No honey, Ms. Greyhaus is from near Dripping Springs. She's supposed to be a master at potions and all," Mama continued, giving the older woman an apologetic smile when she raised her silver eyebrows at 'supposed to be.' "She and her grandbaby are here to help, Mel. Will you let her try?"

I forced my eyes wide enough open that I wouldn't be tempted to close them again and tried to struggle up to a sitting position to greet her as respect demanded. Instead, the ragged edges of the wound around my throat sent shocks of pain across my skin hard enough I gasped, which sadly only made the pain worse.

"Stubborn... Louisa, help her, child! Get across and support her other side!" the matronly witch ordered. The teen hurried around the bed to gently lift my shoulders from that side while my mama did the same. "Here, Shelby, give me a little room so I can get a good look at her." Harvey, who I hadn't noticed in the room, came over and bodily picked up my mother and the chair she sat in and turned her slightly, opening space for the witch to sit on the bed next to me, while leaving me still supported by Mama's arms. "That's better. Now, dear let's get a look at the nasty you've gotten into, shall we?"

She peered into my eyes and had me open my mouth and stick out my tongue. I half expected her to pull out a stethoscope and an arm cuff to take my blood pressure, but she only took my pulse—from my wrist thankfully considering the wreckage of my throat. "Well, physically you're a mess, but we knew that already, didn't we? I understand there would be some understandable hesitation against me taking a blood sample to test back in my home apothecary lab given your boon might take offense to the circumstance. We'll see how far we can get without needing to do so. Be aware it might still be required, but it'll be a last resort. You've got my word on that." The witch cocked her head at me. "That sound all right to you?"

I was surprised she was even asking. They were paying her, not me. I didn't have any right to argue with her recommendations, even if she *did* want blood. Seemed like my blood was more important to the rest of me anyway, wasn't it? Resigned, I nodded carefully, almost more of a 'blink with intent' than an actual nod, but she nodded briskly back as if I'd been easy to follow.

"Good. And call me Rosemary, all of you. No point in standing on ceremony when I'm about to have my astral self all up on your aura as it were." Rosemary turned to the other people in the room, more than I'd realized were there or so I discovered as I did my best to follow the focus of her gaze. What were all these people doing here, spending so much energy on me? I couldn't be worth it. Hell, my best friend hadn't even shown herself since my attack—if Iris couldn't be bothered, why the fuck should they? That sudden, conscious realization of her absence brought the despair crashing down even harder. Once again, part of me wanted everyone to just leave me to my fate and I opened my mouth to try to tell them so, but Rosemary either didn't notice or care that I had something to say. "Now then, I don't know what's exactly in those wounds on either the physical or magical levels, but I definitely need to ward the room in case the magic lashes out while we try to treat her. It'd be best to have other magic limited as much as possible while we're working."

She gave Mama and Harvey a surprisingly sympathetic smile for the stern woman she'd presented herself as thus far. "That does unfortunately include beings of a magical nature, including werewolves and those of your family line, Shelby. The boon appears to our workings as an element of magic itself, no matter how long ago the magic was actually cast upon your family."

Mama's lips twisted showing she wanted to protest, but after a beat she nodded, and rolled after Harvey to join Boss and Terry looming in the hallway, still strangely accompanied by the slight sense of overwhelming size that made me want to look away. "We'll be watching from here, if that's all right?"

"In the hallway is fine, but the threshold of the door will be the boundary line," Rosemary instructed. "Once we begin, please do not try to cross it, even if Melanie appears to be in distress. It is highly likely the infection will fight back, and having to divert our attention to holding the wards will lessen our effectiveness at the job you've brought us here to do." She eyed Harvey again. "Just because some of you probably *can* break the ward line, does not mean you *should* break it. Not until we're finished."

Reluctantly Harvey nodded, as did Boss behind him, his preternaturally handsome face focused and for once lacking all allure as if that part of his identity had stripped itself away in his concern. That, or I couldn't feel anything but the fever and the pain I was already under. Both, maybe?

My mind struggled to focus at all, but I tried to bring my attention back to the witch sitting patiently at my bedside with her working bag now in her lap. The teen—Louisa I thought I remembered her saying, though something about the name tugged strangely at the boon as if I couldn't See her with that name for some reason—helped prop me up on a pile of pillows, semi-upright once and for all, though I wasn't sure how long I could or *would* keep myself that way. "Thank you, dear. I'll let you layer the first spell for the ward, then come keep her stable while I finalize the second and close us in."

"On it." The quiet teen scrambled back out of bed and moved to the exact center of the space orienting herself with her hands spread out to turn a circle, testing the distance all around her from wall to floor to ceiling and back again. Then she knelt and pressed her hands to the thick rug covering the hardwood floors and breathed in and out, closing her eyes as she breathed in again. Then the air in the room *changed*, though I couldn't have been able to describe quite how. The magic hung thick in the air; I could taste it, but something else lingered along with the magic, something almost like a sense of safety, the comfort of my grandma's quilt on a cold day or of leaning against Mama's knees watching a movie, of sitting out on the deck with Iris and Harvey, leaning back and letting the sun kiss our faces.

It felt wild and rich and more powerful than I would have guessed from a teenager, though who knew how long she'd officially been her grandmother's apprentice. Unofficially, a born witch could be training her whole life or so Sadie had mentioned once, I thought.

All at once, something seemed to find that strange new magic offensive, and I shuddered and tried not to vomit as the internal *something* triggered more pain and a strange itching in my skin against the former feeling of safety. That same part of me shrugged off any lingering sense of comfort, convinced it shouldn't be for me, *couldn't* be for me.

Beside me, Rosemary shifted and pressed her lips together. "It's already fighting, Louisa. I think the ward is triggering its defenses." I shuddered again, and she steeled her shoulders. "We'll have to work quickly. In the meantime, Melanie, try to think of something else. Whatever will keep the pain and discomfort as far from your mind as possible." She gently patted my shoulder and set her bag down at her feet, drawing out a small metal bowl and a bundle of herbs. "All right, child, it's my turn now. Get ready to hold her if she reacts again."

The pain spiked again right on cue as she spoke, and as she commanded, I tried to think of something other than how much I hurt. Instead, as if to punish me for daring to think I deserved an escape from the torment, my mind hyperfocused on it, dwelling on every burn beneath my skin, every firing of my nerve. I deserved this. I knew deep within me, in every part of me, that I *deserved* this. And somehow, that was the worst part. I bit back a whimper, but not soon enough, and at the quiet moan I let escape, the girl returned to gently rub her hand up and down my arm, trying to soothe me.

But the closest thing to comfort came from another place, another voice, no, a pair of voices, I realized and managed to turn my head back towards the doorway. Past Rosemary, who lit the sprig of herbs with a quick snap of her fingers in an effortless display of natural gift, I could see Mama and Harvey. Two of the most important people in my world, though damned if I'd realized Harvey mattered that much before now.

Only two of them, though. The absence of Iris hit me like a physical ache, and I keened with the knowledge that I hadn't been as important to her. Couldn't have been. Maybe never had.

Mama spoke, and my heart struggled against despair to make her voice a balm as it had been for all of my life. "We're here, Mel. We're not going anywhere. If you need us, you think about us, and we'll be right there in your thoughts even if we can't come in the room."

"What she said. Keep your chin up—you'll be through this soon. You're stronger than that bitch had any idea of," Harvey added and then winked of all unexpected things, the afterimage of a great bushy tail seeming to wag encouragement behind him. I didn't laugh, couldn't reach through the pain and weight of depression enough to laugh, but I tried to smile at them both.

Mama didn't say anything else, but then she didn't have to—I knew she'd never let me down. Never had, never would. No matter how her hips started hurting in the chair or how dangerous the magic in the bedroom might get to be, she wouldn't move. She'd be sitting right there waiting for me until I could get up and come to the door to collapse into the hug I so desperately wanted.

That dark part of me tried to surge up, to crush that certainty the way it had been crushing my will to survive, to heal with my boon as I already should have. It would win if it could. I knew that and so did the only thing I still could: fight for myself.

I kept my eyes on the door, on those bright brilliant souls who made up some of the best parts of me, and kept my heart on them, too. Nothing else got to have room in me right now, no matter what, no matter how the darkness tried to tell me otherwise. I silently repeated their names in my head one after the other, over and over and over again. Rosemary began to chant and the room filled with smoke both physical and shadowed in the spirit. "Breathe in, Melanie," she told me, and I obeyed as best I could. "Breathe deep now."

She set the bowl on the dresser with the herbs still burning and releasing the smoke into the air, then returned to me. Rosemary pulled a small glass dropper vial with an opalescent liquid inside and carefully let a single drop fall into each of my eyes, causing me to blink though there wasn't any pain or discomfort, only surprise at the sudden wetness. "Now then," Rosemary said, "let us see what we shall see."

I blinked again, and this time, those shadows of smoke seemed to grow clearer until they almost appeared solid. My mind clearing, slowly I realized my Sight had kicked itself into high gear, showing me the magic lining the physical boundaries of our world more clearly than ever before. The power of the wards containing my room rippled in and out as if made of waves tied to Rosemary and her granddaughter's breaths. "I see the wards," I said softly, hazy with the smoke and heartache and pain, though the latter were fading away, numbed by the magic in the air and the potion Rosemary gently tilted my head back to drink. "They're beautiful."

"That would be my granddaughter's doing—she's got a damn near artistic touch to ward spells. Just a natural. Makes them easy for me to add my own to, as well. Here, a bit more," she added, helping me swallow the last drops of the potion. "There now. This will help numb some of the pain of whatever's about to come about. Now, it's up to you whether you watch what I'm doing or not, but it might make it harder for you to feel calm. It's your choice."

I felt floaty, my body only knowing it was on the bed by the way I anchored myself with fingers and toes dug into the quilt beneath me. "What—what would I be watching?"

"The poison, both venom magic induced, drain out of your body. I can't tell you what that poison will appear as, but I can tell you similar infections I've dealt with in the past have been truly disturbing."

The teen shuddered a little, shaking me slightly. "The last cleansing we did, the guy wouldn't close his eyes or look away and ended up barfing all over himself. It was so gross. We couldn't clean him up until we'd gotten the magic cleansed out."

"Yuck," I managed, and closed my eyes obediently, still seeing a faint glow behind my eyelids when I turned in the direction of either of the witches, or I was interested to see, of the people lining the doorway, even Terry, who yesterday I'd have sworn was completely human and mundane. The familiar demon standing next to him remained a strangely comforting block of glittering shadow. "I—I'll try not to look."

Rosemary patted my hand. "It's really for the best. Better you only have to fight it on one front." Fight it, I wondered. What did she mean fight it? Fight what? The despair lurched into focus again but before it could pull me under, Rosemary breathed in deep, almost directly in my ear. "Now, child!"

Louisa suddenly gripped both my shoulders from behind, holding me down firmly as what felt like Rosemary's bare hands seemed to plunge into my neck through the open wounds. I gagged, unable to breathe or swallow as I fought off panic and the urge to open my eyes. Both Rosemary and her granddaughter were chanting now, words I didn't recognize from prior experience with witch rituals, a wild guttural language striking like a blow with each syllable, the consonants hard as stone against my ears. The phantom hands twisted, dragging downwards through my neck and torso to my core and yanking against a binding of smoke-like and stinking ropes suddenly squeezing my chest and stomach so tight I felt they might pull through me like a giant sieve, leaving nothing of me left after the binding filtered out the parts it wanted.

I strained, bowing up against the pressure, hands and feet scrabbling against the bed for purchase, my back feeling as if it would break backwards in two.

There was a scuffle at the door and a low snarl, and Rosemary snapped, "Not one step closer, werewolf. You will not risk her life to satisfy your helplessness. Stand fast or see her breathe her last!"

Even knowing he couldn't come, *shouldn't* come, I reached out my hand to the doorway, begging, pleading for release, for aid. I didn't know what for really, but knew surely he or Mama could grant it. Anything to release me from the awful pressure tearing into my skin.

I couldn't see their tears, but all of a sudden, I could taste them, felt them raining down on my face like a benediction though my ears told me they were still on the other side of the wards, with Harvey cursing and my mother praying to any powers she thought might listen. "Help her," she said. "Help her."

The saline bathing my face fell faster as if a small wave of the sea had been captured and sent solely to bathe away the blood and black gore I could feel oozing its way out of the cuts in my skin. "Just a little more," Rosemary muttered in between phrases of chanting. "Hold on a little longer, Mel. We need a little more!"

With one final rush, I felt the poison leave my body. I fell back against the bed clothes, breathing as deeply as my still shredded throat allowed. There was a moment of relief despite the pain still in the wound, but then all at once the boon *surged* to life as if it had been hovering in the background, impatient and unwilling to wait any longer now that its barrier had vanished. Skin and muscle and vein and tendons writhed at my throat, healing faster than the boon ever had but with so much more pain and sheer unnatural discomfort I could hardly stand it. I cried out and tried to claw at my throat, hardly noticing the multiple pairs of hands coming to hold my arms down and keep me from injuring myself further.

Voices called out my name, telling me to hold on, to keep breathing, that I would be fine, but it was all just noise against the cramping crawling wrongness of parts of my neck fighting for dominance to see which section would heal first.

Then, as suddenly as it began, it ended.

I laid there for a moment in shock, not daring to breathe before a gasp forced its way out of my pristine and perfectly healed body. The gasp turned into a sob, and I rolled to bury my face in Harvey's chest where he'd joined us during the boon's healing against Rosemary's instructions. Though at least he'd waited until the spell work had finished. I was glad he hadn't listened at the end; it likely would have traumatized the teen to have a stranger weeping all over her the way I was weeping all over Harvey. He let me cry, keeping the rest of the room blocked out for as long as I clung to him.

Fuck, it was good to have friends.

I froze, the thought pinging in my brain like an alarm bell. There'd been something missing in my artificial misery, something had felt off and out of true, but I hadn't been able to narrow down precisely what it was.

Now, with the despair gone and feeling oddly weightless, I pushed myself carefully away from Harvey to survey the other occupants of my temporary bedroom. The two Greyhaus women stood arms around each other on the other side of the bed, while Bessie sat stationed with her every present herb bag at the ready in the rocking chair in the corner. Still outside the ward line as instructed were Mama, Terry, and the Boss.

All present and accounted for. All of the people I knew deep down cared for me like family.

All but one. One who, without the sickly sense of helplessness and uselessness lying to me, I knew would be there if at all physically possible. It was enough to make me sick, but I forced myself to turn back to Harvey, the one I knew would have the answer to the question I needed to ask.

"Where is Iris?"

one. Gone gone gone *gone*. The word clanged in my mind like a gong, drowning out Harvey as he explained Iris was missing, as well as Sadie. That no one had seen her since she turned in for the evening the night everything went tits up. *Gone.* There were signs of a struggle in her airstream, and Harvey'd smelled Inna—and Sadie too, though it could be due to how close the pair had been lately.

That or Inna had Sadie in her clutches already when she attacked Iris.

Gone.

I inhaled in through my nose and out through my mouth, part of me reveling in the easy pain-free breathing while the other part tried desperately not to have a full-blown panic attack with a side order of guilt over the fact that I'd let the darkness convince me she'd just... Stayed away. On purpose. As if Iris had ever or *would* ever be willing to leave me to suffer without her. For fuck's sake, she'd been one of the ones to nurse me after every single injury over the past month! I should have known something was wrong—I should have—

I shoved the self-recrimination down as hard as I could. I didn't have time to dwell on that kind of thinking. If I did, I might as well have let the poison win. It hadn't won. I—and all of my loved ones and allies—hadn't *let* it win.

And now, we wouldn't let whoever had Iris win.

She wouldn't stay gone. She couldn't stay gone. I wouldn't allow it.

"How do we find her?" I asked harshly, voice grating against my own ears as I looked around the room at those gathered around me. Boss laced his hands behind his head and leaned against the doorway, eyes bleak and exhausted. Lack of sleep did apparently affect incubi as much as the rest of us. Good to know. "Anyone?" I asked again, full-on begging now and not giving a damn about any sense of pride.

To my surprise, the answer didn't come from Boss, Harvey, or my mama as I'd expected, but from the newcomer in our midst. "There is a chance we could scry this Iris's location," Rosemary offered, exchanging a glance with her granddaughter. "It might not be success-ful, especially after several days gone, but it is a chance."

"What do you need?" Boss asked before I could, eyes intent. This was personal for him, too, though not quite as intensely as for me and Harvey. His people, those under his protection as much as mine, had spent the last month possessed, attacked, killed, and now kidnapped. Inna wouldn't get away with any of this, and by all the demons in the hell he had left behind, we would get our people back.

Rosemary gestured for her granddaughter to speak, to my surprise. "I'll..." Louisa trailed off, nervous at being the center of attention for so many actively angry and semi-predatory supernatural beings at once. She squared her shoulders and cleared her throat, going on as I mused that she *really* didn't look like a Louisa, though damned if I knew why. "I'll need a metal bowl; silver would be best through really anything round and reflective would work. Running water, from the creek preferably, and I'd like to do this in her home if possible. That might help with the lag in time if I'm surrounded by what's left of her."

Terry took off toward the kitchen, still trailing a faint outline of a size I didn't have the time to consider too clearly, while Boss muttered about a bucket and headed out the front door to for the creek as requested. I struggled to move myself to the edge of the bed, ignoring both Harvey and Mama's admonishments to lie still and continue to heal. Rosemary surprisingly didn't protest, but rolled her eyes and pressed her lips together in disapproval. Louisa helped support me as I stood, and she whispered in my ear, "Oma's used to stubborn folks refusing to stay in bed."

"Least she hasn't drugged me into submission," I whispered back, and the teen grinned for the first time since entering the bedroom.

"Well, it's early yet, and there are the missing folks to find." Louisa passed me off to Harvey who'd gotten over his annoyance enough to come and be useful when my legs shook like a newborn kitten's. "After everyone's safe though, the drugging chances are high."

"It's not drugging, girl. The technical term is non-consensual sedation." Rosemary's voice was prim, but I caught a glint of humor in her eyes.

That startled a laugh out of me which happily didn't tear at my sore throat nearly as much as I'd expected it to. Come on, boon, keep it up! The faster I healed, the more help I would be when we finally went after Inna. As if it heard me thinking, my stomach growled long and verbose, and I blushed at the sudden scrutiny from the rest of the room. "Um, I may need food before I'm of any use, y'all."

"I'll get you a sandwich made to take with you over to—to Iris's place," Terry said, appearing in the doorway and holding out what appeared to be an actual silver tureen toward Rosemary and Louisa. "Will this work?"

Harvey leaned away from the silver, likely not stepping back only because of the arm he had around me. "Can you get that out of my face, please, Terry?"

"Shit, sorry. Guess we know it's real silver now," they said with a nervous chuckle, then handed off the dish as Louisa stepped around me to claim it, seeming almost too careful to avoid brushing their fingers on the metal.

She eyed it, running her fingers over every inch, gray eyes like her grandmother's almost glowing in her pale face. "This should work perfect. Thank you; I'll bring it back in one piece, I swear."

Terry smiled at her and nodded, then turned to ask me, "Mel, any preference on that sandwich?"

"Ham, turkey, bacon if you've got it. Protein, mostly? I'll eat damn near anything at this point—need fuel for the healing." I hoped they didn't notice the way I avoid looking at them directly, my Sight seeming to shy away from the image of them.

"You got it! I'll meet you over there in a few."

They and Boss almost danced around each other as the former gave way to let the latter in the bedroom doorway, bucket in hand. "Got the water. Are you ready to head across the way?"

The Greyhaus pair nodded and followed him out the door, not bothering to ask if we were going to follow since it was obvious we would. Mama wheeled over as they left and pinned me where I leaned on Harvey with a look. "I can't convince you to get back in bed, can I?"

"I mean eventually, sure. It's comfy when I can actually feel it, and I'll need a day's worth of sleep once this is all over, but right now?" I shook my head and did my best to ignore the ache at disappointing her. "You know I can't stay on the sidelines until I get her back."

The fact that we all knew 'her' only referred to one of the three women we'd search for sent a quick pang of guilt over my much lower level of concern for Sadie but...but it was *Iris.* If it was Iris and Mama missing, it would honestly be a tossup which of them I could force myself to search for first; they were both that important to me. Iris *mattered,* and when I was honest with myself, Sadie...hadn't. Not really. I'd enjoyed her attention when she bothered to give it, but with her not-so-subtle snide remarks as to my sexuality and digs at my self-esteem the entire time we'd been doing whatever it had been that we were doing, she wasn't someone I'd ever let myself trust, let alone love and respect. I'd do my best to get her back too if at all possible, but Iris was my priority. Period. End of story.

Mama gave me another long look, then sighed and nodded. "I figured, but I had to try. You're my baby, and I have to look out for you even though she's one of mine too, you know."

"I do know, Mama." I carefully slipped out from under Harvey's arm to lean down and hug her hard, breathing in the feel of arms holding me safe and sound. "Are you coming with us or holding down the fort here?"

She pressed a kiss to my head then released me before answering. "Considering that damn footbridge? I figure I'll stay here for now. Maybe make some calls and see if I can get us a lead in case the scrying isn't as effective as I think it will be."

"You think so?"

Mama nodded. "My Sight's all blinded by that girl, and the Greyhaus family teaches their heirs damned well. If anyone can scry her out, I am betting it'll be those two." She shrugged. "But it's not like a backup plan ever hurt anything."

"True enough." I shuffled my feet, feeling steadier on them with every passing moment. "You ready, Harvey?"

I felt more than saw his nod from half behind me, and with another weary smile between Mama and I, we headed out the door after the others. The setting sun shone brighter than my eyes expected after the days spent in Boss's guestroom, and I winced away, letting Harvey guide me as much as support me along. The bridge proved a little exciting for two people to cross together, but his wolfy side left him with better than human reflexes during his less fuzzy phases. I clung to him as he got us across to the community side of the creek. There I broke into a slow jog, ignoring Harvey's grunt of disapproval as he kept pace with me. He didn't argue though, likely knowing as well as I did that time was of the essence. When we reached the trailers and RVs closest to the creek, I realized how quiet the community was compared to how I'd expect a surprisingly nice for early December evening like this one. My residents were in sight, sitting on steps or decks, huddled together in twos and threes, staying off the path and out of the way of our faltering run past them.

Their silence held the air of a vigil, of one community coming together in the hopes our missing folk would be found alive and well, and the danger to our community dealt with once and for all. It was almost heady, that silent show of support and simultaneous expectation, especially after the despair that had weighed down my thoughts for the past few days. I let their faces buoy me up as we jogged on toward Iris's airstream nearer to the front of the community, giving me a reason to keep moving even with my energy at less than its best.

These people, *my* people, believed in me. Even when they bitched and moaned about one inconvenience or another, or when they outright screamed at me for getting in the way of some unsanctioned pet or renovation without permits, or when they ducked my calls and locked the doors in my face when I came looking for money owed. Even then, they knew I would do my job, that I would look out for the good of our strange little community Boss had built here. I was looking out for it now; even if I didn't have any answers yet, I was looking for them and for a way to fix this.

Their trust staggered me, and I held it close to my heart, knowing somehow I needed it more than they could ever guess.

Harvey too seemed shaken and humbled by the scene, though it was Miss Ginger's steady nod from where she sat on one of the picnic tables as we passed that had him gritting his teeth and setting his jaw in determination. We ran the rest of the way to the airstream faster than I expected, both of us riding the rush of support all but radiating from everyone around us.

22

The door to Iris's place stood open, the lights inside bright enough to shine out against the dusk's gloom. I eased my way in, not wanting to get underfoot of either of the witches as they made their perusal of the interior, which was thankfully more cleaned up than I worried it would be. Iris wouldn't like her things staying thrown about by that bitch for any longer than they had to be. I breathed in the familiar scent of the candles Iris usually kept burning whenever she was home and felt a bit of my tension ease. She would be back here soon. She *would*. I had to keep reminding myself of that. She wasn't gone for good.

I scooted my way to the bench and table to the right of the door, claiming my normal spot in the corner and leaving plenty of room for either Greyhaus woman to join me if they wished. It was a small space, and I didn't think there ever had been five people in it at once in my memory. We definitely stretched the limits of the airstream's space, and if the door hadn't been open, we'd likely have had an incident thanks to Boss's allure. It didn't hit me as hard as it usually did in an enclosed space, but I figured that could be due to any number of instances in the past few days. I'd take it, but it was odd not to feel awkward around him. On the other hand, he'd seen me in and out of various sets of bloodstained clothes in his own home for the past few days, and after that, it was hard to keep any kind of distance, be it employer and employee or incubi and man-attracted woman.

I had the terrifying suspicion we might come out of this whole mess as real friends in a way we had never quite managed in my years of working for him, and I wasn't sure what to think about that. Assuming we came out of it at all, which I had decided we would, so there.

Rosemary and Louisa were poking through the trailer, looking for personal items and probably hair I guessed from my limited knowledge of magical rituals. Iris kept things tidy, so it didn't take them long to come back with one of her nighttime scarves and several pictures taken out of frames. Setting the bowl, now filled with water, on the table, Louisa sorted through the photos and went to drop them in the bowl. "Wait—not that one," I interrupted, stopping her hand from letting go of one picture in particular. "It's the only pic she has of her grandmother—she can't reprint it."

"Fair enough," Louisa said. "It's pictures of her we need anyway. You and her would be best of all though, since you're the one searching." She sorted through the others again, frowning slightly as if disappointed in her options. I stood and made my way to the fridge. Tucked away on the side was a much battered, but also much-loved photo of the two of us from back in high school at a Halloween dance. I still had the negatives, as well as my copy, so it could be replaced easily enough. I smiled softly at the image. We'd dressed as a pair of flapper girls which had been the first time Iris got to be herself in public, though everyone else thought it a "drag costume." We smiled in the picture, arms wrapped around each other's waists, and she wore her amulet publicly for the first time as well, instead of hiding it under her t-shirts to keep people from talking. I headed back to the table still studying the picture when I thought struck me.

The amulet. "Did anyone find Iris's necklace after—after you found her missing, I mean?"

"No, no we didn't," Boss said slowly. He was the only one in the room who might know why it was important, and I quickly explained it to the others.

"I got it for her in high school. To—to protect her from physical harm in case anyone found out she was trans and—Well. We're near to Austin, but it's still Texas, and I—I worried." I ducked my head to stare at the picture instead of the others, unable to handle looking at their sympathetic faces. "If it's not here, then she should still be wearing it. It's—it means there's a better chance she's alive. Inna will have a hard time hurting her if that thing's working properly."

Harvey gnawed on his lip from where he stood blocking out the night in the doorway. "If that amulet is supposed to protect her, how the hell'd she get taken?"

"The paralysis isn't technically harm," I said, after thinking about it for a second. "I mean, my boon couldn't recognize it as an attack since it only held me in place. That wasn't a danger in and of itself, so the amulet might still let it happen. Inna'd be able to keep her motionless, hell maybe even pick her up and carry her out of here, and the amulet might allow it if it works like the boon. Inna just wouldn't be able to play happy slashy bitey bitch with Iris like she did with me."

I caught the amused look from Boss at that description of Inna's viciousness, but I rolled my eyes at him. I was tired, damn it—no one could judge me for my vocabulary right now. "Either way, I think that's a good thing, right? Though," I paused and passed over the picture to Louisa, pointing out the necklace in case it would help to know what it looked like. "Will the amulet interfere with your scrying?"

"Actually, that amulet will help," Louisa said, sounding surprised. She tilted the photo to show the other witch. "Doesn't that look like one of Aunt Brande's work?"

Slowly, Rosemary nodded. "It does indeed."

"Is that a good thing or a bad thing?" Harvey asked.

"A very good thing—Brande is one of my daughters. You must have gotten this from our shop, perhaps?"

I shrugged. I couldn't remember where specifically I'd found it, only that it felt right in my hands when I did. "So, it definitely won't interfere?"

Louisa shook her head. "No, much like Inna's spell, our scrying is non-invasive and non-threatening. I don't think it should veil her presence as protection. It honestly might boost me since it was made by a family member. In theory at least."

"Theory's the best we got at this point. Might as well do this," Harvey agreed, and the rest nodded. Louisa submerged the photo I'd given her once, twice, and a third time, doing the same with the scarf, and then laying both carefully to the side, ignoring the way they dripped. Her gaze shifted to me. Without so much as a by your leave, the girl reached out and snagged several strands of my hair, plucking them from my head and dipping them into the bowl as she had Iris's items.

"Hey!" I yelped, but she ignored me, immediately drawn back to the bowl before her. Boss tossed me a hand towel and I mopped the water up as subtly as I could, not wanting to distract the young witch from whatever snared her attention. Rosemary joined us by the table, laying a hand on the back of her granddaughter's neck as if grounding her in her place as Louisa's eyes went wide and then rolled up showing the whites.

"Well, that's just unsettling," Harvey said quietly, and Boss shushed him while Rosemary gave him a quelling look I sure as hell would not have wanted aimed my direction by someone with that much power. Louisa didn't seem to have heard him at all and started humming a little under her breath, skin shimmering to my Sight as magic built in the room. My eyes *itched*. I wasn't used to this much magic in an enclosed space. I might have spent plenty of time around Sadie, but her spells hadn't had this...*depth* to them, I decided. Louisa's magic echoed silently, thrumming at my breastbone like bass in a 6th Street club. It was haunting and intriguing all at once, and I wondered what kind of witch she would grow into. Over her head, Rosemary met my eyes and nodded gravely at my unspoken thoughts.

After ten long minutes of uneasy spine-tingling silence, during which Terry arrived quietly with his gallon sized baggie of sandwiches, Louisa sighed and cocked her head, eyelids flickering over irises finally visible again beneath the barely parted eyelashes. "Barbecue," she whispered, causing all of us to blink in confusion before she continued. "Iris smells barbecue. And...and she can hear the highway out through the door a ways away. It's locked but battered, almost falling off while the roof might fall in on her. And smoke...so much smoke smell coming in through the cracks in the walls. Nothing's burning, but it's so thick around her I can taste it."

"The Smokehouse? Inna's got her at The Smokehouse?" Harvey asked what all of us were thinking. It was too close—surely Inna would have taken her prey a good long distance over the past few days. Unless...

"What if she's planning to come back?" I asked, hating the thought of it. The others looked at me in confusion and then dawning horror. I swallowed hard and kept talking. "She has easy prey here. The past month proved we can't track her actions."

"And no one notices when one of ours goes missing except us," Boss agreed, voice solemn. "Whatever creature she is, she wants fresh prey and attacking humans leads to police presence, news crews. It's harder to stay out of sight. Not like with us."

Rosemary rubbed her granddaughter's back as Louisa blinked, trying to pull herself back to the here and now. "The location might have something to do with *him*, too," Rosemary said, nodding at Harvey. "She's been here long enough to know you act as one of the community's defenders whether you think about it or not. A barbecue place would short out your nose like anything if you'd been able to follow the trail immediately."

"I bet Inna thought you'd go after Iris what with you two dancing around each other lately," Terry added, careful to keep from looking directly at me as if to avoid hurting me with the knowledge. I shrugged and shook my head at them; it didn't matter anymore who Iris did or did not date. If she was happy with Harvey, I could handle it. I *couldn't* handle losing her forever to a monster like Inna. "If she'd succeeded in taking out Mel, then you and Boss would be the next biggest threats, and she hadn't seen Boss much. Might think he wasn't as concerned about the tenants."

Boss shifted at that, unhappy with the thought he didn't care about his people, and Terry ran a hand down his arm to soothe him. "I'm not saying she'd be right—I'm saying you let Mel be the face of the community, *as she should be* as property manager. Not micromanaging doesn't mean you don't care, Papi—we know that. But she might not."

"So, she focused on how to keep me from knowing where she was while she waited for the shit to die down enough to see if she could come back, hit us again," Harvey said, his voice low and almost to a growl.

I'd rarely seen his wolf rise this much outside of the full moon, and I wondered if it was the circumstances, or if something had shifted in him with my attack and Iris's kidnapping. I knew wolves were territorial about the people they chose as pack. I hadn't realized this place, our people, had become so dear for him. Harvey chewed at his lip again and pulled his hat on and off absently as he considered. "She's worried 'bout me specifically—stands to reason she must think I can take her if I find her."

"Can you?" I asked quietly, not wanting to doubt him, but needing to be certain of his abilities before we set him up to face the bitch.

Harvey straightened in the doorway and gave each of us a long look. Then he casually stepped outside and full on *lifted* the front of the loaded down and occupied thirty-foot airstream a solid two feet off the ground.

Without any visible effort on his face through the airstream's window.

I was glad I'd been sitting down as Terry nearly fell on their face before Boss caught them and set them back on their feet—with preternatural grace, because of course Boss did. Harvey held the trailer a few moments more, just to prove he could, and then set it carefully back down and retook his place leaning on the doorframe.

Boss eyed him, then grinned bright and feral. "You've been holding out on us, hmm? I will remember this, I promise you."

"I'd expect you to," Harvey said, a slow smirk growing on his face.

I tried not to let my reaction to the display show on my face. That should *not* have been so attractive, and damn it I didn't need my hormones distracting me with Iris in danger anyway. I shook myself all over and ignored Rosemary's knowing and amused look. I cleared my throat. "So, it's a go for Werewolf versus Whatever-the-Hell-She-Is. Cool. How we doing this?"

We came up with a plan in fairly short order, since the task was a relatively straightforward one. Head to The Smokehouse, get Iris (and Sadie, I supposed) free, and kick the shit out of Inna to make damn sure she didn't hunt people and our people specifically ever again. I mentally thanked my mama's connections again as the Greyhaus women agreed to help without even raising their rates over those for services already rendered. Both swore they'd be able to keep our approach hidden from our quarry and still have plenty of juice left over to heal anyone who might need it after everything was done one way or another. They wouldn't be able to get involved in the conflict itself—completely understandable considering one was elderly and the other a minor. Terry headed back to the big house to keep Mama company and be ready to call in an actual ambulance or doctor if things really went wrong for the mostly human of us. They also had orders to have Mama call the sheriff's office and warn them it might be best if the department as a whole steered clear of The Smokehouse for the night. It wasn't the first such call they'd received, nor would it be the last.

Terry hadn't been happy about staying behind, but whether or not I was right in my growing suspicions about their less than human status, they weren't ready (yet or ever) to tell any of us who or what they really were. I wasn't sure Boss knew considering how determined he was to keep Terry out of the fray. I kept my mouth shut, as did Louisa though she eyed Terry speculatively when they left.

That left five of us to head to the barbecue place, with Harvey providing the muscle, Boss providing stealth and an unsurprising ability to pick locks, and me, hopefully capable of keeping up with the pair of them and of surviving if all else failed.

It's a Smithson family fact that the ability to survive can be worth a lot more than you might think. If you can hold on when you think there's no chance, well that's a little longer you aren't dying. And if you aren't dead, you can still fight back against whatever hurt you.

Or so we kept telling ourselves.

23

The drive over in my beat-up minivan (the only vehicle belonging to any of the five of us that would comfortably hold us all and our respective bags of tricks—or well, as comfortable as an old ass minivan could be) took both less time and more time than I wanted it to. On the one hand, the sooner we got there, the sooner we could get Iris back. On the other, the sooner we got there, there sooner we'd have to deal with Inna. As if in response to the thought, my skin prickled, and my neck ached with phantom pain. Her teeth and claws were no joke, and her odd predatory gift was worse. I shook away the thought. I had to trust Harvey to hold up his end of things even if everything about this situation scared me worse than I remembered ever being afraid. Anyone who said fear of the unknown was the worst terror one could ever feel clearly never faced their loved one in the hands of a known danger like this one.

My stomach churned with anxiety, making me wonder if scarfing down the club sandwiches Terry provided had been the best choice. But, no, I needed the fuel to boost the boon again, and, ignoring the stress-upset stomach aspect, I felt much better for having eaten. As did Louisa—she'd inhaled two herself, understandable after her effort during my healing and her scrying. Rosemary had declined, advising that I needed it more than she did. I wasn't sure I agreed, but I still ate the remaining three sandwiches on my own as instructed by Terry's oddly effective combination of sternness and guilt as they gave their best impression of a Latinx abuela. "After I put forth the effort to make these for you—with real bacon even!—you're going to let them go to waste?"

At least I was the one driving as giving up control of my battered minivan would have been a step further than I could handle mid-stress attack. Boss kept sending me concerned glances from beneath his dark eyebrows, but I ignored them, as I did the push of his allure in the closed vehicle, though it again was less than I had expected it to be. I wondered if he could somehow put a damper on it when he was in defense mode instead of merely existing as his incubus self. I made a mental note to sit him down and finally force an explanation out of him if we survived this. If we were going to be friends, and it seemed like we were, I wanted to know what I needed to do to make both of us more comfortable rather than simply avoiding his in-person presence as I had through the years of my employment to date.

I was more than a little surprised the Greyhaus women didn't seem affected by it in the slightest, but then I didn't know either of their sexualities; occasionally completely non-men-attracted women were more immune. That or the resilience was due to the distraction of their active magical workings; they currently linked hands and pressed their opposite palms to the roof above them, casting some kind of glamor on our approach. Either way, such things were above my paygrade until I'd unlocked their level ten friendship. Besides, you didn't walk up to a grandma or a teen and ask, "hey are you into dudes because it seems like you might not be," my educated guess based on prior experience be damned.

Harvey was just dandy in the closed space with Boss, and I tried not to resent that fact. Granted, he currently pouted over being relegated to the way back, but the Greyhaus pair needed the central location for their casting and Boss's legs stretched quite a bit longer than Harvey's. I patted his ridiculous trucker hat and told him to channel his annoyance into psyching himself up for dealing with Inna, because he'd need all the oomph he could get judging from my reaction to her. Hopefully his enhanced sense of smell and hearing could allow him to approach her with his eyes closed as planned, or he could catch her from behind. He'd wondered if that was quite fair, but it had been Louisa who pointed out hypnotism-induced paralysis was hardly fair either and we could stoop as far as we liked to take out a slashy, bitey, murdering bitch.

I high-fived her for the reference if only out of amusement at Boss's long-suffering look.

I finally pulled up to the stop sign one street away from The Smokehouse and turned off onto the side street at Rosemary's instruction. "This is as close as we can go," she said apologetically. "We can continue to glamor you from this distance, but I cannot in good conscience risk Louisa by getting any closer to the danger."

Louisa winced but didn't object, and I wondered how often they had that conversation. I nodded my support though, seconded and thirded by Boss and Harvey respectively. "We understand completely," I assured her. "Y'all have already done more than most would have. We appreciate all the help—more than you know."

We left them in the minivan, doing our best to make as little noise as possible to help the glamor as much as we could. I locked the door behind us, hoping it kept the Greyhaus women that much safer while they worked. The street loomed dark; the streetlight at this corner perpetually acted up as if the power wasn't any happier with the owner of The Smokehouse's rejection of our town than the residents were. I hefted my shotgun into proper position, keeping the barrel pointed away from my companions as we stalked across the street and around the back of the gas station that stood next to the restaurant. From our approach, we could see few lights on at The Smokehouse since the time it had taken for us to prepare for the attack set us well past closing time. There was a chance the owner was starting the next day's round of briskets, but I hoped that would still be a few hours out. Though shit, considering the lackluster quality of their brisket, we might even have until dawn.

I didn't know if Inna would go for the easy prey over keeping her cover and her victims hidden, and I didn't want to find out by stumbling over a bloody corpse and having to figure out how to either hide it or explain it to the sheriff's department. Yes, our local law enforcement was nominally aware there were things that go bump in the night living within their jurisdiction, but we both preferred not to deal with that fact being acknowledged due to murder.

Deliberate ignorance was less stressful for both sides of the equation.

Boss gestured to the front of the restaurant, slipping off to cover the entrance as we'd discussed, while Harvey stilled beside me, taking in a deep breath, and sifting through the scents around us. A barely audible growl rumbled in his chest, and he nodded towards the back door of the main building. He then pointed me towards one of the ricketier sheds out behind the massive grills and smokers that kept The Smokehouse in business. I mouthed, "Are you sure?"

Harvey rolled his eyes at me and headed to the back door without another word. Best case scenario, Inna would indeed be inside the restaurant, and Harvey and Boss would be a match for her while I rescued her victims.

Worst case... Well, the worst case wasn't worth distracting myself over. If the shit hit the fan, I'd figure out how to clean it up then.

I didn't have the preternatural edge to help me move silently the way Harvey and Boss could, but I hadn't been patrolling the community late at night for years for nothing. We had enough diurnal residents that I did my best to stay as quiet as possible when I passed their homes, trailers, RVs, or otherwise, and I'd been doing it long enough I wasn't half bad at it. For mostly-human anyway. I approached the shed carefully, the gravel barely rustling under my careful footsteps. The padlock and chain on the door were rusty enough I couldn't tell if Inna had placed them there or if she'd lucked into her prison coming readymade.

I avoided the cracks where the old wooden slats fell apart, revealing the slightest hint of light. Whatever lantern or flashlight shone through the boards wasn't too bright, but it would be enough to mess my eyes up if I wasn't careful. I also didn't want to risk the sound of my boots coming through louder in the cracks to alert anything or anyone of my presence. I moved to the corner of the shed at one of the few sturdy spots and leaned in close, listening for any sound within. Someone whispered, so faint it might as well have been under their breath, and definitely too low for me to make out what they were saying. I hoped it meant both of my missing ladies were inside and healthy enough to talk to each other.

Only one way to find out for sure.

I eased back around to the padlocked double doors at the front of the shed and shifted my grip on the shotgun to aim its heavy and sturdy stock at the lock. I took a slow breath preparing myself; I'd only have one chance at this. There was no way to get in there quietly. I had to trust the guys to handle Inna once she was aware of my presence.

"Here goes nothing," I whispered to myself, and brought the rifle stock slamming down onto the battered old padlock with a crash and rattle of the chains that was far too loud for my taste.

I forced myself to focus and wrenched the wrecked lock and chains off the doors, flinging them open with my free hand and easing my way to look inside. Sure enough, the lantern caused me to wince and shade my eyes, but I caught a glimpse of Iris. She sat tied to a chair, gagged with what looked like a ripped sleeve off one of her favorite jackets and looking pissed but otherwise unharmed. The amulet had worked.

The amulet had *worked*.

Relief surged in me strong enough I swayed on my feet and let the shotgun waver toward the ground for all of a breath.

That was long enough for the attack to come and from a source I'd somehow never expected.

The whispering should have been a warning. Only it wasn't whispering, it was chanting.

Sadie's chanting, as I realized as she stood from behind Iris's chair and flung something toward my face, her voice rising in strength and volume as she did so. I had barely enough time to duck, but still felt some of whatever she'd thrown end up in my hair and begin to *burn*.

Whether with actual flames or mere sensation of heat, I didn't have the time to check. I prayed to any deity listening that I wasn't risking third-degree burns as I moved, bringing my shotgun up and firing. Not at Sadie due to Iris being in the way, as I gathered she'd planned for, but at the lantern in the corner just to the right and behind Iris and Sadie. The rock salt, herbs, and silver shavings hit it hard enough to cause the cheap light to explode sending plastic shards and light-bulb pieces flying.

As I'd hoped, the amulet kept any of them from impacting Iris.

Sadie, on the other hand, was not so lucky.

She shrieked, throwing her hands up too late to completely shield her face, the improvised shrapnel tearing into her cheeks, arms, and clothing. I lunged through the new darkness, grabbing for Iris and dragging her out of the shed, chair and all. Once clear and behind the meager shield of the open door, I tore at the gag and rope. Luckily, both were in a similar shape to the shed—Inna hadn't been picky about her restraints, especially with her paralysis and...and Sadie to help. The thought made my stomach roil with betrayal and disgust that I'd let a monster into my bed the way I had let Sadie in. I forced it down, continuing to fight my way through until Iris was free. She stood up from the chair and then turned to heft it by the back like a lion tamer ready to fight off a beast with a stool. Granted, as much taller and stronger than me as Iris was, a chair might prove more useful than I expected.

Echoing her prep, I got the shotgun back up into position just in time. The door in front of us disintegrated at the power of one very pissed off witch with none of my desire to keep this conflict hidden. Thankfully, there wasn't enough left of the door (or the rest of the shed) to send too many splinters into me, something I figured Sadie hadn't realized, but I was definitely going to take advantage of. I would not have been able to hide my eyes the way Sadie had from the lantern bits.

She didn't seem grateful her eyes were still whole, though. Instead, they were red with angry tears and streaked with the blood dripping down her face from her forehead and scalp. The blood clashed terribly with her red hair in the faint light from the streetlight which now, of course, decided was the perfect time to turn back on. Across the parking lot, I could hear crashing inside the restaurant and the kind of roars of rage likely caused by something semi-mortal and pissed, but they were too incoherent to sort out who specifically was doing the roaring.

I forced my concern for the guys out of my mind and stumbled back, trying to keep myself between Iris and the bitch I was so glad I was no longer sleeping with considering where we stood now. I could feel the air sharpening as she prepared for another attack of some kind, the whites of her eyes turning darker as she channeled a power that held nothing of light. I hefted my shotgun again but hesitated to fire. She was still a person, still someone I had trusted with my body, if not my heart. Shooting her at point blank range… Even what I might think of as non-deadly ammo would practically tear her in two with the force of the powder alone. I opted for distraction instead, aiming at the gravel at her feet which exploded into the air around her at the impact of the shot. She shrieked and jerked back, hands once again failing to shield her face as well as they should have.

I backpedaled while I could, doing my best to shoulder Iris's larger form behind me and keep myself from stumbling on the loose gravel. "What the fuck, Sadie?" I yelled as I retreated further. "Why would you do this? Those were our neighbors, our friends, and you… What—sent them to die?"

"This is your fault!" she shrieked back, wiping more blood away from her eyes. "All you had to do was bleed for me when I asked you to, and none of this would have been necessary!"

Her words actually had me pausing for a moment in confusion. "Asked me to—huh?"

That apparently wasn't the reaction Sadie wanted, and she threw another spell sachet toward me with a growl of rage. I didn't have the option of firing to the side this time. Iris was behind me—I couldn't let the spell impact. I shot the sachet out of the air like the clay pigeons Mama taught me how to shoot with, the blow sending both my ammo and the contents of the sachet back directly into Sadie's face.

She didn't shriek this time; only coughed as her eyes widened and she whimpered, the sound almost too pitiful after the volume of her previous screams. Her face paled, and then a strange green started creeping into her features from her ears like a mask overtaking the front of her face.

"Sadie...?" I asked, not daring to step closer as my co-dependent instincts urged. "Sadie, can you talk?"

She collapsed, and I lunged forward to catch her before she hit the ground, barely managing not to whack us both with the shotgun as I did so. Sadie wheezed, the sound ending in a terrible rattle in her chest. "Sadie, tell me. Why did you do this? Tell me!"

On my knees, I shook her, and her eyes fluttered open, locking on my face with an intensity that had me shivering. "He wanted your blood," she whispered, voice ravaged by whatever spell she'd nearly killed me with. I hated that part of me pitied her despite knowing what she'd done. Even knowing the hellish way she was dying in front of me was, in fact, *intended* for me. "Wanted your blood, wanted the boon, wanted all of your family for him."

"Who's he? Why would you do this for him?" I begged, still needing to understand why she'd betrayed us all, betrayed *me* so terribly.

She shrugged and chuckled wetly. "He isn't someone you can say no to once you owe him. Besides, he paid well. And you deserved it," she hissed, glaring at me and then Iris behind me. "I tried to spare you at first, but then, well, *no one* tells me no. No one turns *me* down."

I dropped her back to the ground, Sadie's hate-filled eyes still on me. I looked down at her in disgust and shook my head. "You know, I might have felt guilty for breaking it off the way I did. But you hurt Marvin and Muriel long before I was smart enough to walk away from you. You *chose* to hurt innocents. And fuck you claiming you "asked" me for anything. You wanted this. Wanted to hurt people who'd never done a damn thing to you." I let Iris help me to my feet, a coldness sweeping over and numbing me inside. "But then, you always were a selfish bitch; I just thought I couldn't do any better."

I shook my head as she reached out for my legs, her eyes frantic with an odd mix of hate and longing so clear I could almost feel it against my skin. "Mel, wait. Mel...I didn't give it to him. I didn't." I didn't know why she now, after everything I'd said seemed to want my forgiveness, but she kept talking, desperation in her voice. "I kept it when Inna got it for me, but he hasn't come to collect it. It's in my trailer, but..."

"But what?" I asked despite myself.

"But he'll come for it—for you. He's coming, and there's nothing you can do to stop him..." She let her head sink back against the gravel, then looked back up at me, a wicked light of vengeance back in her eyes, the change in her mood almost giving me emotional whiplash. "You'll burn, bitch. You and everyone at that piece of shit trailer park will burn when he comes. Shouldn't have killed me. Shouldn't have—"

Sadie broke off, her breath escaping all at once as her body stiffened. She went still, the light in her eyes dying with the rest of her.

24

I couldn't bring myself to move for a moment, my mind numb and struggling to comprehend that Sadie, vibrant, powerful, vicious Sadie had died.

I'd once thought she'd be one of those witches to extend her life damn near forever, assuming she wasn't already older than she ever admitted. I hadn't really thought she'd go so dark with her magic, as I knew attempted immortality required...sacrifices, shall we say. But there was always a chance with witches of questionable moral centers, and Sadie had never been anything but ruthless about going after what she wanted, myself included. Everything considered, I'd expected her to outlive me.

I hadn't expected her to try to kill me, either. Today was full of surprises, I supposed.

Fucking hell, but I would have really liked to have a boring anticlimactic day right about now.

Iris shuffled her feet behind me, reminding me of her presence and pulling me out of my shock enough to turn and look at her blankly. She sighed, then reached out and pulled me to her, holding me tight as my knees gave way and keeping me from falling.

Sadie was dead.

Sadie was dead, and self-defense or not, I'd been the one to kill my former lover. I wasn't sure how to deal with it yet, or the information she'd all but spat in my face about the stranger she'd been working for. One without a name or a face, and luckily out of either Sadie's mercy or desire to try to force her employer out of more cash, without my blood. I didn't know why anyone would want it, or why it would be tied to the boon. But now I knew to look—to start trying to piece together the truth with that new information. Now I had the chance to do so.

It still didn't seem worth it, not with three bodies and an exorcised ghost destroyed in its wake.

I shuddered out a gasp and then pulled myself away from Iris, forcing myself to stand firm.

"We have to check on the others," I said, realizing the fight in the restaurant had gone quiet, though I couldn't say when it had done so.

"The others?" she asked, eyes watching Sadie warily as if expecting her to move.

"Boss and Harvey are handling Inna, and there are a couple witches who helped us find you and hide our approach. They—they need to know what's happened here." I shoved my hands into my hair and pulled, forcing my hands to stop shaking. "And—and we need to deal with the body. I don't—I don't know if we should hide it or burn it or say she skipped town... I don't know."

Iris laid a careful hand on my shoulder. "Boss will know what to do. Even if it's wrapping her up in something and carting her back to the Estates for burial."

I shuddered again and nodded. "Can you...stay here, with her? While I check on them? The amulet should keep you safe if she's—if she's playing possum or something."

"I will," Iris replied, then glared down at the body as if it had personally offended her, which, to be fair, Sadie had on multiple occasions. "But I doubt she's going anywhere."

"Same, but considering the past month?"

"Yeah, better safe than sorry." She gave me another brief one-armed hug, then moved to lean back against the sole remaining wall of the shed, which I was frankly shocked still stood strong enough to support Iris's weight. "Go get the boys. I'll be here."

I stooped to pick my shotgun up where it lay by the body and jogged over to The Smokehouse proper, hoping like all hell I wasn't about to come across another body. Or another body that *wasn't* Inna, who could die in a fire for all I cared. Maybe it wasn't the proper Christian attitude a young southern lady was expected to follow, but then, I had a demon for a boss so "proper" behavior was well beyond me by now. Besides, while I knew intellectually Sadie had likely been involved all along and probably even masterminded Inna's role in addition to the other attacks, it still *felt* like everything started going wrong with Inna's appearance in our lives.

It was easier to hate her and blame her, than to focus on my hate for Sadie and the self-loathing for ever letting her touch me that rolled in my stomach like bad leftovers.

The door to the pitch-black restaurant swung open as I reached it, revealing a figure so covered in blood I could smell it. It was only a second figure's quick reflexes knocking the gun barrel to the side that kept me from shooting the first figure right in the face.

"Whoa, whoa! It's us!" Harvey, the blood-soaked figure, held his hands up to show he was unarmed, or as unarmed as a werewolf ever was. "It's us, Mel."

I lowered the shotgun slowly, nerves still on edge from everything that had gone wrong for the past month or more. "You OK?"

"Yeah, it's not mine." He shrugged, then grinned viciously, the pale light from the streetlamp glinting off his teeth. "Inna, on the other hand, is definitely *not* OK."

"Fair enough." A thought struck me, and I blinked. "Y'all see enough of her shifted self to figure out what she was?"

"No idea," Harvey said, just as Boss answered, "A baba yaga, I think."

I blinked again. "A 'Baba Yaga'—chicken house and mortar and pestle and all? Isn't there just the one? It's her name, right?"

"Nope, that's a common misconception. Most people don't live to tell tales about any of them, let alone escape more than one in a lifetime. And they are notoriously anti-social, especially with their own kind. Thus, the use of the word for the species as if it's a proper name in the stories." Boss stepped past Harvey into the dim light, and I was completely unsurprised to see him pristine without a single drop of blood on him or a hair out of place. The dick. He stepped up to me and tilted his head thoughtfully. "It explains quite a bit, you know."

"I do?"

"Mm, yes. All baba yagas feed as much on the manipulation and emotional torture of their prey as anything else." I exchanged a confused look with Harvey, and Boss huffed impatiently before continuing. "Once a prospective victim wandered up to their lair, the baba yaga would give them something to eat. Something that just happened to contain some of their saliva which is where the poison— venom? I never can keep those two straight." He waved the thought away. "Where was I? Oh yes. The poison from their saliva once in contact with their prey would cause them to believe there was no point in trying to escape—that there was nowhere to run and that no one would help them. It eroded their sense of emotional bonds. Eventually most of their victims just allowed themselves to be killed."

Boss's expression was almost pitying as he looked at me. Then he shrugged deliberately. "Then there were the hallucinations. Once someone is seeing shit on top of that sense of artificial hopelessness...I imagine few lasted long after that, no matter what the tales of that young Russian girl say." He shuddered over-dramatically. "A baba yaga in Texas, really. What is this state coming to? I knew a few back down *below*, as it were. Nasty bitches. Made me wary of cute old ladies even worse than the gingerbread witches did, and believe me, that's saying something."

I opened my mouth to ask what in the Grimm brothers hell a gingerbread witch actually *was* beside the obvious, but closed it again, too tired to care.

Something about Boss's explanation was tugging at my thoughts in much the same way as my Sight had been itching off and on all night, especially around the normally unremarkable Terry. I wondered vaguely if a baba yaga's prey actually hallucinated... Or if it was more likely those poor folks had the Sight forced upon them all at once, with no frame of reference for what they actually Saw.

I wondered too just what a substance like that might do to someone who already possessed that ability.

I forced the thought away, deciding I was too tired to care about that either.

"Iris OK?" Harvey asked before either Boss or I could say anything else.

I gestured with the shotgun barrel back the way I came. "Yeah, she's—she's safe. She's waiting for us back at the shed."

"And our resident witch?" Boss asked, voice giving nothing of his opinion away.

I started walking back without waiting to see if they'd follow me, not wanting either to see my face as I said, "Sadie's dead."

"Shit," Harvey muttered. "Should've known Inna couldn't go too long without eating folks once she'd let herself get a taste for it."

"No," I made myself say. "No, I killed her. Not Inna. Iris is watching the body to make sure she stays dead."

Both men froze behind me, and I forced myself to look back over my shoulder at them.

"She'd dead," I said again, and then none of us said anything at all for a while.

It turned out I was right in my vague suspicion that Boss had plans for the body, bodies now, with Sadie too, but I hadn't expected the plans to include the Greyhaus witches. "Too much mess in the restaurant for me to handwave away, Mel dear, even at the height of my strength. Not after a month like this one trying to keep the grounds from rioting back at us due to the unrest of its occupants."

I stared at him in horror at that little tidbit about the property, but he went on as if it was a non-issue. "Besides, blood gets into everything, and I know you know how hard it is to get out of fabric. Let alone out of wood, soaked into the grain because *someone* got carried away when it came to ripping limbs off."

Harvey shrugged, unrepentant and utterly covered in blood. Rosemary Greyhaus took one look at him and rolled her eyes. She chanted under her breath and snapped once, then after a scowl, twice more, and just like that, the blood vanished from his skin and clothes. There was some still in his hair, but it was far less likely to get us arrested in this light, so I didn't bother pointing it out. Rosemary nodded triumphantly to herself, then asked, "All right where's the rest of the mess? You know this will add quite a bit to your receipt. At least another zero or two, I'm thinking."

"Worth it," Boss said, then pointed to the shed where Iris still waited and back to the restaurant. "Two bodies after all, one witchy and one in... Well, in pieces." He eyed Louisa. "I'm not precisely sure either are something your granddaughter should see."

The two Greyhaus witches shared a silent conversation, then Louisa sighed and shook herself all over. "Works for me. Oma, do you need me to do anything from out here while you deal with that?"

"If you've got the energy left for it, toss up a sight and sound ward around this area. I know Mel said local law enforcement is more in the know than I particularly like them to be, but they could still cause complications while we try to get things done and over with." Rosemary patted her granddaughter on the arm and then headed over to Iris, getting the easier of the two body clean ups out of the way first.

I didn't help her with Sadie, couldn't bring myself to. From where I stood a short distance away, I watched both Iris and Boss help with whatever ritual Rosemary cast before conjuring a shroud big enough to wrap my former lover's body in out of thin air. Once Sadie was out of sight, I could breathe easier, and, I hoped, make myself useful.

With only a brief moment of hesitation caused by a sudden rise of pressure in the air I guessed had to do with the younger Greyhaus's ward scheme, I headed back into the slaughterhouse, I meant, The Smokehouse. I felt shoved back out the door by the smell of the blood and offal strewn about the tables. Boss had understated the matter more than I'd thought; or else Harvey had been even more angry at Iris's abduction than he'd let on.

He came up behind me in the doorway and wrapped an arm around my shoulders, pulling me in for a rough hug with his nose buried in my hair next to my ear. He rumbled with contentment, then marched into the scene of his catharsis, the set of his shoulders revealing he was decidedly satisfied with his handiwork.

Huh. I suddenly realized some of the violence might have been for me, too. I wasn't sure what to think about that.

Gritting my teeth against the smell, I propped my shotgun by the door and went to help Harvey move some of the larger pieces into a single location on the concrete floor in order to make Rosemary's task that much easier. It was still an awful mess, easily the most gruesome sight I'd ever laid eyes on, and I'd grown up with a roadkill-eating mini-ghoul living in Mama's garden shed as a cross between a pet and a compost machine. Still, despite the less than enjoyable task at hand, there was a sick sort of satisfaction churning in my stomach at the knowledge my attacker had died and died horribly judging from the mess. "She say anything about being hired?" I asked, dragging her right leg over to the pile of body parts. "Or anything 'bout Sadie's plans or employer?"

"Sadie had an employer?" Boss asked from the doorway, and I realized I hadn't told them what went down in the shed aside from Sadie not surviving it. I gritted my teeth against the bile in my throat and explained. I had to immediately repeat myself when Rosemary joined us to shroud the body pieces and get her blood vanishing snap on while she listened to me.

"Well, that is unsettling to say the least," Rosemary remarked as she watched Harvey heft the shrouded bag of meat. Thankfully the shrouds proved to be well sealed and leak proof so no additional blood got onto Harvey, nor would hopefully end up coating the back of my minivan. Who knew if it would help with the smell much as I couldn't tell so far if the blood scent lingered in the restaurant or seared into my nose hairs.

Rosemary continued. "I knew the witch—can't remember if I told you all, but I did, and she was… Well, the community opinion was that she was more profit driven than is usually smiled upon. Solely looking out for number one. I don't know that I ever heard of her having a loved one or even a 'more tolerated than most' one—just people she used as needed."

Harvey growled low, and I pointedly refused to let my face react to the barebones facts of Sadie's regard for anyone—including me. Rosemary eyed us both but continued. "Most of us know better than to take on work that could lead to death or nonconsensual bloodletting. That kind of thing has an impact on one's magic and can taint it in ways that even the least moral of witches shy away from. There's going dark and death corrupted, and then there's warping the very fabric of your own power until it is more in control than you are. Anyone with sense knows better than to risk it. What little reward you get isn't worth what you lose."

"How would a prospective employer have found her?" I wondered aloud.

Rosemary shrugged. "There's any number of ways—scrying specifically for a practitioner playing within the lines of morality or asking a deity for the name of someone with a proximity to you as the target. Even word of mouth in the community regarding who the rest of us steer clear of is a fairly common tactic. There are too many options to know for sure how he found her. If he's a he—we don't have much to go on, do we?"

"No," I agreed and hated it. "We don't."

She eyed me again, a long onceover as if she saw through all of me to my strengths and weaknesses all at once. "How he found her isn't the important bit—that's what he wanted *from* her. Or from you in this case. You do need to get your blood back, sooner rather than later, you hear me? I don't know much about your family's—boon, you call it? But if it is tied to your family's blood line, a sample of yours could be dangerous in the wrong hands."

"Great."

"Now, I don't know about you all, but I'm feeling a bit peaked after all of this. You have anything else for me, or can we get this show on the road? I'd rather not leave my granddaughter carrying those wards any longer than she must. She's got a touch for them, but she's still only seventeen—not quite old enough to have reached full strength, you know." Rosemary said it matter-of-factly. I certainly hadn't ever heard of anything related to that, but then my limited personal experience with witches prior to meeting the Greyhaus women included only Bessie's hedge witchery and what little general knowledge Sadie had let slip, so I supposed my ignorance wasn't surprising in retrospect.

Boss gave one last look around the restaurant which might actually be cleaner now than it had been when the brawling started. The owner probably wouldn't notice. Hopefully. Maybe? The locals to the area generally knew to ignore strange happenings for the sake of the status quo and their own sanity, but again The Smokehouse insisted they weren't local. "I do think that's everything. Mel, do you think we'll all be able to fit in your vehicle?"

I ignored the implied insult to my baby's capabilities. "I doubt it, especially with the—the bodies, I mean. We'll need two trips." I looked critically at him and Harvey who'd come back from depositing the Inna bits in the minivan. "Unless you boys want to run back? Losing the pair of you would probably make it possible to fit the rest of it."

"Suits me," Harvey said. "The smell in an enclosed space will be rough on my nose."

Boss gave a longsuffering sigh. "I suppose I will join him. But I'll remember this next time."

I rolled my eyes. "Fine. Next time we have to transport bodies and multiple allies, you get shotgun and I'll catch an Uber."

"Done and done." He nodded at both of us, then took off running. He ran only slightly faster than I would expect a mortal man to pull off, but I imagined his stamina would last quite a bit longer. I immediately shook my thoughts away from the inevitable mind in the gutter moment, and smiled as best I could at Harvey in farewell before he headed off, waving to Iris as he passed.

"Well then, ladies, our chariot come hearse come minivan awaits, I guess."

25

Inna's body burned in the second pyre in a month on Asphodel Estates property. This one wasn't nearly as well attended of course, though the surviving harpy sisters appeared long enough to ritualistically spit on the flames before heading back to their trailer, looking lost with only two of them bickering instead of three. I wondered how long the spaces this mess had left would seem so empty before we'd start filling in the gaps between us.

The body I'd seen Inna attacking turned out to be Alex as I'd feared. Arranging their burial—in the small barrow hill that appeared on the edge of the community's memorial grounds and which I swore I'd never seen before—took less research than I expected. Who knew folks on the internet had so much of an interest in Ancient barrow burial practices? Alex didn't have any family they'd admitted to, so the rest of us residents formed the procession following Harvey as he carried the body, one much more elaborately shrouded than the others he'd had in his arms recently. We all carried an item or two of Alex's personal things to lay in state within the tomb. Boss laid two coins upon the lids of their eyes, the coins looked to be actual gold and possibly as ancient as the ritual we followed. None of us asked how he'd gotten them any more than anyone mentioned the mysteriously appearing barrow hill. Some things one didn't question when one's boss and/or landlord was a mostly reformed demon.

Sealing the barrow door over with stones was its own special kind of hell. A hell born of regret: regret I'd hadn't known Alex as well as some of the other residents, regret I'd never seen what Inna was, regret I wasn't fast enough to keep her from taking the wight's life any more than I'd been able to save Marvin or Muriel.

I shouldn't have been surprised that dealing with Sadie was worse, but somehow it blindsided me. We buried her on the south side of Boss's house just at the edge of the property line as no one wanted her in our normal memorial grounds. We laid her a solid ten feet down without coffin, casket, or any other sign of respect—Boss could be decidedly petty at times and was also *not* taking chances. Her grave went deep enough we had to hire a backhoe operator to manage with the rocky hill country soil gone winter cold and hard, if not quite frozen like it might have been farther north. It took longer than I expected to find someone in the know who worked in that specific field. It was only Rosemary Greyhaus's shroud that made the week-long wait possible, something I hadn't realized I would be grateful for. I wanted Sadie buried and gone and would have settled for her body on the pyre with Inna's. However, a quiet word from Louisa reminded Boss and I of the unfortunate connotations of burning a witch in any fashion. So, burial it was.

I knew folks said the dead were at peace, but the last thing her body looked was peaceful when we removed the shroud prior to burial. The spell damage added to the shotgun's salt, silver, and herbs had not treated her face well, and the marks hadn't healed with her gone and unable to direct her own healing abilities. Iris offered to stand at the burial in my place, wanting to keep me from having to look at her body, but I felt like I needed to be there, needed to see the consequences of what I'd done, even if I'd been forced to do it.

Harvey hefted the body again one last time, but unlike Alex's gentle placement in their tomb, Sadie was merely dropped without fanfare into the dark deep hole. The backhoe immediately moved to replace the soil, none of us wanting her in the open air out of some unspoken suspicion she might still come back to hurt us all again as terribly as she already had. Once the hole was filled, I was surprised to see Bessie appear, walking slowly to stand at the head of the grave. Her face bore no expression, but her eyes were hard with grief and anger as she raised her hands and tossed the seeds she carried onto the grave. Within moments, fierce briars and stems of poison ivy and poison oak grew to form a massive living cage over where Sadie lay, weaving one final prison for her.

Bessie stared at us all fiercely, as if expecting one of us to argue with what she'd done. We said nothing, and after a breath, all the fight went out of her. She once again appeared the age she really was, old and so, *so* sad it hurt to watch her walk away again, shoulders shaking with the tears she'd refused to shed over Sadie's grave. I didn't blame her for those tears any more than I blamed her for the one last act of retaliation against the dead woman she couldn't fight any other way.

After she left, the rest of us who'd gathered as much out of spite as grief drifted away behind the backhoe, until only Iris and I were left staring in silence at the vine shrouded pile of dirt.

"It still isn't your fault you know—not the killings, not her death, not that she got her hooks in you in the first place." I opened my mouth to argue on instinct, but Iris kept going, steamrolling over whatever self-recrimination I might have managed. "I know it doesn't feel like it now, hon, but it's the truth. Someday I hope you'll believe it, instead of whatever bullshit she told you."

"There was a lot, yeah," I managed to agree, my voice rough with the tears I was as determined as Bessie to keep locked inside me where Sadie's body couldn't bear witness to them. "I—Iris, I—I can't talk about her. Not yet."

Maybe not ever. It went unspoken, but the words lingered in the air like smoke between us.

Iris smiled at me gently, her dark eyes kind enough I ached, then she laid a hand on my arm. "Fair enough. There's plenty to think over and deal with in the meantime anyway."

I nodded. It was certainly true. Harvey's nose had sniffed out the vials of my blood, hidden in Inna's former borrowed trailer instead of

Sadie's as I'd originally thought. Neither trailer turned up any mention of the person responsible for setting off the violence within our community. Whether it was a man or creature, mortal or supernatural, we didn't know. Nor did we yet know where to begin trying to figure it out.

I hated it—hated knowing there was some unknown enemy out there, obsessed with my blood and bloodline. Obsessed enough to hire someone like Sadie. Obsessed enough not to care about the lives their obsession had cost.

We'd have to continue researching our foe with the help of our allies and Mama's network. Mama herself was a conundrum—none of us could be sure why she hadn't been targeted. She thought the trailer park simply made a better hunting ground for Inna to blend in and study us, as well as keeping her close to Sadie. That location had saved Mama more than anything else. Rosemary, on the other hand, wondered if it might be my lack of children. Magic sometimes worked that way, apparently: weakening in a mother as it was passed on to the next generation. I didn't think myself any stronger than Mama, or... I hadn't thought myself any stronger than Mama *before* the baba yaga bitch had sent my Sight all itching the way it had been. Still, as theories went, it seemed to make more sense to me than Mama's.

I had a third theory, though I couldn't bring myself to mention it aloud. I was the one Sadie wanted to hurt, so I'd been the one she set her partner on. It explained the other deaths too: Sadie never hid her disdain at the thought of her "competition" in Bessie, or the outright animosity between her and the harpy sisters with their blatant dislike of the witch, or, of course, her complete loathing of Iris, though I hadn't realized how deep it ran until she'd outed herself as a transphobe. Alex might have thrown me, but I remembered them calling Sadie out time and again after she misgendered them.

Sadie never did like someone telling her she was wrong.

It was a theory based solely on Sadie's desire to cause pain to a variety of people, and I couldn't help but think it the most likely option.

No matter which of our theories were correct, Mama wouldn't get to take me up on my previous offer of the guestroom instead of the assisted living place any time soon. Only Rosemary's idea offered Mama any clear protection from our hunter, and both of our bloodline living on the same ground was just too much of a risk. I wasn't sure if I was relieved or sad. Granted, a terrible injury on my part would probably be enough to drag her here despite her original decision, but I wasn't that desperate to get her to live with me.

I was happy to brood over my failures alone.

At least, our new Greyhaus connection meant Elysian Fields was now warded to the hilt against anyone entering with "ill intent." I wondered just how many relatives or caregivers with the less obvious forms of elder abuse in mind were in for a rude awakening in the coming days. I could only imagine how tricky the ward scheme had to be for something that nuanced. Rosemary's sister Brooke told me both Rosemary and Louisa slept for two solid days after their spellcasting over there. 'Louisa' still somehow made my eyes cross themselves every time I tried to say it, but I'd decided to let it go for now. I was trying to come up with some kind of thank you above and beyond their basic fee for the work, but what did one get a pair of witches who had everything? I decided I owed them a favor, not that they'd admit it. If worse came to worse, I was pretty handy and I knew a shit ton of contractors if they ever needed help around their homestead. I told Brooke and hoped she'd pass on the message to Rosemary, even if Rosemary might not take me up on it.

The wind picked up, rustling the disturbingly green for December leaves on the vines over Sadie's grave, chilling me to the core and breaking me out of my reverie. Iris still stood patiently beside me, content to keep me company as I let my mind wander. As I came back to myself, she tightened the hand on my shoulder and used it to pull me in to a hug while she spoke softly in my ear.

"And Mel—you know I'm here when you're ready to talk. About anything." There was a wealth of meaning to her words and the soft smile she gave me, but I could only nod due to the lump in my throat.

I wasn't ready and didn't know when I would be. But she'd be there. We might never be what I'd hoped for to each other, but she *would* be there. I knew that one single truth even if I knew nothing else.

Together, we walked back to the homes of Asphodel Estates to heal, and to prepare for whatever would come next.

The End

ACKNOWLEDGMENTS

Sitting down to write this, I realized I should have started keeping a list years ago. It's too late now, but if I miss someone - please know it wasn't intentional, and I am so *so* thankful to everyone who has helped me on this journey over the years. First thanks must go to my family - especially my mom, my sister, and my husband, who all have believed in me often when I didn't believe in myself. Next, of course, the amazing team at Falstaff Books, with a special thank you to Erin Penn who pulled me from the slush pile and finally set me on the path to the publication of my first novel. Everyone involved with the Pitch Wars 2015 group over at FB - y'all have been such a resource and much needed place to vent and ask questions; I am so glad I am part of that group and I wish us all success! More locally, the Herding Cats creative writing group - I heart y'all like crazy and I miss our semi-regular writing retreats. We need to get another scheduled! Also, the Rowboat - y'all know who you are and there will be fic again at some point to thank you for your encouragement. Marie McCurdy - you continue to be the writing partner I didn't know I needed in the best of ways. Kristi Luchi, you probably are my longest running writer friendship, and I miss your face for real. And last but not least, Kym, my bestie, even when we aren't creative in the same medium, your art never fails to inspire and push me to improve.

ABOUT THE AUTHOR

C.L. McCollum (she/they) is a card carrying disaster bi of a SFF author. While living the neurodivergent spoonie life, she writes YA and adult in a variety of SFF subgenres. Her adult debut, 13 COUNTY ROAD 666, is on the road to publication with Falstaff Books. She also will be appearing in THIS HOUSE IS HAUNTED, a YA horror anthology coming August 2024 from Page Street Kids. Previously, she has also appeared in Jolene Haley's "Spooky Showcase" and anthologies with several micro-presses, and has also edited and appeared in the CLICHES FOR A CAUSE self-published charity anthology series. She thinks "What is your favorite book?" is a trick question and impossible to answer, but if you have an hour to kill, she can talk about the hundreds she loves. Currently, C.L. keeps it weird in the Texas Hill Country with the family she loves and their furry roommates. You can find her at home at https://linktr.ee/clmccollum.

FRIENDS OF FALSTAFF

Thank You to All our Falstaff Books Patrons, who get extra digital content each month! To be featured here and see what other great rewards we offer, go to www.patreon.com/falstaffbooks.

PATRONS

Dino Hicks
John Hooks
John Kilgallon
Larissa Lichty
Travis & Casey Schilling
Staci-Leigh Santore
Sheryl R. Hayes
Scott Norris
Samuel Montgomery-Blinn
Junkle

www.ingramcontent.com/pod-product-compliance
Lightning Source LLC
Chambersburg PA
CBHW022031120726
47899CB00007BA/2346